monsoonbooks

MAYA

Nuril Basri is an Indonesian writer born in West Java. He has worked in a variety of positions over the years: internet café operator, secretary to a police attaché, mystery shopper, mini-market cashier, and waiter on a cruise ship. His previously published works include *Not a Virgin* and *Love, Lies and Indomee*. His novel *Le rat d'égout* (*The Sewer Rat*) won Best Gay Novel in Translation in France in 2023.

T0267699

Maya

Nuril Basri

monsoonbooks

First publication in English in 2024
by Monsoon Books Ltd
www.monsoonbooks.co.uk

No.1 The Lodge, Burrough Court,
Burrough on the Hill, Melton Mowbray LE14 2QS, UK

First Edition.

Originally published in Malay by Buku Fixi (Kuala Lumpur, 2019).

ISBN (paperback): 9781915310323
ISBN (ebook): 9781915310330

Printed and bound in Great Britain by Clays Ltd, Elcograf S.p.A.
26 25 24   1 2 3

Buku ini saya dedikasikan untuk orang-orang
yang masih atau pernah merasakan hampa,
terkatung-katung, atau kosong, dalam hidupnya.

I dedicate this book to those who feel, or have ever felt,
hollow, adrift or empty in their lives.

Introduction

I often wonder why the universe, or whatever cosmic forces are at play, decided to cut me some slack. It's kind of weird, you know? My dreams and their plans have never really matched up. I remember standing in front of my trusty mirror, which doubles as my holy altar, and having this little pep talk with myself. Come on, Maya, do you even know what you want from life? I asked, and then I got all teary-eyed. Not because I lacked direction, I was mostly going for a vulnerable look on Instagram. Truth be told, I didn't have a clue about what I really wanted. But one thing was crystal clear – I didn't want to be stuck where I was, especially not in my thirties. So, I slapped my own cheeks like Gordon Ramsay in the 'idiot sandwich' meme, and made a pact with myself: Maya, just go with the flow.

And now here I am at Istanbul Airport in Turkey, waiting for my next flight to Estonia, up there in northern Europe. I've got a four-hour layover ahead of me, so I'm parked in a chair pretending to be some young hotshot executive, hunched over my laptop as if I'm prepping for a major international business gig. In reality, I'm knee-deep in steamy stories on Wattpad. I know it's highly unlikely that someone's going to sweep me off my feet in this transit lounge, but at least I don't look like a sad girl who has no idea where life is taking her, even though that's pretty much what I am.

But you know what? I'm happy I've left Indonesia behind. Jakarta is a mess – a crowded, smog-filled chaos. And don't get me started on my toxic co-workers. Plus, I need some space from the nosy neighbours, the relatives who never quit, and my dear old Mom. This is my chance to reinvent myself.

1

Estonia, it turns out, is downright chilly. A relentless drizzle has blanketed the city of Tallinn all day, making my small, fragile frame shiver despite the multiple layers I've thrown on. Europe is entirely new to me, and I can't resist the urge to take out my phone. There's an irresistible pull to capture a few selfies outside this European airport and share them on Facebook, if only to provoke a little jealousy among the folks back home. But my exposed hands can only withstand the cold for a brief moment, just long enough to snap two pictures.

The guy from the cruise ship, the one who's supposed to pick me up, is nowhere in sight. He promised he'd be here.

Yes, you read that right – a cruise ship. But no, I'm not here to blow cash on luxury cruising, living it up like Nicole Richie. I'm here to work onboard, and no, I won't be navigating the ship or playing captain. My role? I'll be a waitress, serving the passengers.

After what feels like an eternity, my contact finally arrives, and he's as cold as the weather. Without uttering a word, he grabs my small suitcase and tosses it into the boot of his car. We drive to the harbour in silence for twenty minutes, as if he assumes I can't speak English.

Upon reaching the harbour, I get my first glimpse of the ship, and it's far from what I'd imagined. I had pictured a colossal vessel teeming with three thousand crew members and glamorous amenities like a pool and a bar for the staff. But no, I'm about to set sail on a smaller ship, measuring just one hundred metres in length and accommodating a modest one hundred and ten passengers. But hey, no room for complaints, right? My birthday is just a few weeks away, and one of my resolutions is to stop being dramatic.

Stepping onto the ship, I'm greeted by Utpal, a sturdy Indian guy who happens to be the restaurant manager – my boss. 'How's Tallinn treating you?' he asks, while letting me struggle with my baggage.

'Plenty of old castles,' I reply. 'I spotted them on my way here.' Why is he even asking about the city?

'Have you worked on a ship before?' he asks, seemingly forgetting his previous question.

I shake my head. 'But I've worked in a restaurant, a four-star hotel.'

'For how long?'

'A couple of years,' I respond confidently, as I'd anticipated he would ask that.

'Are you prone to seasickness?'

'Hmm ...'

'What's "hmm"?'

'I'm not sure,' I admit. 'I mean, I've been on a ship before, but it was just a ferry, you know? Island hopping. I was on holiday, exploring beaches. In Indonesia, we have like seventeen thousand islands, so if you ever visit, I could–'

He cuts me off. 'I could tell from the moment I laid eyes on you that you're a disaster.'

My mouth hangs open, shocked by his bluntness.

From then on, I'm determined to remain silent. Utpal does the same, leading me to my cabin without a word.

'Your room,' he says finally.

Inside my cabin there are four capsule-style bunk beds, each with its own curtain. In his icy tone, Utpal informs me that I'll start working at 6 pm today, immediately after enduring a nearly twenty-four-hour flight.

***

I have a little secret to confess: I never actually worked in a hotel restaurant for two years. I had a brief internship at a mediocre three-star hotel, and then I sweet-talked the HR guy with a bit of cash and a cheesy grin to provide me with a work certificate, claiming I'd been there for twenty months. I figured he'd prefer the cash.

The idea of working on a cruise ship struck me while I was toiling away as an account manager for an internet and TV cable company back in Jakarta. The job wasn't terrible, but I was terrible at it. I had to go door to door, meeting with potential internet customers and selling our services. But after three years on the job, I rarely hit my sales targets. It's not easy to win over clients, you know? Maybe it's because I'm not exactly a head-turner or perhaps it's because I spent most of my time hanging out at food stalls and playing SimCity on my phone instead of canvassing. Who's to say, right?

But that's not the reason I decided to quit. Besides contemplating the meaning of life, I simply couldn't bear the thought of celebrating my thirtieth birthday among my colleagues. I couldn't stomach the sarcastic comments that would rain down on me that day. 'Oh, thirty already, and still renting a tiny room. So skinny, practically all bones, must be stressed out. No husband, no boyfriend? No one at all? She probably cuddles with a grungy old bolster with a K-pop idol face printed on it. What else? Never hits her sales targets, bound to get fired soon. How pitiful.' Even if they didn't say these hurtful things to my face, my sensitive soul could hear them loud and clear. I'm very attuned to what others think of me.

So, after applying for the waitress position online, I had a series of intense Skype interviews with folks from Croatia. They asked about menus and restaurant services, all of which I could answer confidently, thanks to my extensive YouTube research. In the end, the lady on the other end of the screen told me I had a fantastic personality and a dazzling smile – just what the company was looking for. And voila! I was hired. And now, here I am:

IN HELL.

2

Working in a restaurant aboard a cruise ship is nothing like working in a regular eatery. The moment I step into the dining area for the evening shift, I'm paired with Kanompang, a striking waitress from Thailand. She's got it all – a seductive figure, cascading strawberry-scented hair, and a charming English accent.

Initially, she's all smiles, offering to mentor me like the seasoned pro she is. 'Don't worry, dear,' she assures me, 'I'll show you the ropes. It's a bit overwhelming at first, but you'll get the hang of it in no time.'

But the moment Utpal, our strict restaurant manager, disappears from view, her demeanour takes a sinister turn. 'Don't mess up my station!' she warns with a sudden edge in her voice.

To be fair, I do end up creating a bit of chaos at her station. Just a bit.

It's not entirely my fault that I can't recall which wine is being served tonight. The extensive wine list is a labyrinth of names and vintages, and my training on it was far too brief to be of much help. And it certainly isn't my fault that I lack the physical strength to hoist a massive tray bearing eight plates of the main course. I mean, I'm no Hercules, and the weight of it catches me off guard. It slips from my trembling hands, crashing onto the table with a deafening clatter that draws the attention of nearby diners.

I scramble to pick up the fallen cutlery, my cheeks flushed with embarrassment as I overhear a patron whisper, 'She's new, you know.' Kanompang, however, doesn't miss a beat. With practiced grace, she smoothly replaces the fallen plates, offering an apologetic smile to the passengers as if to say, 'Don't mind the rookie.'

Miscommunication plagues me throughout the evening too.

I mix up orders, serve the wrong dishes, and spill drinks as if I have two left hands. Diners shoot me annoyed glances, and I find myself offering profuse apologies while silently cursing my inexperience.

Dinner service finally concludes at nine, and I'm all set to retreat to my cabin when Kanompang suddenly appears, blocking my path like a sentinel guarding a sacred passage. She enquires about my destination, her tone laced with a hint of authority.

'Bed?' I respond, my confusion evident.

'What a princess!' she scoffs. 'Get your ass back to the restaurant and set it up for breakfast service.'

I'm not sure if this is just how things work or if Kanompang is singling me out. But when I look around, I see other servers doing the same tasks. They move with practiced rhythm, transforming the dining area from the dimly lit ambiance of dinner into a bright and inviting space for the morning crowd.

So, I reluctantly spend the next two hours cleaning the restaurant, changing tablecloths, and setting up the tables to make them look fancy. It's not just about folding napkins into swans or boats; I also have to take orders and serve food. It turns out, this is all part of the waiter's job on this ship.

Exhausted and feeling out of my depth, I try to appear as stoic as Robocop when I finally return to my cabin around 11 pm. But in reality, all I want to do is cry. The room is a cramped sanctuary, the narrow bed feels more like a coffin. It rocks gently with the motion of the ship, lulling me into a surreal sense of isolation and homesickness.

Tears start to well up in my eyes, and I can't help but let them flow, my silent sobs lost in the gentle hum of the ship's engine. I yearn for the familiar comforts of home. But returning is not an option. What would I do? Swim back? I don't even know where I am. How foolish.

This situation brings back memories of that fateful day when I first told my mother about my decision to work on a cruise ship. She exploded.

'Why on earth do you want to work on a cruise ship? What are you searching for?'

I wanted to reply, 'To find something I couldn't discover here. My true self, perhaps.' But my mom would never buy that. She's incredibly practical. So, I blurted out something that made more sense to her: 'Well, I'm looking for better pay. They pay in dollars, you know? Plus, I get to walk around the globe.'

'Is that so?' My mom grunted before retreating to the storeroom, returning with an old globe, the same one I used during primary school geography lessons. She placed the globe on the floor between us.

'What's this?' I asked, puzzled by the unexpected prop.

'Walk around it,' she instructed with a steely expression.

'Seriously, I can't believe you did that!' I exclaimed, my frustration bubbling over. I gave the globe a swift kick, sending it careening into the next room with a loud crash.

'That's a banana goal, like Beckham's,' I quipped, but my mom's glare made it clear that my antics weren't amusing. Although she must have known I'd do something like that. I'm rather headstrong, and I've always had a knack for getting under her skin. But I got it from her.

'Whatever!' She huffed as she left the room, her house dress twirling like the national flag.

'Do you even know what the sea is like?!' she shouted from the far end of the room. 'You could drown, you know? You could die. And if you die out at sea, it'll be nearly impossible to find your body!'

Then she fell silent, giving me the cold shoulder for the rest of the day. If I died out at sea, and the last image I had of her was that sour expression, wouldn't she feel remorse?

So, no, I can't send my mom any messages about how I've been working tirelessly, my arms aching as if I've been constructing an Egyptian pyramid. Complain about how exhausted I am and how I want to return home on my very first day on the cruise ship? That's a terrible idea. My mom won't offer comforting words like a typical mother. But I'm convinced she's telepathic. She'll transmit something like 'See, I told you so!' in the form of a radio wave that only dolphins and my stupid brain can pick up.

Alright, Maya, enough already. Get. Some. Sleep.

3

Four other waiters share our station: two from Ukraine and two from India. On the cruise ship's second deck, Kanompang and I are in charge of Station Three, serving around forty to fifty people during each mealtime. It might sound manageable, but handling this many guests all at once, each with their unique orders, can be a real head-spinning challenge. Thankfully, most of our passengers are in their fifties and sixties, so they're not as demanding as the younger crowd. They may need some assistance getting seated, but they're generally pleasant.

Breakfast service today is nothing short of disastrous. I'm still grappling with jetlag, and the buffet is a total mystery to me. I can't even distinguish between the various types of cheese and cereals. Throughout the service, Kanompang keeps me on my toes, barking orders like, 'Quick, refill the coffee at table two! Hurry up, clear table four before Utpal sees it! Hey, someone at table six wants tea! Come on!' Her constant instructions keep my nerves on edge. As a server, I can't afford to show even the slightest hint of panic, so I just plaster on a smile whenever we cross paths.

Once the meal service ends, my next task is to polish about a thousand plates and pieces of silverware that have just come out of the dishwasher to remove those pesky water stains. Utpal strolls over to check my progress while I'm still hard at work on the banana bowls.

'I've seen people like you before, working on a cruise ship just for the free travel,' he mutters. 'I don't need a waitress like you. You'll be on your way home within a month.'

He leaves after dropping that bombshell. I'm left wondering whether he means it or if it's just his way of being funny or trying to spur me to improve. But one thing's for sure – I don't particularly care for his attitude.

During my thirty-minute lunch break, I find myself sitting alone, poking at my food without much appetite. Lunch is served in the crew mess, a small five by five metre room that serves as our dining area as well as a place to relax. It's furnished with a few stools and tables, and it's here that we watch TV, listen to music and occasionally throw impromptu parties. Frankly, it's not the most inviting space, and the odour of oily coveralls doesn't help.

After lunch, I return to my cabin to freshen up, but I'm not alone in there this time. Two girls occupy the other beds; I didn't have a chance to meet them last night as they were already asleep.

'Sis, are you from Indonesia?' asks one of my cabin mates.

'I'm not if you're holding a grudge against them,' I quip.

'No, we're from Indonesia too,' says the other.

Their little faces light up with excitement as I reveal that I hail from Jakarta.

My two cabin mates introduce themselves as Ida and Yanti, both hailing from Bali. They've been here for a few months, and discovering fellow Indonesians among the crew is a welcome surprise. We share the same sense of homesickness, and the prospect of speaking in our native language provides some comfort. Ida works in housekeeping, while Yanti is a masseuse. They mention two more Indonesians on board, one handling the dishwasher and another in the laundry. Ida and Yanti, with their tanned skin and cheerful personalities, turn out to be much younger than me, just twenty-two years old. What's most irritating is how they make it sound like I'm ancient at 'twenty-four'. After enduring their naive remarks about my slim build, I decide it's time to escape the cabin and head back to the restaurant, where Utpal awaits with his usual dose of shouting.

4

The next few days don't get any better. Utpal shadows my every move as I serve passengers, scrutinizing every action. He observes how I clear dirty dishes, pour wine, and set plates on the table – whether I do it from the left or right side, how often I smile at the passengers, and more. He even remarks on my English accent, which, according to him, is atrocious.

'Quick, tell me, what's on the dinner menu tonight?' he demands, while I'm busy carrying dirty dishes to the dishwasher.

I think on my feet. Last night, I crammed this information. House wine, appetizers, salads, soups, sorbet, four main courses, four desserts, cheese and fruit platter, after-dinner drinks, varieties of tea and coffee. Relax, I'm not that dumb. I hold a bachelor's degree in early childhood education from a public university, with a GPA of 3.0, proving I'm not a complete airhead. I used to cram right before exams, you know, last-minute studying, so I can probably handle this absurdly ever-changing menu. Ha ha, if only.

'Tonight we're serving Sieur d'Arques Vanel Merlot and Vanel Chardonnay from France. Onion galette and cherry tomatoes for the hot appetizer,' I confidently relay. Then he enquires about the entrée, but I'm genuinely unsure whether it's tuna or lamb shank.

His eyes nearly bulge out of their sockets.

'Green salad is always available,' I offer as a last-ditch effort, as I can't remember anything else.

'Do you find this amusing? *Bombohole*!' he snaps.

'I'm trying my best, Utpal!' I reply.

'Not hard enough! You're too much *taka-taka*.'

Solemnly, I look him in the eyes. 'I took this job because I needed the money. Give me a chance.'

He glares at me before shooing me back to my station. I sort of wish he had asked me what I planned to do with the money; I might have said something like getting breast and butt implants. It would have annoyed him to no end, and he'd be right about me being too much *taka-taka*. Whatever that means.

Later, while tidying up spare cutlery in the drawer at our station, I casually ask Kanompang, 'Why does Utpal seem to really hate me?'

I instantly regret asking, not because it sounds like I'm seeking sympathy, but because of her response.

'It's not just him, it's everyone,' she replies slowly.

I put my hand to my chest and mutter, 'Bitch.'

She must have overheard me calling her a bitch because, during dinner, Kanompang makes my life difficult.

'Table two, seat four, lactose intolerant. Table three, seats five and six, gluten-free. There's a vegan at table five, but I don't remember which seat. Table six has someone allergic to seafood, so don't bring the Caesar salad dressing, you know, the one with anchovies. And don't mix up the appetizers and soups,' she adds, pretending to jot down notes.

I try to keep my cool, but I can't remember any of it. What's worse, I don't know what to do about the allergies. I barely know what food contains what. I've only been here for a couple of days.

'What?' Kanompang asks, knowing the game she's playing.

'Just kill me,' I say dramatically.

She almost laughs but refrains. Instead, she heads to the kitchen and reports me to Utpal, claiming that I'm jeopardizing her customers' health by being ignorant about allergies. I know this will only reinforce Utpal's belief that I'm unfit for the job. So, when he approaches me, I turn pale.

Utpal hands me a crumpled book. 'You need to memorize everything in it by the end of the week. Burn it and drink the ashes if you have to.'

It's a restaurant handbook on allergies and other related matters, including details about our menu. I have to study it during my thirteen-hour shifts. How will I manage that? With my brain's capacity, it will take me a month to memorize the ingredients of one entrée, and then I'll forget it within seconds.

* * *

I'm utterly exhausted, both mentally and physically. My body aches to the core, and blisters have formed on the soles of my feet. So, as soon as I return to the cabin, I head straight to the bathroom. I turn on the hot shower and sit beneath it, hugging my knees, and cry uncontrollably. I surrender. If my life were a reality show, I'd wave my hand to the TV camera and plead for mercy. Please, I give up. Just let me go home.

Ida is already in the cabin when I rush out of the bathroom with swollen eyes.

'Sis, are you crying?' she asks.

'What? No.'

'But I heard you,' she says, perplexed.

I must have been crying louder than I thought. 'Yeah, I'm just really drained,' I admit, and the floodgates of emotion open once more.

5

Today, we've docked in Saint Petersburg, Russia. It's a 'lunch-off' day, which means the passengers will have their lunch ashore, and all the restaurant crews get some free time until dinner service. I know I should be studying the handbook, burning it and drinking the ashes as Utpal suggested, but this is Russia! We've visited Sweden, Denmark, Poland and Latvia, but this is the first chance to step foot on foreign soil, and I won't waste it. The cities that drifted past our portholes are now only a distant memory. I can study later.

Over lunch, Kanompang teasingly asks, 'Who are you going to the city with? Your mafioso buddies?' I can't help but chuckle at her name for my Indonesian friends. We do have a tendency to huddle in a group and share black-market kitchen snacks.

'I don't know yet,' I admit, pulling my windbreaker tight against the cold. Every minute is precious; I don't want to waste it hanging around chatting.

Spotting my uncertainty, Kanompang makes me an offer.

'Come with me. I've been to Saint Petersburg before. You can get lost easily if you're not familiar with the city. You've never been here, right? If you go alone, you might get lost or, worse, get robbed.'

Although it sounds like a genuine offer of help, it's actually a cleverly disguised trap. What she really means is: 'I plan to shop a lot, and I'll need an extra pair of hands to carry my bags.' Oblivious to her true intentions, I gladly accept her invitation.

* * *

Stepping onto Russian soil is surreal. The brilliant hues of autumn leaves greet us, a spectacle I've only ever seen on TV. Overwhelmed, I stop to snap photos at every turn, captivated by the simple beauty of this new world.

Kanompang rolls her eyes, commenting, 'So tacky.' But I don't care. This is my moment.

We take an expensive cab to the city centre, but fortunately I have no rubles, so Kanompang pays for everything. She shops for heaps of clothes and perfumes at Zara, while I opt for cheap scarves around the Hermitage Museum and Palace Square, blending in with the budget-conscious tourists.

On the pavement along Griboedov Canal, I lean on the railing and savour the moment, feeling like I'm in a music video. Watching stylish people hurry by, I can't believe I'm in Russia! The only other time I've been to a foreign country (apart from a brief layover at Tallinn airport) was when I visited Singapore, thanks to a cheap ticket with AirAsia.

It's a fantastic moment, and I wish I could tell my mom about it. 'See, Mom, I've travelled. Look at my feet, they're on a different side of the world.' Perhaps she would just purse her lips or audibly say 'wow' in a mocking way.

* * *

We return to the ship at five, and my arms are sore from carrying Kanompang's shopping. I've never been in her cabin before. Her bed is festooned with dolls, colourful Christmas lights, scattered selfies, and about twenty fridge magnets she's collected from each country she's visited, all clinging to the metal wall.

'Where are you going?' she asks, as I prepare to leave her room.

'To bed?' I reply. We have one hour before the dinner service begins, and I'm considering a quick nap.

'You're not leaving until you can tell me all of tonight's entrées.'

Initially reluctant, I eventually give in, and we practice until I can confidently recite the menu, which includes dishes like lamb shank with thyme gravy, pasta quattro formaggi, pan-fried fillet of John Dory, and baked eggplant parmigiana. Kanompang also educates me about allergies.

'Why are you doing this for me?' I ask suspiciously.

'It's my station too, and I'm your captain. If you mess up, it reflects poorly on me as well. So, it's not a favour, it's self-preservation.'

Whatever her motives, it works. When dinner arrives, I'm

prepared to face Utpal, and the guests, with allergies. Maybe Kanompang isn't such a bad 'b' word after all. She's still a 'b,' but possibly a good one.

6

I've had to get a haircut, not because I wanted a new style but because of my dandruff problem. Those annoying white flakes have been falling onto my shoulder like snow in winter. I haven't been able to resist the urge to scratch my scalp these past few days. It has been very embarrassing. I've never faced this issue before, and I've desperately tried to hide it. But, of course, Kanompang, my partner, noticed.

Yesterday, she dragged me to the galley and exclaimed, 'Jesus! You're producing grated parmesan cheese!' She couldn't help but snigger and later informed Utpal about my scalp issue, who promptly ordered me to shave my head bald.

Ida has informed me that the water we use for showering is distilled straight from the sea, with goodness knows how many chemicals to remove the saltiness. She says it also contains chlorine. So, if not dandruff, I might still end up with grey hair – and that is definitely preferable to hair loss.

None of the shampoos available here seem to help with my so-called 'grated parmesan cheese' shoulder situation. So, in desperation, I have asked Ida to cut my shoulder-length hair shorter. I want a style that will make me look like a supermodel. I figure shorter hair might be easier to manage. I show Ida a picture of Cleopatra, and she agrees to give it a try. I trust her, but when I finally look in the mirror, I don't see the Egyptian queen. Instead, Dora the Explorer stares back at me.

I give her a stern look, which clearly intimidates her. She leaves the room without saying a word.

With no other options left, I head to Kanompang's cabin to seek her help. I really don't want to do this, but at the moment she is my only option.

When she sees me, she chokes. 'What's going on with your hair?'

'Can you please help me?'

'No.'

'Please, we're running out of time, and it's almost dinner,' I implore.

She grumbles but eventually gets up. She fetches a pair of scissors from a drawer and instructs me to wait for her in the bathroom.

She strolls into the bathroom with a sly grin, and I sense I am in for it.

'Abort! Abort!' I blurt out.

'Don't be such a scaredy-cat,' she teases, her tone playful. 'Trust me, it's for the best.'

Caught in a no-win situation, I finally surrender. As she snips away, I can't help but wonder if she intends to give me a full-on bald look, just as Utpal suggested. If that happens, it will be my golden ticket home. I could claim emotional distress, and I contemplate suing Kanompang and Utpal for making me go bald, while this ship could take the blame for my dandruff-rich hair.

But when she lets me gaze in the mirror, I am relieved to see I still have some hair left. A few inches remain, and I now sport a chic pixie cut that actually emphasizes my jawline, giving my face a more sculpted look. I can't deny it – I'm starting to like it. As I admire the transformation, Kanompang chimes in, 'Now you look like a boy.'

7

It's the 14th of October, and we're docked in Copenhagen, Denmark. After the lunch rush and a quick clean-up of the restaurant, I manage to sneak away for a couple of hours of freedom. Most of the crew head back to their cabins for a nap or hang out in the crew mess, but not me – I'm determined to see the city.

A brisk wind nips at my cheeks as I stroll through Churchillparken, a beautifully manicured park with fancy green grass. I can't help but chuckle when I find myself sitting by the Gefion Fountain, a massive sculpture of a god riding some beasts. They say tossing coins in can grant you wishes, but all I've got are candy wrappers. I wonder if they'd work.

Next stop is Kastellet, the Citadel, which is shaped like a star. There are these charming orange and red buildings nearby, and all the trees are decked out in autumn leaves. Copenhagen is like a picture postcard. My journey continues to the Langelinie promenade, and what do I stumble upon? The iconic Little Mermaid bronze statue! Tourists are posing for photos with her, but I'm content to sit on the beach, musing about how she doesn't quite look like Ariel from Disney with her regular legs.

Today's a big day for me – I'm hitting the big 3-0. As I watch the mermaid who longs for feet, it's hard to put my feelings into words. But maybe that's okay because some emotions are just too complex, and we can't ever say what we truly feel. One thing's for sure, though – I'm relieved I'm not celebrating in Jakarta. That would mean dealing with colleagues pretending to be nice just for a free meal and my mom making an odd-shaped birthday cake with a 3 and 0 candle. She'd try to look happy, but her eyes would be judging me. I'd pretend to be thrilled but would secretly die of embarrassment thanks to those candles.

I'm so glad it hasn't come to that. Thanks to my job, I've got no time for self-pity or sappy solo birthday parties in my room with cheesy ballads playing. With this gig, I hardly have a moment to spare, let alone for self-pity.

My two hours of freedom eventually run out, and I bid farewell to the Little Mermaid. We're both a bit quirky, but we share something in common: she's dreaming of getting out of the water, while I'm trying to escape the land … and everything else.

* * *

Dinner service tonight goes decently. I may have spilled a bit of wine on the tablecloth, but it's no catastrophe. A casual 'Oops' and a sheepish grin and the guests are happy. The tiredness I felt earlier has faded away. After we wrap up, Utpal gathers us all around one table for the daily debrief. But tonight he's got a surprise – eight cold beer cans to share. We exchange puzzled glances before cracking open the cans and taking swigs. Beer isn't exactly my thing so I nurse it slowly out of politeness.

'Why the special treat?' Kanompang asks.

'It's your paisano's birthday,' Utpal announces, nodding in my direction with his usual swagger.

The rest of the crew lets out a collective 'Ooh' and raise their cans to toast to me.

I'm taken aback. 'What's all this?'

Kanompang probes further, 'So, how old are you now?'

I wish I could say I'm 25, but before I can respond, Utpal chimes in, 'She's 33.'

I quickly correct him, 'I'm 30, not 33! Utpal, what are you talking about!'

Kanompang teases, 'Well, 30 or 33, you're not getting any younger.'

Nina, the other waitress, adds with a grin, 'Don't worry, 30 is the new 21.'

Thanks to Utpal and his big mouth, I'm not just grappling with turning 30 – now I'm suddenly three years older too.

8

We're deep into the Grand Baltic Sea Voyage cruise, and have been exploring northern Europe for eleven days now. Today, I manage to sneak out during our stop in Lithuania and spend some quality time at The Fat Cat Café, hogging their free Wi-Fi and uploading heaps of photos to Facebook. The reactions from friends are a mixed bag – some casually ask for souvenirs (like I'm on vacation); a few snark, 'Ah, Photoshop, huh?' (probably former colleagues nursing a case of envy), while others just drop a simple love or like on my posts.

At dinner service, Utpal decides to grace me with his usual dose of cryptic criticism. 'You work like a blindfolded donkey,' he says. I'm not even going to ask what that means; he's said enough hurtful things, and I've built up a thick skin. Just the other day, he called me a tortoise, which I figured meant I was slow, but a blindfolded donkey? No clue.

Tonight, as we set sail from Lithuania, the sea decides to get feisty. It's been almost a month since I started working on this ship, but I've never felt this miserable. The waves are battering the ship mercilessly – Kanompang estimates they're four to five metres high. The ship sways like a swing, and serving during this time is like trying to tightrope walk on a rollercoaster.

'Don't worry, we've all got sea legs,' Kanompang reassures the passengers, though her worried face doesn't quite match her words.

Sea legs? More like sea disasters. I've already dropped two plates of roasted duck salad, and to top it off I'm feeling queasy. Maybe this is Utpal's way of saying, 'Welcome to seasickness.'

I pretend to be the diligent waiter and carry a stack of dirty dishes to the back area near the kitchen. Once there, I frantically hunt for a trash can. After a quick scan to make sure Utpal isn't lurking, I face the trash can and, with all the grace of a sick walrus, proceed to empty my stomach's contents. People in the cold and hot galleys are horrified – it seems I've given them an unexpected show. I thought I just needed a good purge to feel better, but I didn't anticipate terrifying everyone in the process.

With a wiped mouth and shaky legs, I return to the restaurant, sporting my practiced level-six smile, as if nothing happened. Five minutes later, I'm back at the kitchen, searching for that trusty trash can.

'Blargh ... blargh ...' I retch.

'You've got to rest,' one of the kitchen guys urges.

'I'm fine.' I brush him off, washing my mouth at the tap before returning to my station to serve dessert. However, some passengers have already left their tables, unable to endure the relentless rocking of the ship. My stomach holds on for another three minutes before I make yet another dash for the trash can. Of course, Kanompang catches me this time, grinning like she's won a prize, and immediately summons Utpal.

'Go to your cabin,' Utpal commands with his usual bossiness.

I shake my head and try to muster some strength. Despite Kanompang's annoying tendencies, I can't leave her alone to handle the guests at a time like this. She'll be overwhelmed.

'Whatever,' Utpal concedes.

Call me stubborn, but I manage to hang in there for another forty seconds until a colossal wave broadsides the ship, and I sprint to the back, spewing out whatever remnants my stomach still holds. On wobbly legs, I lean against the coffee pot cabinets near the cold galleys. Some junior chefs are busy with orders.

'Don't drink,' one of them advises. 'It'll make the seasickness worse.'

'Huh,' I mutter.

Feeling drained, I settle on the kitchen floor. The kitchen guy is understandably concerned and rushes over to help me up. As he supports me, he suddenly exclaims, 'Oh my God, you're a girl!'

9

I wake up feeling much better after having taken two Dramamine pills the night before. The seasickness has finally loosened its grip on me. But here's the deal – we don't get any weekends off on this job. It's work every day for the entire ten months of my contract. So, bad night or good night, it's robot-mode the next day.

In the kitchen, I bump into the guy who mistook me for a boy. 'Thanks for yesterday,' I say, though I'm still a touch salty about his gender confusion. I can't really blame him though. I rarely chat with the kitchen crew. Maybe this is what Utpal means by blindfolded donkey.

'No problem,' he grins, revealing his small teeth and two prominent fangs. 'I'm Oleksii.'

'Maya,' I reply.

'I thought you were Andrew,' he says, which only perplexes me more.

'What?'

'Yeah, Kanompang told everyone your name is Andrew.'

'Just for the record, I don't have any, you know, manly attributes.'

His eyes widen, 'I figured that out last night!'

I roll my eyes, 'Is it the short hair?' I ask, trying to figure out his confusion. 'It's the witch that gave me this cut,' I say.

He scratches his head, 'Sort of ... and, well, you're not exactly ...' He trails off, obviously hinting at my not-so-prominent chest area.

'My bra's there for a reason!' I retort.

He blushes, 'Well, I couldn't see that. You know, it's hidden.'

Ugh! If not for his timely assistance with saltines, I would've smacked him. Do I give off a tomboy vibe? Sure, I don't have a curvy figure or a pair of C cups, but I definitely don't have anything bulging in my pants. I blame this waitress vest that made my chest so invisible.

Walking away from Oleksii, I reflect. Sure, he's cute in a comic relief kind of way. Not your average macho type of guy. A bit on the short side, but it doesn't really matter to me. Later, I learn he's a sous-chef, not just a 'kitchen guy'.

Speaking of guys, I haven't had much luck in that department. Sure, back in the day, Westlife posters decorated my wall, and later the brooding members of My Chemical Romance. But real-life boyfriends? Zilch. It's not that guys never liked me, but their subtle signals always zoomed over my head. Or so I'd like to think.

The truth is most dudes I've known are just ... average. The kinds who live for the 9 to 5; date because they're supposed to, and lack any real fire or ambition. Bland. And me? I'm somewhere in between special and ordinary. I'm that person who won't be missed if absent from a party, yet won't cause any ripples if present. I often wonder: do people even notice me?

So, while I haven't found Mr Right or even Mr Alright, I'm fine on my own. There's a party for one, with just my music, romantic novels and tasty crisps. Haven't found a guy who gives me that 'butter flutter' feeling. Maybe, just maybe, my emotional compass is a bit off.

Sometimes, I wonder if there's something missing inside me. Or do you think maybe I'm just not looking hard enough?

10

Life on the cruise ship settles into a routine. I wake up, work, eat and sleep – rinse and repeat. Sometimes it feels like we are living in a floating bubble, disconnected from the world outside. The days blur together, and I find solace in simple pleasures like camaraderie with my fellow crew members.

I continue to interact with Oleksii, whose playful banter always gives me some reasons to smile. We talk about the most mundane things to the most absurd, and he has a knack for making me laugh even when the sea threatens to rock my stomach.

One evening at 11 pm, after a busy dinner service, I get very hungry. I haven't eaten anything. So, in the crew mess, I begin preparing a simple meal of melted cheese over bread cubes. As I wait for the cheese to melt in the oven, Oleksii approaches.

He looks tired, his eyes heavy with fatigue.

'Long day?' I ask, faux concern in my voice.

He nods, taking a sip of his own tea. 'Yeah, the kitchen was a madhouse today. How about you, Manis?'

I chuckle at his use of the Indonesian term. 'Manis' means sweet, and the first time he called me that I turned as red as a dragon fruit. It has become our little inside joke.

I tell him that I just witnessed a funny incident. An elderly lady at one of the tables was covertly filling a plastic bag with salt from the shaker. When I caught her in the act, she simply muttered 'I need salt', while her husband sitting beside her looked away in embarrassment. To spare their blushes further, I pretended not to see their peculiar salt-collecting operation. It's just salt, after all.

'It's a ritual,' says Oleksii.

'What is?'

'They throw salt into the sea for good luck or to repel a curse,' he says again.

'Huh? What's the point? The sea is where the salt comes from.'

Oleksii leans in closer, his voice lowered. 'You know, they say the sea air makes people do crazy things.'

I raise an eyebrow. 'Crazy things?'

He nods, a mischievous glint in his eye. 'Oh, you'd be surprised. Lonely hearts seeking adventure, forbidden romances in the moonlight, and secret rendezvous in hidden corners of the ship.'

I can't help but laugh. 'You watch too many movies, Oleksii.'

He winks. 'Maybe, but truth can be stranger than fiction, Manis.'

The microwave beeps, signalling that my meal is ready. I retrieve my hot bowl and sit down at the table, with Oleksii joining me. Other crew members in the mess are either watching TV or engrossed in their smartphones, similar to what Oleksii is doing now. While I blow on my hot bread cubes, he becomes preoccupied with his phone.

'Maybe she's busy,' I suggest, trying to console him. He looks a bit upset. He has told me about his girlfriend who recently gave him some distance.

'Busy with other men,' he continues, his expression sombre.

I'm not sure how to respond so I continue eating.

Oleksii then tells me about the challenges faced by seafarers and their relationships back on land. He explains that the long periods away from home often mess with their relationships.

'What do you mean? Like cheating? But not everyone does that,' I say.

He shrugs. 'True, but it's a reality we live with. When you're out at sea for a long time, sometimes the only comfort is found in the arms of another. The same goes for those we leave on land.'

'We're not controlled by our genitals,' I offer, trying to make a point. I mean that not everyone spends their time solely focused on sex; there are many other meaningful aspects of life that influence our decisions and actions.

'You're naïve. We are driven by the force! And here on the ship, it's the place with the strongest force!' Oleksii declares, his tone passionate.

'What force?' I ask.

'The horny force,' he replies with a grin.

'Bullshit,' I laugh.

'There's not much else to do here. Look around; it's a small ship with no entertainment for the crew.'

'That may be true. But, well, I'm not driven by the force. I'm here to work and earn money,' I explain.

'You're not driven by it yet. When boredom starts eating you, you'll see,' Oleksii predicts.

I laugh at his last statement and finish my meal quickly.

'I thought you were sad,' I say.

'Oh, I can be sad and horny at the same time!' he says.

I laugh some more.

'I'm off to bed,' I say, as I place my dirty bowl in the washer. 'May the force be with you,' I add before leaving.

'May the force find you soon,' Oleksii replies with a chuckle.

I ponder his words, realizing how complex life on the ship can be. And there's so much to understand, including myself. The force? Does it exist? And me, naïve? That's nonsense.

However, my night isn't over. As I walk back to my cabin, I encounter Kanompang, who is tiptoeing around nervously. I casually ask her where she's headed.

'Laundry room,' she replies, thrusting her laundry bag in my face. I'm curious why she smells so pleasant at almost midnight, but I don't have time to ask further. She hurries away as if trying to avoid being caught. What a strange girl.

Inside my cabin, Ida and Yanti are engaged in a rather uninspiring conversation about their past lives in the village. I undress and get into bed.

'Hey, guys, have you ever had sex?' I interrupt their conversation with a relaxed question.

Their response is immediate silence, as if my question is too frightening.

'Sis,' Ida finally says, gently reminding me that I'm broaching a very taboo subject.

'What?' I ask innocently.

Without saying another word, they close their curtains, like we're playing hide and seek. It's a very Indonesian response, shy-shy style.

As with dating, I've never given much thought to sex. Even though I'm already thirty, I've never engaged in sexual activities, not even kissing. I suppose I'm not ready, or perhaps I'm just too lazy to pursue it. What's more, according to my religion and my father's beliefs, it's a sin to have sex outside of marriage. My dad, he's quite a devout Muslim. He wanted me to pray five times a day and wear a hijab. I like my hair, so I explained to him that not wearing a headscarf doesn't make me a bad person or a sex maniac.

As the ship sails through the dark waters of the Baltic Sea, I drift off to sleep, my thoughts swirling like the waves outside.

11

We've been sailing around the Baltic waters for a few weeks

now, visiting northern European countries like Riga and Gdansk. Europe starts to feel pretty ordinary after a while, just places we pass by. Every thirteen days, passengers disembark and new ones come aboard. Some are cheerful, and some seem downright annoyed. Whenever Kanompang rakes in a lot of tips, she shines like freshly polished crystals. And when she doesn't, she starts pointing fingers at me for delivering lousy service at her station.

I've nearly memorized all the restaurant menus, so Utpal sometimes sends me to the bar to assist the bartenders. The bar work is more laid-back. I take drink orders and serve them with elegance, carefully avoiding spilling anything from those pesky martini glasses, which, by the way, I've spilled quite a lot. Besides the live music in the bar, I get to snag some of those delicious chocolate cookies meant for passengers. That's what makes it worthwhile.

The only downside is that when I'm assigned to the bar on Deck Four, it means longer hours. I only make it back to the cabin around midnight. But it's not such a big deal because it means passengers get to know me better, and that often translates to more tips. And who doesn't like money, right?

* * *

After my shift at the bar, I stand before the crew's notice board to check the 'port manning' schedule. If your name is on that list, it means you can't go ashore even when we're docked in a new country. You need to do the ship watchkeeping. No matter how envious you are of other crew members having a blast on land, you have to stay put. We need people onboard in case of an emergency.

Next to the port manning schedule, there's a sign that reads: 'Dispose of used condoms in the trash bin provided, don't throw them down the toilet!' At first, I thought it was a joke, but remembering what Oleksii said, I guess it's no joke at all. It means people on this ship are having sex, even though I haven't experienced it. Why else would they need such a sign, right? Those clogged toilets must be a recurring issue. Oleksii was right, I can be pretty naive.

Still pondering that, Kanompang suddenly walks by me, heading swiftly towards her cabin.

'Hey, where are you coming from?' I ask.

'Stop being nosy!' she snaps, her voice strained, and before I can enquire further, she vanishes behind her cabin door. What a strange girl (part two).

Afterwards, I simply do my usual routine. I enter my cabin, strip down and crawl into my top bunk. I'm too tired to bother with a shower or wash my face. It's nearly midnight and I'm utterly drained. The curtains on Ida and Yanti's beds are drawn, so they're probably already asleep.

Just as I'm about to drift off, I notice my bed rocking. At first, I think it's the usual sway of the ship – a gentle, soothing motion like a cradle. It's pleasant and helps me fall asleep. But tonight, the vibration persists, and it feels different – constant. I believe it's coming from Ida's bunk beneath mine. Could she be having a nightmare? I try to ignore it, but the shaking doesn't stop.

Concerned, I climb out of my bed and slide open the curtain

on Ida's bunk, intending to wake her. My intentions are pure – I'm genuinely worried she might be experiencing sleep paralysis or something. Who knows, there might be sea ghosts, right?

My mouth is halfway to uttering a casual 'hey' when it takes an unexpected detour and releases an involuntary shriek born of utter surprise. Ida does the same, squealing while scrambling to cover herself. And the man on top of her looks just as startled. Thankfully, he doesn't yelp; he just grunts.

12

A second after the incident, I immediately close the curtain. My heart skips a hundred beats as I climb back into my bed. The vibrations from Ida's bed stop at once, and I hear the cabin door open and close. The man must have left.

I can't get the picture out of my head. I've never seen humans having sex before, not as a live show right before my eyes. Sure, I've seen chickens do it, but they're poultry. Ida doesn't look anything like a bird! And the man on top of her … who the hell is he? God, I'm so confused about what to do. Should I apologize or something? I keep the curtain closed and wait for sleep.

In the morning I successfully avoid Ida, even though we share the same cabin, and hurry off to work. I don't know who should be more embarrassed. I suppose she should be, right?

In the crew mess, during lunch break, I sit in front of Kanompang, and my mouth, which is like a leaking bucket, immediately bursts out.

'Hey, imagine if you caught your roommate doing "ahem-ahem", what would you do?'

Kanompang immediately raises her eyebrows, then says, 'Well, since you're kind of clueless, it's not entirely your fault.'

'You mean?'

Without caring, Kanompang puts kaldolmar, a Swedish food made from cabbage, into her mouth. Then, with her mouth full, she adds, 'You know people close the curtains on their beds for privacy?'

'But it's a bunk bed! Her bed is beneath mine! My God, I could feel the shaking, my God. I thought there were high tidal waves. I was just checking on her because she's an innocent-looking girl. If I have a burning question about sex, she plays coy and avoids it. So I didn't expect to see what I saw last night. I mean, she refuses to talk about sex, but she's actually doing it?' I grab my own hair. 'Do you know what I'm talking about?'

Kanompang keeps chewing on the kaldolmar. I also like kaldolmar; it is minced meat and rice.

'Sure, I know things,' she replies.

'After all, what were they thinking about? Playing "riding a horse" on the lower bunk bed? I was above them. It's not just her room; it's mine too!'

Kanompang is still chewing her food.

'If she wanted to do "ahem-ahem", she should have told me first. I mean, I could have left the room before, I wouldn't have minded. I know it was her right to "ahem-ahem" as much and with whomever she wants, but I also have the right to be shocked and annoyed. A traumatic experience, you know?' I keep on talking to cover up my anxiety.

'What a motormouth. You've never had sex, huh?' Kanompang accuses instead.

'What? Of course ... of course, I have.'

Kanompang says the word 'sex' out loud, making me uncomfortable as people look our way.

'Bullshit,' she says. 'Your boobs haven't grown because they've never been touched.'

My face turns even redder and I get ready to leave. 'Talking to you is a waste of time.'

'You can try with Oleksii; he has a big crush on you,' she says.

'What? What are you talking about?'

She doesn't answer – too busy shoving kaldolmar into her annoying mouth.

I finally meet Ida in the cabin. Since I'm the older one, I think I should be the one to start the conversation. I am going to apologize for opening her curtains without permission.

'Sis,' she calls me in a low voice before I even have a chance to speak.

'Yeah?'

'Don't tell anyone, okay? About that thing.'

'Oh, okay,' I give her a thumbs-up. Crazy, doesn't she know that everyone already knows?

'Next time if you want to do that again, tell me first, okay?' I ask, but it comes out more like a demand.

'Y-yes,' she stammers.

'It's not a big deal; I mean, I'm from Jakarta. Something like that? I'm used to it. I'm not surprised. Everyone does it, right? It's nothing new, so take it easy. Don't be shy or nervous like that. I do it all the time too, believe me. I'm not such an innocent girl, you know? I'm quite experienced in this area. I'm really worse than you ... I don't mean you're bad. Anyway, I'm from Jakarta. You know how it is there, right? It's the city; it's wild.'

Oh my God, what the hell am I talking about? I just want to make her feel okay, to console her. I try to make myself sound terrible so she won't feel bad. I'm not sure if this method is healthy or not, but it seems to work. She immediately seems less embarrassed.

'Really?' she asks sincerely.

I wink at her just like Oleksii did to me. I know Ida is still feeling a little uneasy.

'So, who was that guy?' I ask discreetly, as if we are in a sisterhood.

Ida goes silent for three seconds before her mouth turns into a burst dam. She starts babbling incessantly about this man, someone from Serbia who works in the electrical department. To comfort her more, I even ask for details about their encounter and what his size is. And just like that, Ida spills everything, including the part where she shaved her pubic hair to make it look cleaner. I can't help but giggle with amusement, and my heart is pounding.

After she finishes her story and I run out of questions, I climb into my bed. And there, on the bleach-scented sheets, I begin thinking about sex. I guess I really should start considering it.

Damn it, Kanompang, do I really look like I'm still a virgin? I'm not a self-righteous girl. I kissed a boy before. In elementary school. When I lost in a marble game. Hey, that counts as a kiss! But since then I've never kissed anyone. I was just a really ordinary girl. I told you I never had a boyfriend. I spent my adolescence kissing the boys on my bedroom posters.

I've been so focused on myself, not aware of my surroundings, in a place where the sexual tension is very strong (to quote Oleksii). It feels like I've been blinkered. I know I shouldn't feel this way, but I can't help but feel a bit disturbed that I may succumb to peer pressure. It seems like everyone is doing it, even that 22-year-old Ida with a tall guy from Serbia! My God, am I finally addressing my adolescent insecurities?

13

'Ayde! Ayde! Don't block the road!' Utpal startles me.

Lately, Utpal has been even grumpier than usual. He shouts 'Ayde! Ayde!' or 'Babalu! Babalu!' at anyone who does the slightest thing wrong. He looks for reasons to scold me all the time. However, because I am getting better at my job and I keep receiving endorsements from the passengers – 'Oh, Maya is really fun', 'Maya is really cute', 'Maya is like my son' – it somehow leaves Utpal with fewer reasons to insult me. I guess basically he just likes to get angry, and if he can't find a target for his anger he gets cranky.

Anyway, you know I have been working on the ship for more than a month. Utpal hasn't given me an evaluation for my work yet, but I feel like I am starting to settle in. After a while my body aches less and I no longer cry before bed. My body is compromising. Even the grated parmesan is gone.

Tonight I find Kanompang acting very suspiciously. Well, she's always suspicious. But this time it's different. I see her hiding something at our station. And I know what it is.

'Where did you get this extra food?' I ask, while changing the table linens, referring to two servings of lamb shank with thyme gravy, tonight's special for passengers.

'Don't be noisy, you do piče!' she grumbles while turning her head toward the other waiters. It's clear that she doesn't want to share the food.

So, I threaten her that I will report her if I don't get my share. She glares at me.

'I'm courageous when I am hungry,' I add.

'You are also thirsty ... thirsty for sex,' she responds.

'What the heck!' Then it's my turn to look at the other waiters. 'Shut up!'

After cleaning up our station, Kanompang and I sneak into the crew mess, carrying big plates of lamb shank, covering them with napkins so the CCTV doesn't pick up what they are. We find a corner table and quickly start gobbling up the delicious mutton with mint jelly I stole from the jam cupboard. This is such a luxury. The crew doesn't get the same food as the passengers.

'Relax, no need to be so tense,' Kanompang says, licking her fingers when we are done.

'Somebody will see us, and we'll get into trouble.'

'No one will dare to touch me,' says Kanompang indifferently.

I frown. 'Who do you think you are?' Wasn't she the one who hid the food before?

'Where do you think I got this lamb shank from?' she asks.

I stutter. Of course, she got it from the kitchen. But who gave it to her? I don't have any idea.

'Hurry up and have sex so that your miserable life isn't so tense,' she adds.

'Why are you so interested in my sex life?' I ask.

'I can sense when someone is desperate for it,' she says and then stands up, leaving her dirty plate for me to clear.

After removing the evidence of our gourmet dinner, I take a walk down the hallways of the other crew's cabins. Usually, I go straight into my cabin and snore, but tonight, I feel a little adventurous.

In the hallways, I notice that some of the cabin doors are not completely closed. I peek in and see that the people inside are doing interesting things. In one cabin I see a group of European workers playing a guitar and singing their hearts out, with a bottle of liqueur amidst them. They invite me to join, but I politely refuse with a smile. Then I look into another cabin and find the kitchen staff from India watching a Hindi film, very loudly. Then I spot Kanompang tiptoeing over to the farthest corner cabin and disappearing into it. Curious about whose cabin Kanompang has gone into, I am about to try the door when Oleksii grabs me by my arm.

'Gotcha! You're caught,' he says with a grin.

'Shh!' I hush him immediately.

'What are you doing sneaking around like a thief?'

'Whose cabin is this?' I ask.

'Why do you want to know, Manis?' My heart flutters a bit when he says that, but I can't be distracted. He should stop calling me that; it's inappropriate. I take a quick look at the small sign on the door and see the name of the head chef emblazoned on it.

'No problem, I already know,' I say.

'What do you want with the German shepherd?' Oleksii calls his boss a dog. Maybe because he is mean?

'I want to ask something about tomorrow's dinner. I don't know if they're going to use béchamel or espagnole sauce.'

'Really? Aren't you just stalking your paisano?'

'Shut up. She's not my paisano; I'm from Indonesia.' Paisano means compatriots. I have not yet finished my speech when I have to clamp Oleksii's mouth shut and push him into his cabin because it seems like the door to the chef's cabin is opening.

I quickly close the door to Oleksii's cabin. I've never been in a male crew cabin before. It turns out the cabin also consists of two bunk beds. His cabin is a little messy but not dirty. The cabins can't be dirty because we have a weekly crew cabin inspection by the safety officer. If he finds a cabin is not to his liking in terms of cleanliness, we will be subjected to an annoying warning.

'Which is your bed?' I ask Oleksii in a very bossy tone.

Oleksii points to the bottom bed on the right with a crumpled blanket. I go straight to it and find an open laptop. Oleksii grabs the laptop and tries to close it.

'You've been watching porn, haven't you?'

Oleksii grins and giggles. He's not the type to be shy or to try too hard to hide things.

'Let me watch it too,' I say impulsively.

'Really?'

'Yes, I watch porn all the time,' I reply, lying through my teeth. What happened to me? I must be under the influence of lamb shank. In my defence, I'm just trying to be someone new. More relaxed, more fun and more sexual. Silently, I find myself wishing Oleksii would question me again, offering an: 'Are you sure?' – a chance for me to reconsider my hasty declaration, but no, Oleksii immediately reopens his laptop and presses the play button.

'Oh ah, oh ah' blares out from the laptop. I try not to look shocked. I've seen Ida do it, even if only for a fraction of a second. But truthfully, I have never seen anything like this. So many details – it's terrifying. I don't know why I feel so embarrassed to see it. I had never even watched my own genitalia so closely. Oleksii giggles. I can't stop myself from frowning and wanting to shut my eyes.

My heart feels like it's about to fall out when the cabin door opens and a man walks in.

'What are you guys watching?' the new arrival asks in a relaxed voice while settling his butt down beside me, and then he starts watching too. 'Oh, porn,' he continues matter-of-factly.

He doesn't sound too excited but he watches it anyway. The three of us sit on the bed in silence. Then the new guy looks at me all of a sudden, and there are ripples on his face.

'You're a girl,' he says, his surprise evident as he quickly moves his tall body away.

'No! I am a woman,' I reply, looking at him.

His green eyes blink rapidly. I blink too. Then, I raise both my eyebrows. Has he never seen a girl before or what? In such a shocking situation, I immediately seize the opportunity.

'Okay, I'll go, I'll leave you guys to it,' I say, trying to look cool as I stand up and then hastily exit the cabin. After closing the door, I let out a sigh of relief ... my God. What an adventure!

14

'I know where you go every night,' I whisper to Kanompang at breakfast service.

She smiles at one of the passengers and offers a simple good morning, completely blanking me.

'You take private cooking lessons every night with the head chef,' I say again, when I am sure none of the passengers is listening.

'So noisy, you do piče!'

'Aren't you afraid of getting caught?' She doesn't answer. 'Don't you feel guilty? He already has a wife. Don't you feel sinful?'

She sighs, then rolls her eyes in annoyance.

'If you feel good, it's not a sin.'

Ugh, this person, really.

***

Nothing of interest happens today except that every time I go to the kitchen, Oleksii tries to talk to me. He utters strange little sentences like, 'Let me know if you want anything to eat tonight.' Obviously he means food. After all, he works in the kitchen, and people have access to food in the kitchen. However, I can sense the innuendo. Oleksii is the kind of person who's able to say everything in a very sexual way. He is a degenerate.

I'm wondering if what Kanompang said about Oleksii is true, that he has a crush on me?

Oleksii. Hmm. He's a little short, but he has a very cute smile and undoubtedly has a good sense of humour. I think it may be okay to try it with him. By 'it' I mean sex.

You know that thing that Kanompang said? I've been mulling it over for several days. What if she's right? That I actually need this to unwind? I mean, I feel kind of peer-pressured (as I mentioned before). But isn't this pressure kind of stupid because I'm the only one pressuring myself? Kanompang put this idea in my head, but she's the God of wrong things. Her pressure is not important. The most excruciating pressure is when it comes from someone you actually care about. Other than that, I also realize that I'm no longer in Jakarta. I mean, hello, look at me now in international waters with international co-workers. Shouldn't I be leaving behind all those shy-shy values and terror that people will judge me if I'm feeling sexy? I mean, it's only sex, and everyone does it. This is the place where the sexual force is the strongest. I mean, I don't want to leave the ship the same girl who boarded it. I need to tweak my mentality a bit. Though I can't lose myself along the way too. I've weighed all that jazz for a week now and

I've come to the conclusion that I have to get laid. At least once. And Oleksii ... well ... he seems like an okay-ish candidate.

I don't want to get to know him too much because I don't want to invest any feelings. It's not that I don't want commitment or anything. I don't know if I want to. What I am going to do is just an activity. Nothing more than that. I just want to know the taste. And I think Oleksii is quite the right person. He has a cute butt, a pretty flat stomach, and his arms aren't too bad either. Okay, I do objectify him in my head. But so be it; all men do that to women. As a prelude to my transformation into an international woman, I conclude Oleksii is a good choice.

When dinner is over, I am (again) tasked with polishing hundreds of plates. Oleksii is not far from where I am; he is tidying up his cold galley.

'So, does the offer still stand?' I ask casually.

'Oh, sorry, it's expired. Now if you want something, you have to pay,' he says with a giggle.

'Never mind, then.'

He laughs. 'I'm kidding ... okay, what do you want to eat? I can't make anything complicated; everything's cleaned up. But I can improvise.'

I pretend to think for a moment. Then I say in almost a whisper: 'I want to eat something else.'

Oleksii goes silent for a moment.

What the hell am I thinking? Where will I put my face if he refuses? Of course he will refuse. He has a girlfriend that he contacts every night. Gosh, I must have been possessed by that demon named Kanompang.

'Okay.' Surprise still registers on his face.

He's agreed? I parrot an okay and my face is totally burning.

'I'll pick you up at eleven,' he says. 'Or do you want to sneak around like your paisano?'

'You just wait in your cabin,' I say with false bravado … and a tremble in my voice.

15

I finish my work quickly and return to the cabin to shower and get ready. Ida doesn't seem to be sleeping. She watches me dab some perfume on my neck.

'Sis, do you have a date?' she asks.

I nod.

'With a boy?'

I turn to her, my eyes narrowing flirtatiously, 'With Oleksii.'

Ida's eyes widen; she closes her mouth. I want to ask her if she's slept with Oleksii, but I don't really want to know the answer. I mean, it doesn't matter, it's none of my business. I remind myself: keep it casual, no emotions involved.

'Okay, I'll go now,' I say, as I exit the cabin.

'Good luck!'

I pretend I am going to the laundry room, which is located in this corner of the first deck, trying to act relaxed just as Kanompang did that one time. To ward off other people's suspicions, I simply wear a crumpled nightgown. My chest is throbbing uncomfortably when I stand in front of Oleksii's cabin, and I have acute second thoughts. Then I slap my conscience down, 'Don't be such a coward!'

I knock. In less than two seconds, the door opens. Okay, I am just going to tell him that I want to cancel this. The reason? Because I don't want to do it in his bed. Because there must be someone else sleeping in this cabin, right? It's not his private room. Duh. Of course I can't make passionate love while there's someone on the bed above. I remember what happened when Ida was having it off below me. I don't want anyone else to suffer like I did. That makes sense, no? Right, so, I will tell Oleksii that I want to cancel this event.

However, that doesn't happen. Oleksii immediately steps out of his cabin and leads me to the next-door one. He opens the door to the chef's cabin and pushes me in. Once we are inside, he locks the door.

I blink.

'What are we doing here?' I ask.

'I rented this place,' he replies with a sly smile.

Crazy!

***

The interior of the chef's cabin is surprisingly spacious and well furnished. Dark wooden walls adorned with framed art, plush carpets, and a larger bed than the standard crew cabins. It's evident that the head chef has certain privileges.

Oleksii's hands fumble behind me as he starts playing some mellow music from a nearby speaker. The warm lighting of the cabin creates an intimate ambiance, and for a moment the anxiety I felt earlier seems to dissolve.

I realize that Oleksii has taken this quite seriously; he seems as nervous as I am. Perhaps this isn't just a casual fling for him, or maybe it is and he's just really good at setting the mood. Either way, it makes me wonder about his intentions and feelings.

'You really went all out, didn't you?' I murmur, trying to lighten the mood.

He chuckles. 'I always believe that if you're going to do something, you might as well do it right.'

We both share an awkward laugh. There's a palpable tension in the room. Both of us are unsure of how to proceed.

'What if the chef finds out?' I ask, glancing around the luxurious cabin.

Oleksii smirks. 'Let's just say I have my ways. Besides, he owes me a few favours.'

My nerves creep back in, and the horror of the situation becomes all too real. I take a deep breath, reminding myself of the reasons I made this decision: wanting to experience something new, breaking out of my comfort zone, and embracing this new phase of life.

Oleksii steps closer. He takes my arm and then invites me to sit on the bed. I imagine Oleksii will push me back onto the bed and try to have his way with me. However, he is remarkably restrained as all we do for the next three minutes is sit side by side and hold hands like two schoolkids.

'Do you want to watch something?' I ask, looking for the television remote.

Oleksii shakes his head. 'We don't have much time.'

'What?'

'I'm only renting this place for two hours.'

I feel like stuttering with my eyes. Then Oleksii grows bolder and he kisses me on the cheek, which makes me flinch because it comes as a shock to me.

It's completely wrong. It's wrong times a hundred times over. Oh, Maya, you weak, lousy, stupid girl. I don't really want to do it, but I don't know how to stop it. It's like slipping off a steep snowy ridge.

Oleksii, still holding my hand, directs it to his crotch. I am deathly silent but my chest is pounding like a war drum. O-Em-Gee, what is he doing? To be precise, what the hell am I doing? I pull my hand away and slink back like a frightened cat.

'Oleksii,' I squeak.

'I know,' he says.

'What do you know?'

'I know you've never done it.'

To me, he sounds half teasing.

'I've done it before!' I argue.

Oleksii grins. 'You look nervous.'

'I'm nervous because I've never done it with a Caucasian.' I try to calm myself by lying. Good job, Maya.

'Really? Are you nervous because of that?'

'Yes, of course.' I try to convince myself.

'Why?'

'You know, don't you? White men, they ... have ... that bigger stuff.'

Oleksii's face immediately turns smiley.

'You've never seen a European one?'

I shake my head quickly.

'Do you want to see one?'

However, Oleksii doesn't wait for my confirmation. He stands up and unbuckles his belt. And what I see next is him pulling his pants down and his penis hanging in front of my face like a bell. As an innocent girl who has never ever seen a penis in person before, my reaction should be to close my eyes and scream. However, what I do is just the opposite. I watch the penis carefully. He's uncircumcised, and his pubes, like his hair, are blonde. The penis looks soft and pursed. Maybe because it's still sleeping.

Then Oleksii shakes it in front of me.

'Wiggle-wiggle-wiggle,' he says.

I cover my mouth, trying my best not to laugh.

Soon the penis swells, and then it stands upright like the Eiffel Tower.

'Do you like it?' he asks.

I look up and see the expression on Oleksii's face: a very mischievous grin. I don't know how to answer. Do I like it? I don't know.

'Perfect size for you?' he asks again.

I don't know if it's the perfect size for me. It's my first time seeing one in person. I don't know what to compare it to. Baked eggplant parmigiana? I shrug my shoulders. I mean, I have no idea. Or I am confused. However, Oleksii misunderstands it.

He thinks I am expressing something like: 'Meh, it's like a baby carrot.'

'You have to hold it, it'll feel bigger.'

'What?'

'Just hold it, don't be embarrassed.'

'Hold it?'

Oleksii thrusts his hips forward slightly, aiming his missile. It is intimidating and scary. I move away again. Oleksii then sits down. The penis is still standing to attention.

'Just dip your toe in even if you're afraid of swimming. Dip and start. If you don't dip, you will never be able to do it,' he says.

'You mean it's like swimming?'

'Yes, it might feel shocking at first but soon you'll be diving in for more. I know you're scared.'

That's an acceptable analogy for my tiny shrimp brain. If what Oleksii means by 'dipping my toe in' is equal to holding his penis, well, maybe I can do it.

So, in my toe dips. I hold it. Grab it, more precisely. It feels warm, and it throbs. And Oleksii is right. It's bigger when held.

'Stroke it.'

'Wait, what?'

'Stroke it!'

'How?'

'Here ...' He moves my hand.

I stroke it about ten times before Oleksii starts to groan, and I immediately yank my arm back.

'I have to go.' I jump up and run straight for the door.

Making my way back to my cabin is not easy on my unsteady

feet. I don't know what I'm feeling right now. Everything is so mixed up. All I know is I hold my chest and whisper to myself:

'I'm no longer a little girl.'

* * *

Back in my cabin, I feel confused and supercharged at the same time. Ida refrains from asking what has happened, but it is clear from her face that she is very curious. I look at my reflection in the bathroom mirror. My face is bright red, and it feels like I have come more alive. I hold my cheeks (Gordon Ramsay 'idiot sandwich' style), then remember my palms have held something earlier. Ew, I hastily wash them with soap. I then take a shower. And it gives Ida the wrong message. She sees me drying my hair, and her mouth is already foaming with questions. However, I don't want to give her any information. So, I just wink at her twice. Then I climb into bed.

I think of the totem. The almighty penis. I've touched it, squeezed it, stroked it, felt it throb in the palm of my hand. And this makes me feel ... feel like I have become a complete person. Is this the achievement I have been looking for? Is it a sign that I have become optimal? I feel a bubbling energy. I don't know what this energy is. Does this mean I have treated my penis envy? Maybe I should ask Sigmund Freud about that. Yes, there's definitely something wrong with me if touching a man's genitalia can be categorized as an accomplishment!

But before finally falling asleep, I smile. I just dipped my toe in. I am making changes.

16

However, the next day is a complete disaster. Kanompang clears her throat over and over every time she sees me. At first, I don't understand what it means. Then, when I go into the kitchen to put the dirty dishes in the dishwasher, I see the head of the kitchen wandering through the hot galley and shouting: 'Chakabumba!' He repeats it many times. I frown then return to the busy restaurant.

'You look radiant,' says Kanompang.

'Not at all, I didn't even shower,' I reply.

'Oh, but you look glowing.'

'What do you want?' I become suspicious. She's never had any positive comments for me, so this is very strange.

'Nothing.' Kanompang shrugs her shoulders nonchalantly. Then drifts away mumbling something like: 'Probably dissatisfied.'

I grab Kanompang's hair and walk her to the back of our station to hide from Utpal, but I let some passengers witness us.

'Ow, what the hell?' She fixes her hair.

'What's with you? What did you say? What did you mean "dissatisfied"?'

Kanompang looks up at the ceiling. 'Didn't you just "chiki-chiki" last night?'

'What's that?' I frown.

'Chiki-chiki with Oleksii.'

My eyes burst open. 'What?! I did not chiki-chiki with

Oleksii, whatever that means!'

'Okay, whatever you say ...' She is about to walk off, so I quickly stop her.

'How do you know all this?'

'What do I know?' Kanompang puts on an innocent look. 'You said you didn't chiki-chiki.'

'I did not!'

'So, what happened between you and Oleksii last night?'

'Nothing!'

Kanompang flashes a devilish smile, then feigns picking up the dirty dishes from table two. I rush to the dishwasher, venting my frustration on the pile of dirty cutlery I've gathered. The atmosphere in the kitchen feels tense. Maybe it's all in my head, but I sense that everyone's eyes are on me. I catch fleeting glances from the pot-washer and the guys in the hot galley. From the pastry kitchen I can faintly hear the chef's repeated shouts of 'chakabumba!' Through all this, Oleksii remains conspicuously absent. Damn that guy.

Back in the restaurant I catch Nina's insincere smile as she serves the passengers at her station.

'Nina, what does chakabumba mean?' I whisper. She waits until she's done flashing her smile to the guests.

'Who told you about that?'

'Doesn't matter,' I reply, pretending to hand her extra napkins as a pretext to linger at her station.

'It means having sex.'

'Ugh,' I mutter, my face flushing.

She smirks. 'Did you chakabumba last night?'

'No!' I nearly yell.

'Wow, take it easy ...' she responds, eyes wide.

Mumbling an apology, I quickly walk away.

This is fast becoming my worst day onboard ship. Every trip to the dishwashing area or the cold and hot galley is marked by the infuriating chant of chakabumba! And even if the chef's crew haven't joined in, their small, judgmental smirks don't escape my notice. I swear, when I find Oleksii, he's going to wish he was never born.

* * *

In the afternoon, I corner Oleksii when I'm certain there is no one around. He doesn't look as cute as usual, well aware of what is coming when I glare at him, smoke metaphorically billowing from my ears.

'I didn't tell anyone,' he explains, without me even asking.

'Bullshit.'

'I swear to the Gods of the sea, if I did, our ship will be battered by a storm.'

'Don't say such things! Then, how did the chef find out about this? We didn't do anything!' I stomp my foot in frustration.

'Yeah, I didn't say anything to him, but I rented the cabin.'

'Ugh!' I pulled my hair in frustration. Stupidly I hadn't considered that. I really should have cancelled it yesterday. I want to scold Oleksii, but I don't want to be rude. I just growl and storm off.

Damn it! It is because I wanted to find something different in my life that I've become the subject of gossip. What should I do next? I feel like I want to curl up and disappear.

***

And within hours there is a storm. Our ship pitches back and forth, preventing passengers from leaving their cabins for dinner in the restaurant. Consequently, we have to handle a lot of room service. Whenever I cross paths with Oleksii, I shoot him an accusing glare. This storm is all thanks to him and his big mouth. I won't trust him anymore, and maybe I won't trust men in general. They're all gossips.

17

The next three days officially become my worst days on the ship. The confined spaces start to feel suffocating, and I feel trapped because there's no escape. Every time I go to the crew mess, it seems like everyone is watching me, possibly thinking, 'That's the chakabumba girl.' I want to scream, 'I DIDN'T CHAKABUMBA WITH OLEKSII! NOTHING HAPPENED!' but I manage to restrain myself. Perhaps I should post a notice on the crew's announcement board to set the record straight?

'Why are you so bothered?' Kanompang asks on embarkation day.

Embarkation day involves the departure of previous

passengers and the arrival of new ones. We greet them at the reception desk and take turns escorting them to their cabins, often carrying their expensive handbags.

I clench my teeth. I feel like quitting this job. It's too embarrassing. If my mother found out, she'd probably disown me (in a frequency only dolphins can hear).

'How can I not be anxious? Everyone is talking behind my back!' I reply.

'Don't flatter yourself. No one is talking about you,' Kanompang reassures me.

'Your boyfriend won't stop shouting "chakabumba" all the time. How can I not lose my mind?'

'Don't mind him. He's just having fun.'

'You need to distract him with your melon tits to keep him quiet!' I exclaim, frustrated. Kanompang bursts into laughter. She then escorts a limping old man to Deck Five, while I accompany a cheerful couple from Idaho. They look adorable together, and I show them how to use the toilet and the in-room safe for storing diamonds and other valuables.

'Oh, we don't need that, dear. We've spent all our savings on this cruise,' the wife says, laughing. I burst into giggles, thoroughly amused. Oh my God, if Kanompang knew this, she wouldn't want to serve these passengers. Their money was spent on the fare, which means no tips.

During my second round of escorting, I bring two glamorous-looking female guests to their cabin. One of them has short silver hair, similar to mine, while the other is on the voluptuous side with thick hair reminiscent of Farah Fawcett during her *Charlie's*

Angels days. You wouldn't guess they were both in their fifties.

I compliment them on how cool they look as I guide them to their cabin on Deck Four. Along the way, I explain the location of the restaurant and the bar, and inform them about the upcoming safety drill.

'You're a sweetheart. What's your name?' Farah Fawcett asks, lowering her glasses slightly.

'Maya,' I reply, showing my name tag. 'Where are you guys from?'

'California.'

'Wow, Hollywood! That's why you look like superstars.'

They blush and giggle.

'Actually, I have some Asian blood. You can't really see it, huh?' the plump Farah Fawcett asks.

Actually I could see it, and her hair wasn't really blonde, of course, but I didn't want to be too candid.

'Really? I can't believe it!' I end the compliment with a small laugh. 'If we meet again at the restaurant, I'll be your server.'

'Oh, wonderful! Which station are you?'

'Station Two. On the corner.'

'Great! See you there!'

I don't know if they mean it, but I respond with a cheerful: 'Yay!'

I meet Kanompang again in front of the reception desk, and she immediately whispers to me, 'I've told the passengers I escorted to sit at our station.' The idea is to be friendly and encourage them to tip.

'I can't stand this feeling. I feel like I'm about to explode,' I say, wanting to mess up my hair.

'Why? Because you want to chiki-chiki again with Oleksii?' Kanompang teases.

'Stop talking about that chiki-chiki nonsense! I didn't chiki-chiki at all. I just held his penis!'

Kanompang's eyes widen in surprise. 'Oh ... big? You liked it?'

'That's not the point, you witch!'

'I don't get why you're so upset. If you felt good, you shouldn't feel guilty. Sex is natural, everyone does it. And trust me, everyone will soon move on.'

'Everyone? You said no one knew!'

She lets out an 'oops' and then quickly grabs an incoming passenger to escort.

18

I ignore Oleksii on this new cruise. I don't even want to look him in the eye. It makes me furious that he doesn't seem like he wants to apologize, which I think he should, for reasons not entirely clear to me. Maybe I am just a maniac for forgiveness. I want him to feel guilty about what happened. He does call me 'Manis' a few times when I go to the cold galley to get some soup, but what's that? That's not an apology. He finally stops doing that after I ignore him. Can't he read my mind? It's just an apology, what's so hard about that? Honestly, on the one hand, I regret what happened with Oleksii, but on the other hand, I can't help but be amused when I think about it.

The itinerary for this cruise is slightly different. We sail around Spain for a while, then stop at Dover in England. I don't have time to get down at those places, but I enjoy the journey because the guests are funny. Especially Farah Fawcett and the glamorous pixie-haired woman. They never miss the chance to sit at my station and share some banter with me.

On a Spanish-themed night, I get an assignment at the bar to take after-dinner drinks orders. Even though the extra work keeps me there until midnight, I'm happy because sometimes I can get extra tips from semi-drunk passengers. Tonight Farah Fawcett, who is mostly downing margaritas, laughs as she approaches me. 'This is my favourite waitress!' she shouts. Then she asks me to dance with her while the musicians play a tango.

'Uh, I can't dance!'

I mean not only am I working but I genuinely can't dance.

'I'll take the lead,' she says, as she snatches the tray from my hand and throws it onto the bar counter. She grabs my hips and motions me to move. I've never danced before.

'You are amazing,' she says, as I trample her feet.

* * *

Something funny happens on the afternoon we anchor in St Antonia, Spain. Ida runs in to the restaurant like a madwoman, her face as pale as toilet paper. She finds me deep in a bag of dirty napkins I've been collecting.

'Help,' she whispers frantically. She's never run to the restaurant before so it must be important. 'There's something,' she says, tugging at my uniform. She's almost crying now.

'What? Come, show me.'

She pulls me with her up to Deck Three. With her master key she opens one of the cabins. All the passengers are out for a city tour. I don't know why Ida is so worried, the room looks just fine to me. I mean, I don't actually know the ins and outs of housekeeping, so I don't know what is unusual. She hastily locks the door behind us and, when she is sure we are safe, she pulls the blanket down the bed. I see a purple object vibrating and squirming on it. My jaw hits the floor.

'Oh my God!' I gasp for air. 'Where did you find that?' I ask, pointing to the generously sized purple dildo dancing on the bed. When I turn, Ida is shaking with fear. Her vibrations are as strong as that of the dildo.

'I was just curious,' she replies.

'What did you do?'

'I just pushed the button on the bottom.'

I timidly pick up the dildo and feel it vibrating in my hand. I've never held a dildo before. It's both disgusting and fascinating. I look for an off button but can't find one. The only button is to activate it and I have pressed that many times.

'I'm toast …' Ida is really scared. She probably thinks that because I'm from Jakarta I know about sex toys and such.

'Where did you find it?' I repeat the question, trying not to panic. She points to the drawer on the nightstand. When I put the dildo back in the drawer, the whole thing rattles. Damn, not a good idea. Why is it vibrating so violently? And which bored, rich granny is staying in this cabin anyway? Okay, this is not the time to judge.

I take the dildo back out of the drawer then hold it tightly ... just because. I don't know why I do that. My whole arm vibrates. I throw the dildo back on the bed.

Then Ida grabs the vacuum cleaner nozzle and steps forward.

'What are you gonna do?' I snap.

'Beat it to death,' she replies.

'You think it's a fish?!'

She freezes.

'Let's just wait until the battery runs out,' I decide.

I don't know when the battery will run out. I literally have no idea. I am just saying it out of desperation. Ida and I wait, standing by the edge of the bed holding hands and praying. I can hear her murmuring some mantra non-stop. She must be terrified of being fired. I restrain myself from asking her why she was being so nosy in the first place. Because if I were in her position, I would probably have done the same.

We watch the purple dildo continue to writhe and squirm. And after ten very, very disquieting minutes, the artificial totem is finally at peace. I breathe a sigh of relief, and Ida cries with joy.

'Quickly, put it back where it belongs, and don't press any more buttons,' I say in a shaky voice. After the thing goes into the drawer, Ida and I look at each other and we both burst out laughing. I suddenly realise whose cabin it is.

After that incident, I never look at Farah Fawcett in the same way again.

***

I find myself working in the bar again. The party isn't so crowded, so I have the chance to steal some cookies and devour them quietly in the pantry. At some point, Linda Nor, the woman I know as Farah Fawcett, approaches me and whispers: 'How are you, kitty?' She is obviously drunk. Her breath reeks of alcohol and her face is flushed red.

'Just fine, Mrs Purple Dildo,' I reply.

Of course, I don't say that. I just smile sweetly like a kitten.

'I need more drinks because I'm so pissed.' Then Linda shares her frustration with her boyfriend in England, who has accused her of having an affair on the ship. 'He thinks I'm a maniac.' Linda Nor rambles on endlessly about this and that, including how she doesn't really like men from her country. 'I like tall, smart and adventurous men,' she says. 'My boyfriend lives in London. I fell in love with his accent. He's got a ton of tattoos too, and even though he's in his fifties, the sex is really great. But his job is so boring – he owns a bar.'

As a good waitress, I listen to her story with great empathy and respond with many 'ohs' and nods. Guests love to be heard.

'Oh gosh, I talk too much,' she says before collapsing onto me.

The bald bartender who is on duty tonight comes up to me. 'I have many customers; take her to her cabin, Number 322.'

I want to refuse, but he's not listening. So, it is with a heavy heart and great dexterity that I manhandle Linda to the elevator, then drag her along the corridor. She doesn't wake up even though

I accidentally bump her body here and there. Using her own key, I open the cabin door. I drop drunk Linda Nor on the bed just like I threw her purple dildo on it earlier in the afternoon. But instead of sleeping, she wakes up and her eyes widen. Maybe she is just pretending to be drunk so she didn't have to walk to her cabin.

'Wait, don't go yet,' she says, staggering to the nightstand. She looks around and slurs, 'Damn it … someone broke my dildo.'

I am immediately nervous. Maybe she knows Ida and I are the culprits. Maybe she wants to scold me. Just as I picture myself getting fired, Linda reaches towards me and hands me a banknote.

'Take it, take it, don't be shy.' She forces it on me.

I take it and thank her. I close the cabin door and make a hasty retreat before she notices that her rubber totem has my fingerprints all over it. And when I check the money, I am shocked. She gave me a one-dollar bill.

19

More than a thousand passengers have come and gone. I can't believe it's already my third month here. I no longer think things are so bad. Apart from the incident with Oleksii, which was both sickening and embarrassing, Kanompang's prophecy turns out to be accurate. Gossip is fleeting, and soon another scandal breaks out, pushing my chakabumba incident into the background. After all, it isn't really a scandal considering that I am single and Oleksii isn't married. Unlike Kanompang who got into a heated altercation with the head chef and ended up crying on the open deck to the point where the hotel manager had to intervene.

The chef has accused Kanompang of trying to sabotage his family, suspecting her of revealing their affair to his wife to instigate a divorce, allowing him to be exclusively with Kanompang.

Kanompang swears she's never contacted his wife. Yet their heated exchanges continue. I merely observe from behind the buffet table, pretending to clean the condiment bowls, silently enjoying the drama.

Kanompang has now refrained from talking to anyone for several days. She serves guests robot-like, without even the semblance of a smile. Her demeanour concerns me, but not because I am worried about her mental well-being. Rather, I'm concerned that her sour attitude will deter guests from tipping us. How self-centred of me, I know.

Moreover, there's a doctor on board rumoured to be spending her nights in the captain's quarters. With all these intense scandals erupting, my fleeting affair with Oleksii has quickly become yesterday's news.

As for Linda Nor, beyond her infamous purple dildo, she seems to be quite an intriguing individual. Although I've only known her for two weeks, we share a unique bond. Occasionally, she approaches me to share details about her day, concerns about her appearance or to voice her opinions of other passengers. 'We were walking outside, and my skirt was fluttering. Do you think my thighs are too big? There's that guy from Room 503 who keeps winking at me. Isn't he ashamed of the wrinkles on his skin? Can you check out my ass? These pants suit me, right? See the colour of this lipstick light up; I love being daring.' Listening to her is enjoyable. Linda possesses a free spirit. Despite being 50, she has that youthful energy. She remains unmarried, frequently switching boyfriends at her whim. In many ways, I view her as the epitome of cool, and perhaps, subconsciously, I think of her as my role model.

After a day docked in Porto, Portugal, we set sail for Lisbon, where this cruise journey concludes. As I anticipated, Kanompang doesn't receive many tips this trip. However, guests approach me, discreetly handing me five- and ten-dollar bills, as well as euros and pounds, whispering their gratitude. 'Thank you for taking care of us,' they say, ensuring Kanompang, who seems perpetually under a raincloud, doesn't overhear.

'This is for you,' Linda Nor murmurs, slipping something into my pocket. 'I've written down my email address. If you find some free time, drop me a message, okay?'

I nod in eager agreement. Once all the guests have departed, I retreat to my cabin to count my tips. Linda generously gave me twenty dollars in small change.

20

I won't go into detail about how I got through the last two months because it's quite boring, and you might stop reading this. All I have done is serve passengers day and night as we sail through Europe. However, at the end of each month, I feel ecstatic to find my bank account has grown with various currencies. Passengers come and go, blessing us with endless entertaining stories. I've had my share of experiences too, like watching one guest throw up on a table and hearing another nervously exclaim they've forgotten to wear their diapers and request to be taken to the nearest toilet.

I've been working here for more than four months now, and the only change I've noticed is that I'm getting thinner. My weight keeps dropping due to lack of sleep, and perhaps my body is silently feeling tired. What worries me isn't that people might think I'm anorexic, but rather the size of my chest, which seems to have shrunk like pancakes. It's not that I want to have big breasts like Pamela Anderson, just normal ones. Oh my God, why do I have such thoughts? I seem to be losing my mind, probably because I hang out too much with Kanompang, the melon-breasted woman.

After the incident with Oleksii, nothing special has happened in my life. You might think that after such a ruckus I would have turned into a wayward woman thirsting for male genitalia and hunting incessantly for these ancient artifacts, but no, that hasn't happened to me. My life has simply returned to normal. Oh, I once held a penis, that's an experience, okay, so what? My life is empty again, but not entirely meaningless.

Working on a cruise ship with crew from different nationalities is much different from working on land. We're basically stuck here, forced to gather in the same bowl and tolerate each other. On land, you could easily take a different route if you didn't want to bump into a co-worker you disliked. You could choose a different restaurant for lunch, for example. That's not possible on the ship.

We can't even choose who we want to be friends with. We literally live together twenty-four hours a day, every day of the year. And I'm stuck with Kanompang, who is now permanently on edge.

She's a mess, having broken up with the chef. Her eating habits are out of control (we often hide extra food from the buffet, even stealing jams to snack on in the cabin), and she flirts with everyone, seemingly intent on getting the chef's attention, but it only makes her look cheap. Worst of all, when she gains weight, as seen from her slight belly, she cries incessantly in her cabin.

After four months, we dock once again in Lisbon, Portugal. The last passenger is unloaded, and we won't be carrying passengers for four weeks now because the ship needs to be inspected and repaired, a process called 'dry dock'. I don't know what to do during dry dock. From what I hear, the crew complains about it because we won't receive any tip money from passengers for the next four weeks. However, I think it will be fun because the restaurant crew can finally take a break. No passengers means no restaurant, which means no service.

Unfortunately, that's not the case.

Utpal gathers us round for our 'dry dock assignment'. I was hoping for four weeks of holiday, but that's just wishful thinking. Which company would want to keep paying its workers to relax?

Two waiters are sent to help on the deck, doing tasks like repainting the ironwork and mopping the wooden floors. Two others are sent to help in the kitchen (My cabinmate Nina will get to peel potatoes.) Kanompang is assigned to help at the reception because she looks gloomy, so she's not given a heavy job. As for me, since I have a BST (Basic Safety Training) certificate, Utpal sends me to meet the safety officer to become a 'fire patrol'.

'I don't know what to do,' I tell the tall and handsome safety officer who's been waiting for me. Utpal has informed him that he will send someone from the restaurant to help.

'You can use a fire extinguisher, right?' he asks.

'Yes, I can. I can even use that long hose.'

'Oh, there's no need for that. If there's a big fire, you just need to contact me via the HT. Can you use an HT?'

'No,' I reply.

'Why did Utpal send you?' he says. 'You're so small.'

From the way he looks at me, I suspect he's checking to see if I'm a man or a woman.

'Don't underestimate me. I'm very strong,' I respond defensively.

The safety officer barely suppresses a laugh before explaining what a fire patrol must do for the next four weeks. 'The main point is, if someone is doing hot work you should be there to watch them. However, usually, no one works at night, so you can sleep during that shift.'

Hot work. What does hot work even mean? Maybe it means that if I find someone making love, I have to spray them with a fire extinguisher? Ha ha. That would be fun, but of course it isn't.

21

You won't believe what hot work is! During the dry dock process, various parts of the ship are inspected and repaired. Vendors replace things like carpets, ceilings, doors, hinges and more, including stripping and repainting surfaces. So-called 'supervising the hot job' involves watching the people from the construction company cut, join, weld and grind metal parts. Sparks scatter, and the smoke can trigger the alarm. My duty is to keep an eye on this. The work is hot and smoky, and I feel like a steamed rice cake!

'Fire patrol ... fire patrol ... chief officer.'

'Chief officer, go ahead.'

'Check hot job Deck Three aft, starboard side.'

'Aye aye, sir, okie dokie.'

This means I have to go to Deck Three at the rear of the ship, on the right side. The job is actually quite interesting. I feel like an FBI agent inspecting bombs, except when a fire starts blazing and smoke fills the air, I panic about whether I should start spraying everything with a fire extinguisher.

I use the fire extinguisher once when a fire does start to devour the paper on the wall, causing construction workers from Lisbon to shout at me in Portuguese.

'You don't want this ship to explode!' I say with a pounding heart as they continue to babble in a language I don't understand (me spraying the extinguisher until it runs out – a very fun thing to do).

Wearing oversized coveralls, an old safety helmet and a disposable face mask to prevent coughing, I wander around the ship to monitor ongoing hot work. It can be a tad boring if nothing unusual happens, and I find myself sitting and watching the sparks which start to hypnotize me. However, I think it's still better than the other waiters' new assignments.

My night patrol shift lasts from midnight to four in the morning. Just as the safety officer mentioned, it's very quiet. I only need to check the laundry room once every hour, and I can sleep on a couch for the rest of the time. Inspecting the laundry room on Deck One takes about five minutes, just to check for smoke or sparks from the engine if they become too hot. That's all. Even though I have plenty of down time, I'm reluctant to sleep; I can't relax when I feel like I'm working. Plus, curiosity gets the best of me, and I have the authority to explore the ship.

Other than the restaurant, crew mess, cabins and bars, I'm not very familiar with the ins and outs of the ship. Armed with a small flashlight, I begin to explore, pretending to look for fire spots when I'm actually just curious. I start by checking the hot, noisy engine room, then I sit in the passengers' library, a surprisingly cool place, to check out the DVD collection and I even try to play the grand piano in the lounge. I also visit Decks Six and Seven, discovering a Jacuzzi for VIP guests on Deck Six and Zodiac RIBs on the top deck. The ship has never been this quiet. On a normal day, it is bustling with people around the clock. Today it feels like a dead ship moored in Lisbon.

Few people work at night. It's just me, the fire patrol, one person in the gangway who checks people going in and out of the ship's door, and a deck cadet attending the bridge in the control and steering room. Other crew members finish work at six in the evening and usually spend their free time in Lisbon, gambling in casinos, shopping at the mall, visiting cafés or even going to brothels. I don't have that chance because of my midnight patrol.

'It's a shame you're on fire patrol like this; you can't hang out with us,' Kanompang says as she prepares to go shopping at the mall.

Often, I just sit at the stern, feeling the icy gusts of wind on my face while gazing at the night lights in Lisbon, or I stare out into the dark sea where jellyfish the size of buckets float close to the surface. Tonight, however, I decide to go to the bow.

'What's this?' I whisper to myself when I see something like a large round compass mounted on the rim of the ship.

'It's a gyroscope,' someone answers from behind me.

I squeal and turn around, then pat myself on the chest.

'Sorry, did I startle you?' he asks.

'You think?' I reply sarcastically.

We fall silent. He looks at my outfit, the thick windproof jacket, helmet and small flashlight.

'Are you the fire patrol?' he asks.

'What do you think? Am I a thief?' I respond rhetorically.

He doesn't smile, just extends his hand. Oh, he wants to get acquainted. I shake it hesitantly.

'Maya,' I say.

'Maroje,' he replies. His voice is deep, and he's so tall while I'm like a little pea. Actually, I know him; he's the one I watched porn with in Oleksii's cabin. I hope he doesn't recognize me, although that's unlikely. Since the incident with Oleksii, it seems like everyone knows me. Even though they've never said hello, I can feel them stealing glances and whispering, 'That's the girl who chakabumba with Oleksii and watched porn in the cabin with two guys.' You have no idea how hard the last months have been for me mentally. But of course, I've come to terms with it. I'm a strong international woman. It's just sex, which doesn't matter at all. So, I shouldn't have low self-esteem because of it. Why am I even thinking about all this when I should be chatting with Maroje? Stupid.

'Nice to meet you,' I say casually.

He nods without saying a word.

'What are you doing?' I ask. 'It's late.'

'I'm on duty, in the control room.'

'Oh, you're a deck cadet.' I should be reporting to him.

He nods again.

'Don't worry, there's no fire at all, I've checked. That's why I can walk around like this,' I mutter defensively.

'There's no need to worry. I trust you.'

My face immediately turns red. What he said is actually a normal thing, but it embarrasses me for some reason. 'Okay, I have to stroll around this ship. I mean patrol,' I say too quickly. He nods, and then I flee.

22

After I've checked out the laundry room and played 'Twinkle-Twinkle Little Star' on the grand piano by the bar, I circle the boat on patrol and decide to head to the bow again just like yesterday. Only this time, I am the one who finds Maroje first. He is standing with his hands in his pockets like a solid wall, looking out at the ocean, lost in deep philosophical thoughts.

'Anything interesting?' I ask.

Maroje turns around. Unlike me, he doesn't startle. 'Only water,' he replies.

I lean against the guardrail and look down. 'There's a lot of water,' I say, then continue, 'if you stare too long into the abyss, then it stares back at you.' I try to quote Nietzsche and sound deep. Unfortunately, Maroje does not respond at all. He seems distant.

'Do you want to jump?' I ask casually.

'No, it must be very cold.'

'Indeed,' I say, tightening my jacket. Lisbon in November is not somewhere you want to go if you're looking for warmth. 'Have you always liked the sea?' I continue.

Maroje shakes his head. 'Everyone I know is a sailor; I don't know anything else. I've heard about the ocean since I was little.'

'You can find out for yourself if you want to know something else,' I suggest.

'Maybe. But I'm used to this …'

We just stand there for two minutes watching the small waves crashing against the hull. The Lisbon wind pierces my skin.

'Where do you come from?' I ask, trying to continue the conversation.

'Dubrovnik, Croatia.'

After letting out an 'oh' I pause for a second. I don't know where it is. I honestly don't know much about other countries. It is only after working on this ship that I know such places exist. I need to stop spinning in my own shoes.

'What's on your mind?' Maroje asks, probably because he sees me mumbling.

'Huh?' I turn to him, then blink my eyes several times like a puppy. Finally, he's had the initiative to ask a question. 'Oh, that, yes, I was imagining how Dubrovnik would be,' I answer dishonestly.

Maroje seems interested. He starts to look at my face with a different expression. I think he is attracted to me! Oh, crazy, how can that be? I mean, I don't understand if someone is attracted to me or not. What are the signs?

'Have you ever watched *Game of Thrones*?' he asks again.

I shake my head. What is *Game of Thrones*? I don't want to ask because I don't want to look stupid.

'Some of the scenes were shot there,' he explains.

I 'oh'ed again, then nod. I take my phone out of my jacket pocket, pretending to be busy replying to some chats, then quietly type 'Dubrovnik' and 'Game of Thrones' into Google. Okay, it turns out to be kingdoms and castles.

'Are you a prince?' I blurt out, trying to joke.

'Why do you ask such a thing?' he is surprised.

'Because there are many castles in Dubrovnik?' I ask him back with less certainty, looking for confirmation instead.

He snorts briefly. 'No, I'm not a prince,' then the corners of his lips rise slightly, he smiles.

He doesn't seem to be someone who enjoys joking around or readily showing his emotions, but when he smiles, it's really magical. I think quiet and mysterious people are bursting with interesting things. The fascinating detail of their lives are just waiting to be revealed. Besides that, Maroje is also very handsome, like Keanu Reeves in *Speed*. Clearly, there's something wrong with me because I feel challenged to pursue a conversation with him and subconsciously want to provoke his smile again.

'Well, you could be one of them,' I say.

'One of what?'

'A prince.'

'I don't have blue blood,' he replies seriously.

'You know, don't you? You can be a prince ... for someone. You don't have to have a castle or blue blood. But you can be a prince in their life.'

Maroje holds my gaze for a few seconds, and it makes my heart beat faster. The corners of his lips rise slightly again. Since I think it is a green light, I bare all my teeth, giving him a brilliant level-six smile, the smile of a waiter.

23

Clearly, it had been an inappropriate and foolish move. Lying in my cabin after my shift, I reprimand myself. How could I have teased Maroje like that? What will he think of me now? It's not that I have feelings for him; it's just that he's pleasant to look at. His facial features are strikingly attractive, especially his nose and lips. Even among the other Europeans on this ship, Maroje stands out. Ugh! And I don't want to look tacky and cheap in front of beautiful people.

Regardless, it's too late to worry about my reputation now, so I might as well dive deeper into the mud. Maybe I'll even flirt with Maroje again. I'll need to do it a few times just to confirm if it's really a mistake.

Unfortunately, I can't find Maroje the next night. Instead, there's only Denis, another deck cadet. I don't particularly like Denis; his blond hair and youthfulness make me feel like his aunt. 'Hi, I'm the fire patrol now,' I greet him, reporting to the bridge with forced cheerfulness. I have no idea why I'm acting so jolly, perhaps it's just a habit from working in the restaurant.

'Yeah, good job. Charge the HT battery over there,' he replies, then returns to fiddling with his mobile phone, completely ignoring me like I'm insignificant sea foam.

I go on my rounds, checking the engine room and examining the giant chains. I visit the chemical room, and I make use of a spacious and elegant toilet meant for passengers. Finally, I head to the gangway, the ship's entrance, where I come across Kanompang and several others who have just returned from the city centre and are about to reboard the ship. Kanompang is laden with shopping bags. 'We had dinner out, Chinese food, yum. We did a lot of shopping too, look at these,' she boasts, displaying her bags.

'I don't care,' I reply, my annoyance showing. By this point, I'm yearning for the same working hours as everyone else. They finish their duties by six in the evening and have the opportunity to leave the ship and spend the night in Lisbon. I don't want to go to a casino or a brothel (duh!), I just want to explore Lisbon, spend my tips, and enjoy some Chinese food as well. We've been here for a week and all I've done is circle the ship, gazing at Lisbon from a distance like a seagull in the harbour.

***

At breakfast the next morning I run into the safety officer in the crew mess, and he can clearly see my frustration. My eyes are red from lack of sleep, and I look like a skinny vampire.

'What's wrong?' he enquires.

I haven't said anything yet. 'Hmm,' I snort instead.

He remains silent for a moment. 'Tonight you can take a break from patrol.'

My eyes widen in surprise, and without saying another word, except for a quick thank you to ensure he doesn't change his mind, I grab a green apple and exit the crew mess, screaming with joy on the inside.

This afternoon I venture out to Lisbon's city centre, Chiado, on foot. Eager to immerse myself in the city, I avoid public transport. This turns out to be a stupid choice as the distance wears me out. My legs are trembling when I finally arrive.

Lisbon is a quaint mix of historic buildings built on steep hills. Some buildings are vibrant – painted in hues of pink, turquoise and yellow – while others are timeworn. The roads leading to Chiado, a shopping district, are steep. High-end stores line the streets. Benetton, ZARA, Pull & Bear and more. Tourists are everywhere. I wander through Chiado, going in and out of boutiques and glancing at the menu prices in elegant restaurants. Eventually, I have a late lunch at a Chinese buffet restaurant that sets me back ten euros. The sun starts to set by the time I've had my fill of the buffet, so I decide to head back to the ship.

Lisbon doesn't overly impress me. There's nothing about it that stands out except for the beautiful streets made of cobblestone or mosaic tiles. It's not that I haven't enjoyed it, but I suppose sightseeing isn't as enjoyable as when you have someone with you. Maybe it's not about the place itself, but more about the company and the shared experiences.

I decide to buy a cheap baseball cap for five euros as a souvenir, something to remember this trip by. Suddenly, a very attractive man approaches me. He's incredibly good looking. H.O.T. Capital letters.

'Ni hao,' he greets me.

My attraction is immediately replaced with annoyance. 'What the heck? Just because I look Asian doesn't mean I'm from China.'

'Oh, sorry, where are you from?'

'None of your business,' I reply, not quite sure why I'm being so rude. Maybe it's because I don't want to be the typical Indonesian who acts overly sweet in front of foreigners, regardless of the situation. But really, I don't care.

'Hey, chill, man, no need to be rude,' he says, his tone completely changing.

I walk away without looking back, but this person doesn't seem to accept rejection.

'Do you want some good stuff?' he persists, still following me.

I look at him out of the corner of my eye. What does he want?

'It's free, you can try it first. If you don't like it, you don't have to pay.'

For a moment, I think this man is trying to sell himself. And when he says 'good stuff' I think he means his 'stuff'. Oh God, I feel ashamed of myself for having such dirty thoughts. After the embarrassment fades, irritation takes its place. Do I look like a drug addict? Maybe it's because of this cheap hat!

'No, thanks,' I say curtly with a forced smile and continue walking. But this guy really doesn't understand the word 'no'. It annoys me for some reason, maybe because it reminds me of myself?

'Come on, try it first, it's free.'

'I said NO!' I snap.

'Hey, relax, man,' he says, changing his tone again. 'You fucking Asian!'

Honestly, I'm a little scared now because this guy has suddenly become creepy.

'Leave her alone,' someone says from behind me. I turn and see Oleksii walking towards me.

'Back off, midget,' the man says.

'Don't call him a midget!' I suddenly feel the need to defend Oleksii.

'Oh, yeah? What are you gonna do?' the man challenges.

Out of nowhere, a deep, warm voice emerges. 'Leave them alone.'

I search for the source of the voice and find my Croatian prince approaching.

Creepy drug dealer and Maroje exchange a brief glance. Without further ado, the dealer walks away with his hands in his jacket pockets, muttering curses under his breath.

'You guys okay?' Maroje asks both Oleksii and me.

I want to say that I'm terrified, to play the part of a delicate, spoiled girl, in order to coax Maroje into protecting me, but it would be too embarrassing. Even by my standards, that would be crossing a line.

'Yeah, I'm fine,' I reply as nonchalantly as I can. I don't even look at Oleksii. I haven't chatted with him in a long time, and I thought he knew I was avoiding him. But it's not like I still hold any resentment towards him. He's actually not that bad.

'Alright, bye,' Oleksii mumbles.

'Yes, thanks, by the way,' I respond in a similarly vague tone.

Then I continue on my way, and sure enough Maroje falls into step beside me.

'What did he want?' Maroje asks.

'He? Who's he?'

'The guy who approached you earlier.'

'Oh, he sells drugs,' I reply.

'You have to be more careful,' Maroje advises.

'Hmm,' I say indifferently. I mean, he doesn't need to say it, I already know I need to be careful. It's a basic instinct for any sensible human being: to be cautious. It's just that, no matter how cautious we are, some people are determined to harm us. The problem isn't with me.

'By the way, what are you doing here?' The tone of my question comes across unintentionally curt as if I'm bothered by his company. Stupid mouth.

'It's my day off, so I decided to take a little walk.'

'Did you buy anything?' I ask again.

He looks around and approaches a street vendor selling roasted chestnuts. I wait for him as he hands over two euros.

'I bought chestnuts,' he says, offering me some.

I chuckle. 'You're weird.'

'What?' he asks, genuinely puzzled.

'Ha ha, nothing, you like nuts ...'

'You're not on patrol?' he asks.

'I skipped it,' I reply with all my teeth showing and wink at him conspiratorially. He chuckles.

'Anything else you want to do?' he asks again.

I shake my head.

'Let's get you back to the ship.'

'I thought you were going to gamble or, you know, go to some entertainment place, a bar, with the others,' I say.

'No, I prefer nuts,' he replies, matter-of-factly.

Is he trying to make a joke? I turn to him, but he doesn't crack a smile. So maybe he's being serious. I end up laughing out loud, and I can see the corners of his lips lift ever so slightly.

We decide to head back to the ship on foot, and this time it turns out to be a good decision. Walking along the coast from downtown to the dock where our boat is moored feels somewhat romantic. Well, maybe not in the traditional sense of the word, as he doesn't sing me a song or recite poetry about the beauty of the moon. But in his own way, offering to accompany me home is quite gentlemanly, like a knight without a horse. Perhaps he really is a prince. I need to redefine my idea of romance. Do I actually want someone to be romantic with me? Yuck!

Well, actually I do. But I'm too embarrassed to admit it.

'So, how many days off do you get?' I ask.

'One a week.'

'The captain gives you a day off once a week?' I can't hide my annoyance.

'No, the safety officer does.'

'What a privilege,' I grumble. I immediately plan to ask the safety officer the same thing. The ship will be moored in Lisbon for two more weeks. I need to secure two more days off.

'What are you thinking?' Maroje asks.

'Nothing.'

'You're lying,' he says flatly.

I turn to him in surprise. 'Yeah, I was thinking of asking for another day off next week.'

He nods. 'Maybe we can go together.'

My heart skips a beat. This is a metaphor of course.

'Yes, yes, we can,' I stammer, clearly failing to sound nonchalant about it.

My God, did Maroje just ask me out on a date? Did he invite me to go out with him next week? It feels like a dream. And before I can even process it, the chapter ends.

24

A week goes by, filled with the usual routines: intense work, sparks flying like firecrackers, thick smoke choking my throat, and other mundane tasks I've grown accustomed to. The only exception is when a water sprinkler breaks, dousing everything in sight and I scramble to find a massive bucket. There isn't much else interesting to report.

I muster the courage to beg the safety officer for another day off. I explain politely that I've noticed the deck workers are getting a weekly day off, and it doesn't seem fair given how hard I work. With a grunt of reluctant approval, he finally grants my request.

On that magical Thursday, Maroje knocks on my cabin door. He stands there with an expression that's difficult to read and asks, 'Are you ready?'

I reply with a quick 'Wait a minute' while offering a smile. Fortunately, I've already brushed my teeth. After a quick dusting of my face with baby powder and a pat to smooth my clothes, I grab my purse and check if I have enough euros. Then I spritz on some cheap-but-nicely scented perfume I brought from Indonesia, focusing on my neck. Maroje watches me do it all without saying a word.

'What?' I ask, self-conscious. He remains silent. Oh my God, he's so handsome, and I can't help but accidentally stare at him all the time. 'Let's go,' I say, feeling somewhat embarrassed. I sneak off the ship because I don't want the other crew members to see us, while Maroje walks casually. We start walking closer to each other once we're a safe distance from the ship, as if there's something wrong with being seen together.

'Where do you want to go?' I ask. Even though we planned this outing last week, we never actually discussed our plans. Whenever we bumped into each other on the ship, we'd exchange polite smiles like civilized co-workers.

'Do you want to see the castle?' Maroje suggests.

'Yes, sure,' I reply.

'It's a bit uphill,' he warns.

'If I get tired, will you carry me?' I tease. He doesn't say a word but nods seriously.

As it's still early in the morning, the air is fresh and the sun bathes the backs of the buildings in golden light. Lisbon looks as beautiful as gold itself. So we decide to take a leisurely stroll.

We head to Castelo de Sao Jorge, also known as Saint Jorge Castle, a half-hour hike from Chiado to the top of a hill. The path consists of asphalt and rocks, flanked by old residences. Around the castle area, merchants sell hand-painted ceramics, mosaics and other Lisbon souvenirs.

By the time we arrive, I'm gasping for air and massaging my knees. Maroje buys the entrance tickets, and I'm pleasantly surprised when he tells me I don't have to pay. Handsome and generous.

We spend an hour exploring this 14th-century castle, climbing from one tower to another, feeling the cool stone walls, admiring the architecture, and observing peacocks in the garden. We also take in the panoramic view of Lisbon from above, gazing at the sea of red-tiled roofs. However, I can't help but find it all a bit boring. I mean, the castle was once a royal residence, but it's still just a house with latrines, bathrooms and so on. If I were a princess, I'd definitely want to live in a house with modern amenities. I'd prefer an auto-flush toilet that can spray and dry my buttocks. I wouldn't want to use a chamber pot and make a maid clean up after me. Living in a castle must have been quite challenging. If I ever had a four-storey house, I'd want escalators instead of stairs so I wouldn't have to climb them. I'm not particularly interested in being a princess though. Can I be Maroje's wife if he's a prince?

'What's on your mind?' Maroje startles me from my thoughts.

'Huh? Nothing much,' I stammer.

'You're lying again.'

Can he read my mind or something? 'Hmm, I'm just feeling a bit bored,' I admit.

'Let's get out of here,' he suggests.

We exit the castle complex and start descending the hill, passing colourful old Portuguese houses. When we reach the city centre, Maroje asks a one-word question: 'Eat?'

'Yeah, okay, I haven't had breakfast yet. What kind of food do you want?' I ask.

He doesn't answer, instead leading me to an Asian buffet restaurant. He seems to know what I'm craving.

Throughout the day, I do most of the talking. I tell him about my various jobs leading up to working on a cruise ship and share other stories. Occasionally we exchange glances, and although we don't say much it's not boring. Being near Maroje, even in silence, brings a sense of tranquillity. Sometimes I catch myself gazing at his pretty face, to which he responds by turning slightly towards me, raising his eyebrows as if to ask what's on my mind. It truly warms my heart.

Is this normal? I've never been on a date with a guy before, except for outings with co-workers. Those were completely different because we usually chatted non-stop. But with Maroje, I don't think he's much into gossip. Could this be the Croatian way? Oh, I don't know.

When we're tired of the city centre, Maroje takes me to visit Belem Tower, a fortress built on the banks of the Tagus River. It used to be a prison and is now a museum. The tower has a cute boot-like shape, and there's already a queue of tourists waiting to enter. I'm not keen on waiting, so I decide to buy a frozen yogurt from a nearby food truck instead.

'You know?' I suddenly ask when we find a place to sit.

'Yes?' Maroje responds.

'Maybe you want to talk about something?' I'm hinting for him to take the initiative and start a conversation.

'Something … like what?' he asks in his deep voice.

'Anything you'd like to talk about. Anything.'

Maroje falls silent for a moment, perhaps pondering. 'I don't know what I want to talk about,' he replies in monotone.

I burst out laughing, and my yogurt nearly flies out of my mouth. His innocence and the seriousness in his tone of voice strike me as amusing.

'Do you want this?' I offer him the frozen yogurt.

He shakes his head, so I take a spoonful and try to feed it to him. He purses his lips tightly.

'Aaa …' I say, encouraging him. He finally opens his lips slowly and accepts the bite. His face immediately turns red.

Seeing him embarrassed makes me chuckle. Perhaps he's never done anything like that in public. Neither have I.

Maroje escorts me back home afterwards, and we walk along the great river. A chilly breeze begins to blow in the late afternoon, but the sun's rays still dance on the surface of the river like a shimmering sea of fireflies. I tighten my jacket.

'Will you be my girlfriend?' Maroje suddenly asks. It feels as though the question has come from the echo of an uninhabited cave in another world.

'Say that again?' I'm not sure if I heard correctly. Really?

Maroje falls silent again, perhaps he was just practicing or maybe it slipped out accidentally or maybe he's actually crazy.

'Will you be my girlfriend?' he repeats.

I hear it loud and clear this time and decide to stop walking. I look at Maroje, trying to gauge his sincerity.

'Are you drunk because I gave you a spoonful of frozen yogurt?' I can't help but laugh.

'How can I get drunk on frozen yogurt?' he responds, taking it seriously.

'I'm just kidding,' I say, patting his arm.

'I'm not kidding. Will you be my girlfriend?' he repeats.

'Maroje, I don't want to lie to you. I'm 30 years old,' I confess.

'Will you be my girlfriend even though you're 30 years old?' he corrects his sentence.

I blink.

'Maroje, you're only 24 years old.'

'Will you be my girlfriend even though you are 30 years old, and I am actually 23 years old?'

I blink again, my heart having leaped out of my chest a while ago, and I'm not quite sure where it is anymore. What? He's only 23 years old?

'I ... I don't know,' I stammer.

25

I feel like I'm logging out of the real world every time I run into Maroje on the ship. My ears get hot, and my chest heats up when he's around me. Of course, he doesn't say anything; he just glances at me with that unbelievable and unreadable look of his, but I guess that says a lot. In return, I can only look down coyly like an innocent country girl. I haven't accepted his request for me to be his girlfriend. I don't know what to do. Seriously, I am so confused.

'Do you really like working as a fire patrol?' Kanompang asks me as I make my rounds and pass the reception desk, where she hangs out doing nothing but clipping her nails.

'What?' I'm not really focused.

She immediately frowns. 'Are you in love or something?'

'Huh?'

She rolls her eyes.

'You look macho,' she tries to irritate me.

'Thanks,' I reply absently.

'So, who is it?'

'Who? What who?'

'Boy or girl?' she asks again.

'What?'

'Don't be shy. I'm used to it. Maybe that incident with Oleksii traumatized you and changed your direction. It doesn't matter to me, don't worry. So, who's the girl?'

'A guy!' I snap.

Kanompang immediately rolls her eyes again. Then she smiles slyly. 'I knew it.'

'What did you know?' Damn, why am I so easy to provoke like that?

'I thought you had a crush on someone.'

'Shut up!'

She immediately smirks and tries to guess: 'One of those stinky welders, huh?'

'No! I don't want to tell you who it is,' I reply.

'I know who it is. I can watch you all the time, you know? We got CCTV here,' she pauses. I get a bit worried. 'You mingle with those welders from Portugal every single day. It must be one of them. There are no other possibilities. Some of them smell really funky, do you realize that? You probably don't. You're in love. They're always sweating; tell them to take a shower.'

'Not a welder!' I snap again.

'Don't be shy; just ask him to take a scented bath and you can introduce him to me.'

'No, no! Why the hell are you smelling other people's body odour anyway?'

'I have a nose. But maybe your nose isn't working? That's why you can stand kissing those macho welder boys.'

'I didn't kiss them. Not them, okay? But Maroje! And he doesn't stink at all. And I didn't kiss him either!'

Kanompang's eyes narrow. I feel like I am being investigated. She sighs, giving a pitiful face that is actually very mocking.

'Be patient, okay,' as she pats my shoulder.

'What do you mean?'

'I hope your feelings will go away soon.'

'Why do you say that?' I really don't understand what that means.

'I liked someone too. I know how it feels when one's feelings are not reciprocated. I felt so … shattered.'

'Have you really felt that way?' I asked.

'Never,' she replies. 'I was just saying it to cheer you up.'

'Why do you need to comfort me?'

'Maroje? Darling, one can dream, but you're obviously not in his league.'

'Bomboclat!' I blurt out. 'He asked me to be his girlfriend, you know?'

She snorts. 'No way.'

'Yes way! You big ass!' I snap and fly from that damn reception desk.

What is Kanompang thinking? That I am delusional? That I am not worthy of Maroje? How bad am I? I am not bad at all. Other than the fact that I am small and twiggish, I think I am okay. Ugh, talking with her drains my positive energy. It is my fault for chatting with her.

Fuelled by annoyance and frustration, and with a burning desire to prove something to Kanompang, or maybe to the world, or perhaps to anyone, possibly even to myself, I march to Maroje's cabin at the speed of a cheetah. Without bothering to knock, I push open his bedroom door and find Oleksii standing there in his underwear.

'Totem,' I squeak.

'What?' He is as surprised as me.

'I'm looking for Maroje,' I correct, as my shock eases. I can see Maroje's head popping out of his bed. Ignoring Oleksii again, who then gets dressed and heads out of the room to cook, I approach Maroje and look at his newly awake and confused face. He's so handsome up close. Every detail of his face is Ultra HD. I am ready to spit out what I have decided to say.

'What's wrong?' he asks in a sleepy voice.

I smile and say: 'Yes, I do.'

He looks confused.

'Yes, I do,' I repeat.

He grows more confused.

I become impatient and repeat it again. 'Yes, I want to be your girlfriend.'

And Maroje miraculously lets out a kind of yapping sound like a happy puppy. Then his eyes widen, and he pulls me into a hug. The movement is so sudden, I don't expect it. I kind of assumed he would just give me a flat facial expression while saying: 'Oh.' So, an actual reaction is a surprise for me. I laugh and can see Maroje is smiling too.

We cuddle up on the bed for a while, excited and breathing heavily. My heart's racing. I put my hand on his waist for the first time and realize he is so strong. Then I cannot stop being grateful. I guess I am a very lucky girl, aren't I? Why did I have to wait so long to say a simple 'yes'. Why must I overanalyse everything and be pushed to the brink before I can muster the courage to make a decision? What a fool I am.

I let myself get lost in this euphoric mood for a while. I should show this euphoria to Kanompang just to shut her up.

But then, after a few moments, the ecstasy goes stale. The roar that is lodged in my chest has subsided. And the only thing I can think of is: 'Oh, well …' which is really moronic because I should have been overwhelmed by heavenly feelings. What's wrong with me? Then I force myself to smile again. I am very happy. Extremely happy. I keep reassuring myself until I actually become happy in the end.

26

I share with my family that I have a boyfriend. My mother remains unimpressed, and my younger brother mirrors her indifference. I thought they might have expected me to have one considering my age. However, my mom isn't the type to fixate on boyfriends, marriages or prospective sons-in-law. She seldom probes such matters. That's one perk of being her daughter. Maybe she's content with me not being married so I remain under her armpit all the time.

Sharing the news with Kanompang and the rest of the ship's crew is a different story. When I confide in Kanompang that Maroje and I are officially dating, her immediate response is to hand me a cup of chamomile tea. 'This will calm your nerves. I pity you for entertaining such stupid thoughts,' she remarks.

Despite my insistence, Kanompang remains sceptical. I feel like throwing my cup of chamomile tea in her face. Unlike her, both Ida and Yanti believe me without hesitation. Their faith in my words, especially after the memorable purple dildo incident, has grown. Like the genuine girlfriends they are, they eagerly ask for the juicy details and share in my joy.

Actually, I get annoyed with myself too. Why do I need validation from others about my relationship with Maroje? Why the urge to broadcast our relationship? It's our bond, not anyone else's. With that realization, I choose to fully enjoy the relationship, dismissing external opinions. What Maroje and I share is unique. Neither Maroje nor I have ever dated. He is as confused as me. Whenever we cross paths, he blushes a shade of magenta and appears bewildered. Once, on the deck, as he is stripping paint off some metal, I approach to invite him to lunch. Seeing me coming makes him flustered, causing him to repeatedly drop his tools. 'Yes,' he murmurs, barely audible, catching his breath.

Actually, I want to see myself as a tiny/fragile lover who deserves to be protected. But I can't do that because Maroje is even more nervous than me. Is it because I am older than him? Don't know. What I do know is it sucks when I think about it. I train myself not to overthink it. I just want to live in the relationship happily. Yes, Maroje is a little stiff, but I am happy to have a boyfriend. Everyone wants one. I don't allow myself to criticize his flaws or the things I don't like about him. I realize I am not that picky. I am an older girl who's successfully captured a much younger and very handsome man, who is probably the prince of Croatia, and I've forgotten to be grateful. Yes, that's me.

I suppose dating is a time when two people tolerate each other. And I try to do just that.

27

We seldom have the luxury of going on proper dates. Our interactions mostly involve sharing meals in the crew mess, during which he observes my food choices.

'You really love rice,' he remarks.

'Yes, no rice no power,' I respond awkwardly. 'And you enjoy pasta and bread, right?'

He nods, and I've seen him enjoy canned tuna and crusty bread with the same enthusiasm as I would with gado-gado or laksa. I love watching him eat, so full of appetite. It's no wonder he's so tall. Sometimes, as a good girlfriend, I bring him drinks, which he readily accepts. It's not too challenging, as Maroje usually welcomes whatever I bring, whether it's concentrated juice, tea, coffee or even some wine. I've banned him from drinking water from the distiller to avoid a sore throat, so I often sneak special bottled water meant for passengers just for him.

In return, when I have night patrol duty, Maroje willingly accompanies me, sacrificing his sleep. Our conversations revolve around exchanging information about the day's events. We spend twenty-four hours on the same ship, and there's not much happening that we're unaware of. Besides, Maroje isn't one for gossip, so there's no juicy news to share. Our discussions typically revolve around topics like ship maintenance:

'The paint on the aft port side of the fourth deck hasn't dried yet,' he reports.

'So I should be cautious there?' I enquire.

Maroje nods.

Fun.

However, he's not always that rigid. One Tuesday night, as we inspect the lifeboats on Deck Six, a cold wind sends shivers down my spine. Without uttering a word, he leaves my side and returns with a steaming mug of Milo and an oversized windbreaker. In appreciation of his sweet gesture, I don the jacket, even though it makes me look enormous, like an oil barrel. 'You're so sweet,' I tell him, causing his face to turn beetroot red as he shifts his gaze elsewhere.

After a few more days, we finally have a day off together. We opt to return to the city centre, although I had initially wanted to visit Sintra to explore other castles. Maroje had suggested that Sintra was more colourful and pleasant, but time constraints led us back to Chiado and lunch at Burger King. I indulge in chicken nuggets, reflecting on the absurdity of sailing from Jakarta to Lisbon only to feast on them.

'Let's take a selfie,' I propose to Maroje, a first for us. Until now, I hadn't thought about capturing our moments together on camera. This far into our relationship I've been too captivated by his flawless face. However, I realize I need to preserve these memories. Maroje moves closer to me and I snap the first photo. 'Smile,' I instruct for the second one. His smile seems somewhat odd, revealing his teeth, which I find slightly eerie. 'Don't smile,' I quickly follow up.

While at Burger King, I use the Wi-Fi to upload our photos to Facebook. I don't expect much of a response but to my surprise the post garners numerous likes in a short period. 'Oh, wow,' I murmur to myself.

'What's wrong?' Maroje asks.

I show him the photos on Facebook and point to the number of likes and comments: twenty-five likes and six comments in just five minutes. The comments include: 'Wow, you've caught yourself a white man' and 'Who's the handsome guy? Please introduce us.'

'I want to tag you,' I tell Maroje.

'Tag?' he questions.

'You do have Facebook?'

'No.'

I decide not to press the issue or express my surprise with comments like, 'Why not? Facebook is cool.' Instead, I let it go, understanding that he might prefer not to socialize. However, I can't resist suggesting that he create an account. He promptly hands me his iPhone, leaving me momentarily stunned. 'You can also create an Instagram account,' I add.

This whole dating experience is new to me, and I often find myself questioning what I should do and feel. Maroje never broaches the topic and he appears content with our silence.

'So, how many siblings do you have?' I finally ask.

'I'm an only child,' he replies, offering nothing more. (Insert the sound of crickets chirping in the background here.)

I could rant about various subjects, from my family to my life in general, but I'm concerned that it might bore him, and I don't want to push him away. I take his hand, and we stroll around the city centre, observing tourists dining at proper restaurants instead of indulging in chicken nuggets. However, they aren't as fortunate as I am. I mean, look at us! I'm hand in hand with my lover, and we resemble a pair of doves! (Even though many of the tourists are with their partners too, I deny this to feel a bit exceptional. I want to believe that we possess something extra special! LOL.) I glance at Maroje and smile.

'What?' he asks, his typically flat voice now sounding slightly softer.

I shake my head, and he snorts. Within moments, the corners of his lips turn up. That's the thing about smiles: they're infectious. I guess, without realizing it, I'm beginning to feel it. Didn't he feel it before? I mean, the fondness – I like him. And maybe there's something more than that, something I'd dare call love.

28

I never realized I was searching for love all this time until I finally found it. As I mentioned, it was never my top priority, and I didn't delve deeply into it. What I sought was self-discovery, understanding who I was, and what I truly desired in life. I was confident that these revelations would bring a sense of completeness to my life.

Describing this newfound feeling is challenging. It's pleasant, yet it doesn't entirely fulfil me. Nevertheless, my emotional repertoire has expanded, adding new moods to the mix beyond my usual confusion, feelings of being lost, and uncertainty – emotions that have become my trademark. There's a brand-new sensation, a sense of need, desire and longing. It's the feeling of being a part of something, of being wanted, and not alone. *Rasa*.

I don't know how Maroje feels or what he thinks about our relationship. Perhaps it's not yet the right time for me to know, or maybe it's a topic that feels too far removed for discussion. Or perhaps, deep down in my heart, I'm not truly interested in knowing. It's not that my heart is indifferent, but rather I'm allowing myself to fully immerse myself in this new experience. I'm savouring it like a traveller sipping a glass of water, enjoying every drop without questioning its source or contents.

There are moments when a flicker of emotion stirs within me as Maroje and I cross paths, and he greets me with his deep, low voice. Maybe it's the nature of both of us – he's reserved, composed, and keeps his feelings concealed, while I'm passionate, perplexed and inquisitive. I want to converse, while he simply wants to savour the moment.

Two weeks pass in the blink of an eye. Maroje hasn't invited me to his cabin, possibly because Oleksii is often there, though it doesn't bother me. Instead, he prefers to visit my cabin. Each time I'm not on patrol, he arrives like the attentive boyfriend he is, bearing gifts of food. Often it's snacks made by Oleksii in the pastry kitchen. I find it quite endearing. For seafarers like us, food is essential, and food smuggling is a common practice in the restaurant department.

Maroje sits beside me on the edge of the bed, holding my hand until it's sweaty, all without uttering a word. Only his rhythmic breathing fills the air. He quickly releases my hand when Ida or Yanti enter the cabin. Both pretend not to notice our gestures, which, in reality, involve nothing more than hand-holding.

It's exhilarating but unfortunately the excitement can't endure as long as we'd like. Another month passes swiftly. The dry dock repairs on our ship are now complete, and crucial parts have been fixed. With a fresh coat of paint, the vessel regains its beauty and is ready to set sail once more. Challenging hours await and, with a heavy heart, I must relinquish my role as a fire patrol officer.

My intimate moments with Maroje will be reduced as well. We can only meet shortly before midnight, after I've finished all my restaurant duties. However, there's a silver lining to this change – I get to interact with passengers again, which means more tips to save (even though at this point, I'm uncertain what I'll use them for, perhaps a wedding with Maroje? Do I truly want to marry him? I don't know, ah!).

29

Tonight, the ship undergoes testing to determine its readiness for the upcoming journey. We sail around the great river, and everyone cheers, shouting, 'Goodbye, Lisbon! Goodbye!' It's a little amusing because we return to Lisbon the very next day to pick up passengers who will board from this port.

Utpal gathers the restaurant crew and offers a rather unpleasant observation, 'Enjoyed the good life, did you? A whole month of leisurely roaming around, doing nothing. I hope you still remember how to serve the passengers.'

We spend the night rehearsing a gruelling waiter-guest roleplay. I wish I could have spent that night alone with Maroje.

The following day we anchor at a different dock where passengers can easily embark and disembark. The atmosphere is lively, perhaps because we haven't seen any guests for a whole month.

'Are you ready? What took you so long?' Kanompang peeks into my cabin once more.

'Just a minute,' I reply. I think she might be upset with herself for gaining weight, leading her to lash out at everyone. It's evident that she's also irritated, especially now that it's confirmed I'm actually dating Maroje. She seems to think I don't deserve it.

I can't rush because my hair isn't as pixie-like as it used to be, and I need to style it in a way that still looks attractive, using a couple of black pins for my bangs.

'The guests are coming!' she snaps, as I struggle with the pin for the third time without making it look ridiculous. Annoyed, I snort, throw the hairpin on the table and let my bangs remain messy.

The passengers board the ship at three o'clock in the afternoon. I haven't forgotten how to flash that big, charming smile and deliver the courteous greetings that come with the job. I hope the passengers won't realize that it's all part of the service.

After guiding them to their cabins and gathering them for a tedious evacuation drill – 'When you hear the whistle blow seven times, gather at the designated muster station and prepare to board the rescue boats' – the ship sets sail at five in the afternoon. Strangely, I start to feel a bit nauseous. I head to the kitchen to ask for saltine crackers and a green apple, but unfortunately only Oleksii is there.

'Why don't you take some Dramamine? It's going to be a rough sail tonight,' he suggests.

'Dramamine makes me drowsy,' I reply curtly before leaving with what I asked for.

I'm not particularly fond of the 'welcome dinner', which is the first dinner of every cruise. During this dinner, the ship's captain dines in the restaurant with VIP guests at a special table, and we must serve that table flawlessly.

Guess what? That's precisely what goes wrong tonight. There's some confusion when the main course is served, and I forget who ordered what. Balancing three plates (hot pasta and steak) in my hands, I take a chance by placing a plate in front of a passenger I hope is the correct one.

'Oh, I didn't order this,' he says, and the ship's captain shoots a disapproving glance in my direction.

Later, as I carry dishes to another table in the galley, Utpal is ready with his mocking remarks. 'I saw you dancing on the table! Bombo!'

In my defence, I tell him I'm feeling a bit seasick. He appears incredulous, and that's when Oleksii intervenes, saying, 'She really is seasick.'

'I don't need to be defended,' I murmur quietly.

After the chaotic dinner, we clean up the restaurant and prepare it for the breakfast buffet the following day. I head to the crew mess and find Maroje sitting alone in the corner.

'I made you some tea,' he says, pushing a white ceramic mug

towards me. I cradle the mug in my palms to check its temperature, and it's still warm.

'Were you waiting for me?' I say.

He doesn't answer, and I suddenly have the urge to go 'aw, so sweet', like when people watch something romantic on a reality show or in a chick flick. It's just that I'm not watching other people; it's happening to me.

30

The progress in our relationship and how I feel about it boosts my self-esteem and improves my outlook on life. I no longer feel as worried or as tired as I used to. I often reassure myself: *It's okay, no matter how challenging today may be, I'll meet Maroje by the end of the day, and he loves me, so everything will be better*. I know it might sound a bit cheesy, but that's genuinely how I feel. He gives my life a newfound purpose. I'm no longer a confused girl; maybe I'm even a happy one.

However, as with many things, happiness can be fleeting. On the third day of our first cruise, right after the lunch service and while I'm changing dirty linens, Kanompang suddenly shouts: 'Did you turn off the vacuum cleaner again? Dammit!'

'What's wrong now?' I reply, trying to ignore her. She's irritable because she has to vacuum the entire restaurant floor, which is a very tiring job.

'Someone keep stepping on the cable,' she complains.

'No one stepped on it,' I say, busy laying tables and smoothing down tablecloths.

'But the vacuum cleaner is off!'

I pause to listen. The vacuum cleaner has indeed stopped humming. 'I think the lights are off too,' I inform her.

Kanompang immediately drops her vacuum cleaner hose and rushes towards me.

'The ship's engine is off,' she tells me, her face tense.

Only now do I notice that the atmosphere has suddenly grown very quiet.

'Oh my God, we're going to die!' Kanompang grabs my arms and shakes them vigorously.

'What do you mean?'

'We'll perish in the waves, oh my God, oh my God!' She continues shaking me back and forth.

'Get a grip,' I say, struggling to break free. 'Sit over there; I'll go check it out.' I walk to the kitchen to see if anyone is there. The washer area is deserted, as are the hot and cold galleys. I head with a little more urgency to the reception area on Deck Three, where some guests have gathered, clearly wanting to know what's happening as well. I still don't believe this is anything serious. I know from the endless safety drills that seven long whistles is the signal for us to prepare to leave the ship, and there has been no whistle. It's probably just a regular blackout, right?

On my way down to Deck Two to check on Kanompang, I cross paths with Maroje. 'What happened?' I ask him.

'Don't know yet,' he replies, before hurrying down to the engine room below, looking somewhat nervous.

Back in the restaurant, I find Kanompang sitting on the carpeted floor, hugging her knees in a corner. I squat down next to her. 'Don't worry,' I say, trying to calm her down.

'What do you mean? This is a bad sign, you know! You've never experienced this. A ship's power shouldn't go out. It means something is wrong. You know what happens when the power goes out? The engine stops working, and the stabilizers also go dead. If a massive wave hits the ship, it loses balance and could capsize. It's happened before.'

'Did you capsize?'

'Do you think I'd still be here if that happened?' she asks sarcastically.

I just shrug. I thought that before the boat capsized, we would have all put on our life jackets and boarded the rescue boat, as we learned in Basic Safety Training.

With the power cut, the restaurant becomes oppressively hot. I stand and gaze out at the ocean through the window, seeing the waves crashing against the hull. Kanompang is right. When the ship stops, as well as the eerie silence, the swaying becomes more pronounced. I already know enough about currents to realize that if the current comes from behind the ship it won't be a problem. But when the ship is going against the current, or the current is hitting it from the side, the swaying becomes even more intense. Just like it is now.

Fifteen minutes later, the lights come back on and the ship starts moving again.

'Oh, thank goodness,' I mutter, glancing at Kanompang, whose face has turned ashen.

* * *

The atmosphere at dinner is different. Some passengers appear relaxed, while others engage in hushed conversations.

'Offer them plenty of wine so they won't be too surprised or angry when there's an announcement,' Utpal advises.

'What announcement?' I ask.

'Shut up,' he orders.

'Damn.'

'We're going home,' Nina whispers.

'What do you mean?' I ask.

'Don't too much taka-taka, pour the wine into the glasses as instructed,' Kanompang interjects.

Announcements aren't made until the main course is served (lamb kofta, pasta quattro formaggi and quiche jardinière). When we finally clear the dirty plates and prepare to serve dessert, the captain stands up and announces that the ship must dock in the next port and, temporarily, will be unable to continue the voyage. He explains that one of the radars has malfunctioned, and a replacement has to be imported from the United States.

You can probably guess what happens next. There's an outbreak of noise as everyone starts asking questions. Meanwhile, we waiters navigate through the chaos, offering desserts along with tea or coffee. I know there will be an eruption of anger soon. Still, the captain assures passengers the cruise fare will be refunded in full, and they will be provided with a free replacement tour.

'What a shoddy ship! I don't even know if I can go on the next cruise. Maybe I'll be dead by then,' mutters an elderly woman as

I approach her to offer coffee. She might have a point.

31

Tonight, we dock in La Coruna, Spain, and the passengers disembark, grumbling all the way. After they've all left, the crew re-boards the ship, and we set sail for Lisbon. The journey will take a day and on the way Utpal informs us to pack up our belongings and prepare to return home from Portugal.

'I don't want to be on this ship anymore. I'm so grateful we're going home. I'm not coming back to work here,' Kanompang declares.

'Really?' I ask.

'We'll never see each other again. Goodbye!'

I pack my few possessions into my small suitcase. Within two hours, I've packed everything. After returning my vest and apron, the hotel manager asks me to sign a contract termination letter. The original contract required me to work for ten months, and I only have three more months left to complete it.

'How long do you think it'll take to repair the ship?' I ask the hotel manager.

'Soon, I hope. Why? Can't wait to come back?' he raises an eyebrow.

I shrug. I don't know if I 'can't wait to come back'. I'm still somewhat shocked by this sudden order to return home. All the restaurant crews, except for Utpal, are being sent home. Only a few kitchen crews remain to cook.

'What's the issue?' I ask him again.

He just smiles and doesn't provide any details. 'The remainder of your salary will be transferred immediately.'

I roam through the empty ship's cabins, descend to the crew mess and head to the bow in search of Maroje. Unfortunately, he's nowhere to be found, not even in his cabin. Only Oleksii is lying on his bed. Maybe he's watching porn again.

'He's in the engine room,' Oleksii informs me before I even ask.

I can't go to meet Maroje there; he must be busy with some job relating to the ship's problems. I don't want to risk disturbing him. All I can do is wait for him to finish.

In the cabin, Yanti and Ida are packing their things.

'Are you both being sent home too?' I ask.

'Of course, yes,' Yanti replies cheerfully. 'I've been missing home so much.' She's been on the ship for almost nine months, and it's taken a toll on her. Ida, on the other hand, remains silent. She wants to stay on the ship longer because she needs the money to pay off her family's debts. I sit and watch them pack.

'Do you know why we're being sent home?' I ask.

'One of the engines has failed,' says Yanti. 'It's broken, old,' she says in a high-pitched voice, ending with a laugh. It's worrying that we're now sailing back to Lisbon with just one engine.

I climb into bed and start daydreaming. Going home so early wasn't part of my plan. Yes, I wanted to go home before, but that was mainly because I was exhausted and struggling with my job. Lately, things have been more enjoyable here. I'm dating Maroje, and the thought of our separation weighs heavily on my mind. After tomorrow, we probably won't see each other again. He'll return to Croatia, and I'll go back to Indonesia. There's going to be a considerable distance between us, unless I discover a magic door.

'What are we going to do after this, with no work?' I ask Ida and Yanti in a hushed tone.

Ida remains silent and gloomy. Meanwhile, Yanti begins excitedly discussing her plans to buy land for flower farming. She mentions that flower farming in Bali is very profitable, as the flowers are used for prayers and other purposes. I wonder if I should suggest to Maroje that we buy a piece of land in Bali and grow flowers so we can live together happily?

32

Seeing Maroje for only a few hours before we dock in Lisbon is a bummer. He's been working in the engine room all night, looking wiped out, covered in oil and grime. We meet on Deck Five by the Jacuzzi, a crisp February morning with the sun taking the edge off the chilly breeze.

'You're not going home?' I ask.

He shakes his head. My romantic daydream of us leaving for Lisbon Portela Airport together, complete with a teary-eyed goodbye, seems impossible now. It's just not going to happen. I curse the world for separating us like this. If we must part, I want it to be something grand, like in the movies, not a quiet workplace departure.

'When's your contract ending?' I ask.

'In three months,' he replies. He's got dreams of becoming a ship's captain, and I can't ask him to ditch that for me. It's only been three weeks since we started dating, after all.

He takes my hand and gives me a long hug. 'I can wait three months,' I say, trying to soak up the sun despite the heavy feeling in my chest.

***

The journey home is a pain! Delays, layovers, and Kanompang's constant chatter. Thank God for Yanti and others, or I might lose it. Between layovers, I scavenge for Wi-Fi spots just to check if Maroje has messaged.

When I finally get home, my mom's reaction is surprisingly subdued. She doesn't seem shocked or relieved to see me back in one piece, she just continues ironing clothes. My brother's no different. He asks casually, 'Why are you back so soon? Got fired?' Their indifference stings.

I spend a whole week sleeping and eating. I'd forgotten how nice it is to rest. My body's tired from six months of hard work, and my mom tries to help with herbal drinks, we called them *jamu*. They're bitter as hell, but they seem to work.

Maroje finally replies to my messages after four days.

'How are you?' I ask.

'A little tired,' he responds. I quickly start a video call. He accepts.

'Hi,' I say, looking at his tired face lying on the bed. We don't say much, just stare at each other for a couple of minutes.

'I miss you,' I finally admit.

He doesn't say anything but smiles slightly. Then the video call cuts off.

'My data plan ran out,' he texts. 'I miss you too.'

I grin and hug my phone, rolling around on the sofa.

'Who are you missing?' my mom asks, bringing a glass of sweet herbal drink.

'No need to be nosy,' I reply. 'I want to eat uduk rice, please.' It's been ages since I've had local food, and I rattle off a list of my favourites. Traditional food is what I'm craving.

With decent savings of around seventy million rupiah from my monthly salary of twelve million, I give a third to my mom for some house repairs. I figure I can take a break and enjoy life for a while. Working as a cruise ship waiter hasn't been that bad, despite the long hours, a nasty boss and the seasickness. It enabled me to explore the world and, of course, to meet Maroje. He's been one of the best things in my life.

On the seventh day I visit a nearby photo studio, print a 10 x 12 of Maroje and me and hang it in my room.

'Who's this guy?' my brother asks.

I smirk, 'My boyfriend, Maroje.'

'Ah,' he says and walks away. It's not the enthusiastic reaction I was hoping for.

33

A month drifts by in a whirlwind of sheer boredom. My days are an unimpressive mix of TV marathons, munching on snacks, and some questionable online shopping decisions ... including a pillow with Maroje's face on it, because, well, why not?

'Ugh, I'm so bored,' I sigh, hitting the off button on the TV remote.

'Get out, meet your friends,' my mom suggests, diligently sewing a loose button back onto a shirt.

'I don't have any,' I mumble. The only people I could meet are my former work buddies, and let's face it, they're only interested in souvenirs – souvenirs I don't have.

In a moment of sheer desperation, I turn to Facebook, sending out friend requests to my shipmates. I track down Ida, Yanti, Nina and, yes, even Kanompang, who seems to be having the time of her life sunbathing on the beaches of Phuket. I also find some folks from the kitchen, reception, and one pending friend request from Oleksii. After some inner turmoil, I click 'confirm'. Hey, I'm not one to let things get too awkward.

As I chat with them, trying to fend off the relentless loneliness, I notice something – they don't respond as quickly as I'd hoped. Why? Because they are out there, living their best lives. In malls, bars, cafés, restaurants – you name it, they are there, savouring every moment. Unlike me.

Nonetheless, I realize that I've made some progress. I'm no

longer the same confused mess I once was. Maroje's presence has brought some clarity to my life. I think maybe I want to be with him for ever. All I know for sure is that I miss him, even if he isn't the most communicative person. One thing is crystal clear though – I want to get back on that ship.

So, I decide to spend my afternoon drafting an email to the HR department of my ship's parent company. After hours of carefully crafting the perfect message, I finally hit 'send'. Within fifteen minutes, I receive a reply:

'Hi Maya, it's great to hear from you. We're thrilled that you're interested in returning to work with us. However, due to ongoing repairs on the ship, we can't provide a definite date for the next contract. We'll be in touch once everything's shipshape. In the meantime, enjoy your well-deserved holiday!'

Not willing to leave anything to chance, I message Kanompang on Facebook Messenger.

Maya: 'Hey Kanompang, reply to my message!'

Kanompang: 'What? Go away!'

Maya: 'When are we going back to the ship?'

Kanompang: 'I'm not going back to that wreck! Are you insane?'

Maya: 'Well, I want to go back, so … when?'

Kanompang: 'You're crazy. You just want to go back and be with your lover, right?'

Maya: 'Of course I do. So, when?'

Kanompang: 'I don't know.'

Maya: 'You've had three contracts with them, you must know.'

Kanompang: 'Urgh, you're a pain. Usually, they give us two months off. They'll contact us when it's time, okay? Satisfied?'

Maya: 'Not quite. So, you're not coming back?'

Kanompang: 'Not in a million years. I have a boyfriend here. I'm getting married. You should find someone too. You're getting old, already 33.'

Maya: 'I'm 30, you devil.'

Kanompang: 'Yeah, whatever.'

Maya: 'Thanks. Goodbye!'

So, Kanompang says two months. I still have another month to unwind, be jobless, and not stress about my future. Just as Utpal would say, this is living the good life.

34

The month passes with so much joy. I spend my time going to the cinema, eating at restaurants with my brother and mom, and I even attend the Java Jazz festival alone. No need to pity me. I don't feel lonely at all by myself. Quite the opposite, I have never felt this free.

Regarding Maroje, I usually text him first. I check on him all the time and tell him what I'm doing. I send him photos and voice recordings, and I ask him to make video calls. 'How's the ship? What are you doing? Is the food okay? I went for a haircut earlier; it's short, I hope you don't mind.' He responds to all the messages when he has free time. And when I know he is going to sleep, I text him, 'Good night, Sweetheart' ... every day.

It dawns on me that the two months of vacation time will end in three days, so I begin to wonder: *Why haven't I received any notification from the company yet?* In fact, even Maroje says that the ship is fully repaired and ready to depart in a few days.

'Did you get a call to be on board?' I ask Kanompang on Facebook Messenger.

'Not yet.' She doesn't say anything else.

Three days pass, and I get a message from Maroje.

Maroje: 'Aren't you going back to the ship?'
Maya: 'What do you mean?'
Maroje: 'Some people are already on board.'
Maya: 'What?!'

That can't be possible. I immediately check my email but there is not a single message from the company. My phone is always on, so there's no way I'd have missed any calls. I leave some messages for Kanompang, but she doesn't read them. However, when I check her Facebook page, she's just updated her status: 'Here we go again – travelling to Portugal from Bangkok.'

Damn it! Something feels wrong. I send the HR an email,

not caring about grammar or the damn semicolon. I ask about Kanompang, who has already left her country to be on board again. And then what about me?

I get a reply after six hours, almost in the evening. You can't imagine how anxious I am.

'Hi Maya, how are you? We are very sorry, but for this season, the restaurant team has already fulfilled its worker quota. The vacancies for waiters will only be available next season, in about six or seven months. However, if you are interested, we can try to place you on another ship, so you can be on board again immediately.'

Freaking hell! What is going on? I have to wait six months to get back on the same ship? That's half a year. What do I do for half a year in Indonesia? Without a job? What will happen to Maroje and me? Oh my God.

I immediately text Maroje about this: 'I don't understand why I wasn't asked to get back on the ship for this season. This is stressing me out.'

When he reads my message, he just sends me a sad face emoticon. I don't think he can do anything about it either. I contact Kanompang again, this time with a barrage of messages. She finally replies to them when she arrives at the airport in Lisbon.

Kanompang: 'Shut up!'
Maya: 'Why wasn't I called back?'

Kanompang: 'I don't know, I'm not the one who owns the company!'

Maya: 'You must know, you always know! You told me so.'

Kanompang: 'I wasn't the one who gave you a work evaluation sheet. I don't have the authority not to want you back. There are other people who can do it.'

I'm silent for a moment.

Maya: 'Utpal?'

Kanompang: 'My taxi has arrived, bye! Enjoy your long vacation, bitch.'

Maya: 'Wait!'

Kanompang: 'What else?'

Maya: 'You said you wouldn't go back to the ship again! Why are you licking your own spit!'

Kanompang: 'Hello, I need money for my wedding.'

I can't believe any of this!

35

What did I do wrong to Utpal? What did I do to the universe? To God? Why did He leave me stranded back here? On a sickening bed in my cramped bedroom. In Jakarta. At home with my mom.

In Indonesia! What am I supposed to do now? What? Then I scream and scream. My brother peers into the room and raises his eyebrows. I scream at him for no reason.

'If you're looking for your pirates' documents, Mom hides them in a drawer in her bedroom.' And then he walks away.

What's that? Why did my mom hide my seaman documents? I get up from the bed and throw bananas at her. This must be her. She must have sabotaged my departure.

'Mom!' I snap.

'Hmm?' she hums in a soft and carefree voice. She is frying floured *tempeh*. 'Don't shout, I'm cooking with very hot oil,' she says again, as if to threaten me.

I growl. 'I was not called back to board the ship. It must be you, right?'

She squints her eyes, scrutinizing me from afar. Judging me. She used to do this each time I was angry, as if to secretly say, 'Are you okay, or not?' but in a very condescending way. I don't like it when she does that. Intimidating and cunning. She knows that I am being illogical.

'You want fried *tempeh*?' she asks instead.

Even though I shake my head, in the end I devour the dish with some chilli. Then I start crying while venting how annoyed I am that I will be unemployed for six months. (Still while eating the *tempeh*, of course, because it's the eyes that cry, not the mouth.)

'Are you upset that you won't be able to see your boyfriend again?' asks Mom.

How could she possibly read me like that? I hardly ever speak to her about Maroje.

'Yeah, that too,' I squeak. Then I look away.

She falls silent, but I can tell she is preparing something to say. I wait for her to open her mouth.

'Mom, what do you want to say?' I ask, losing my patience.

'What?' she asks back.

'I know you want to say something.'

'Not really,' she argues. 'Even if I say anything, you won't listen, will you? You're always so wrapped up in yourself.'

'Ugh, what! I'm not like that.'

Actually, yeah. She knows me well.

I want to ask her opinion, but I can guess the short story she's about to share. She will tell me to look for work in Jakarta and forget about the white man who lives far away. The exact two things that I don't want to do. I mean, work/travel abroad with a salary in dollars, plus having a very handsome boyfriend? How could I let all of that go? That's pretty much the All-Indonesian Dream.

36

I send Maroje a WhatsApp: 'I can't go back to the ship. Have to wait for next season.'

'I can't do anything,' he replies.

Even though what he says is true, it pisses me off. I mean, can he really not say something sweet and encouraging? Like: 'Be patient, let's find a solution together.' That would calm me down a bit. Maroje seems to be drifting away? Yes, he's always cold, I know him. But these last two days, I feel like he is withdrawing into himself. Is it because I can't come back this season? Or because there is someone else on board? What the hell am I thinking? Of course, there are other people on board. New waitresses, for example. Or maybe Kanompang, the demon, has planned to snatch him from me. That's plausible. Argh! This makes me really uneasy. Anxiety envelops me throughout the day, and my tiny head keeps on speculating about this and that.

'Is there someone new? I want to know.' I finally get the courage to send Maroje this message.

He simply replies to my message with one word: 'No.'

He doesn't even try to convince me otherwise, and it drives me even crazier. You won't believe what a crazy thing I do next. I send a message to Kanompang. A very threatening message. 'Slut, don't you dare steal my boyfriend.'

The message is read but not answered, which makes me fume. As if she is about to do what I tell her not to. I can even imagine her evil laugh as she reads my message.

'Maroje, what are you doing?' I send the message again after the two previous messages go unanswered and unread.

'Work,' he answers after two very, very painful hours.

I cry again, confused. Should I be aggressive or should I play it casual?

'Do you love me, Maroje?' I ask again. And the message is not read at all.

'Maroje, please answer my messages. I really need you.'

The message is ignored. And I cry because I am so frustrated.

In between sobs I keep sending a series of threatening messages to Kanompang: 'I know where you live in Bangkok, I will terrorize you.' And send a completely different message to Maroje: 'Forgive me. I did not mean it. Of course, I trust you. I hope you are fine. I miss you.'

To which he replied: 'Yes.'

While Kanompang does not reply at all.

'I think of you, do you think of me too?' I ask Maroje again in the night, to which he answers with the same Yes. It feels like I am talking to a SpongeBob Magic Conch Shell that can only respond with Yes or No.

For the next three days, I spend my hours bawling my eyes out like I'm watering flowers.

'I don't want it!' I snap at my mom, who has just brought me a tall glass of avocado juice served with thick condensed chocolate milk. She doesn't deserve that reaction, but I just want to shout. I feel like she's bothering me a lot even though she's not doing anything wrong.

'Oh yes, you want it,' she says, placing the glass next to me.

Then I start bawling again, half because I feel bad for her and half because I am still venting my grief.

'How long will you be a pile of dirty laundry?' she asks, crossing her arms in the doorway. I want to laugh because she says such a funny thing. It's also very annoying, interrupting my mood.

'I want to go back to sea,' I say, sobbing.

'Go, lah …' she waves her hand, indicating that it is a trivial matter, and she wonders why I bother about it.

'I can't go!'

'Cannot? Why?'

'Because … because I can't work on the same ship.'

'But you can work on other ships?' she asks again.

'Yes I can, but …'

'Then go.' She narrows her eyes. 'Do you remember your purpose of working on the ship?'

'I remember, but …' I start to get dizzy and look away.

Are you going for someone else or for yourself? I read her like she reads me.

I cover my head with a pillow and scream. My mom leaves the room. My attitude is not something strange for her.

I stop crying and recalibrate my thoughts. Oh, come on. Why am I crying for a man? Why am I begging for attention? It's very sad, isn't it? I have only known him for a few months. Why have I become so dependent on him? Yes, he is my boyfriend, at least I think he is, but he ignores me. Whoever he is shouldn't affect my way of life. I mean, of course I want to get back to work on the ship. Remember, not because I want to be with him, but because of myself. I want to see the other side of the world, and of course I want to get a lot of money. Tch, Maroje doesn't deserve to steer my emotions like this. Who does he think he is? He has no control over me. I am determined and very realistic. I can't be enslaved by feelings. I feel perfect, healthy, strong, and know what to do next!

I am an independent woman who doesn't 'need' anyone. I can get through this! I am great! This is the moment when the phoenix rises from the ashes! I am great!

I am great …

For ten minutes.

Then I collapse and cry again because I miss Maroje and want to hold hands with him. I want to read chats from him and hear his voice again. Damn that douchebag! He asked me to be his girlfriend and showered me with special treatment! All those sweet looks! Then he dumped me. I feel like a pile of dirty laundry.

So, I guzzle the avocado juice, which I suspect contains a sedative, then send Maroje a message: 'Hi' which is actually full of questioning. Just a plain 'hi' without any punctuation. The message goes unanswered even though I know these are the hours he is in his cabin. Then I send another message: 'Fuck you.'

37

Tonight, I sit in the living room and listen to a soap opera on television – it's my mom who watches it – while I write an email to the company's HR. It doesn't matter if it is a barge, a coal carrier or a tuna fishing boat, I want to sail soon. The important thing is to leave and escape from the current reality. I know this is not a noble motivation, but it is the truth.

This is the reply I receive:

'Dear Maya, we apologize for not being able to give you any certainty as to when a position will be available for you. We did have vacancies some time ago, sadly they are no longer available. We will keep you on the list for departure in the next season, which is still six months away.'

I'm devastated.

I grab the sofa cushion, bury my face in it and scream.

'Shut up!' my brother shouts from his room. Instead, I growl louder, like a tractor.

When there is a commercial break in her soap opera, my mom finally talks to me.

'Well then, just consider that as a vacation for six months, it's not bad.'

'No, it's bad, Ma! I belong at sea. My soul is already at one with the ocean. I'm a mermaid.'

My mom rolls her eyes as if to say 'whatever'. Definitely the influence of soap operas.

38

I scour the internet for two weeks, hoping to find another cruise company that will hire me. But I soon realize that the interview and departure process will take a long time because, of course, they don't have ships that leave all the time. I am about to give up and look for work elsewhere when I rummage through my seaman documents and find a slip of paper with an email address on it. It was given to me by Linda Nor of the purple dildo. On a whim, I send her a brief email.

'Of course, I still remember you. You are my favourite waitress. I'm in London now. With my boyfriend. Last night he came to my apartment, and we had an incredible night together.'

Then, I vent about my job, and how I won't be able to return to the ship anytime soon even though I am so desperate to sail. I tell her I am so stressed that I want to drown myself in a well. In addition, I tell her about Maroje because Linda likes to gossip about boys. We end up being friends on Facebook and chatting on Messenger. Linda is half a century old, but she has a very flirtatious and lively Facebook page. We spend the rest of the evening chatting, and for me it is like finding a long-lost aunt.

Linda Nor: 'You know what? Fuck him. Forget about his little dick!'

She was talking about Maroje.

Maya: 'But ...'
Linda Nor: 'The only way to get over him is to find another dick. A lot of dicks. All at once if you prefer it like that.'
Maya: 'Linda! I'm not looking for a replacement.'

I have never even seen Maroje's. The only thing I had ever seen was Oleksii's.

Linda Nor: 'You are an innocent girl. A bit vanilla.'

Maya: 'I'm not! I'm a wild Jakarta girl!'

Linda Nor: 'Honey, that's not an achievement. If you can be a wild girl in London, then I will acknowledge your reputation.'

Maya: 'I can be even wilder if I were in London, and I would outshine you.'

Of course, I am joking when I say all this.

Linda Nor: 'Then come here …'

Maya: 'I wish! How could I afford a trip to see Big Ben when I don't even have a job?'

Linda Nor: 'Let's find a way so you can come.'

39

I check my mobile phone. Who am I trying to fool? There is no message from Maroje. Not a word. With a heavy heart, I pretend to be strong. Consumed by idleness, I turn to Google, searching for answers to my unemployed and heartbroken state. The search results lead me to the story of a thirty-four-year-old man who faced a situation similar to mine, claiming he wanted to end his life. Although I'm miserable, I haven't reached that point of despair. I hope I never will.

To distract myself, I start researching London. Should I just go there? I still have some savings, but I feel it would be a pointless trip. Just when I am contemplating this, Linda texts me.

Linda Nor: 'How are you doing?'

Maya: 'I'm feeling like a desperate, broken-hearted, temperamental and sad old lady.'

Linda Nor: 'LOL. Have you thought about coming here? This is where your stress can melt away. I'll take you to the bars, and we can have bottomless cocktails.'

Maya: 'I really want to go there, but it would be a waste of money.'

Linda Nor: 'Then look for a job here.'

Maya: 'How can I do that? It's not that easy to get a work visa. I need a sponsor, a company that will hire me and provide a work contract.'

Linda Nor: 'It's hard to be Indonesian!'

Maya: 'Indeed …'

Linda Nor: 'But we can work it out. What do you want to do? I have many friends here. I'm quite popular, you know?'

I suddenly feel a glimmer of hope, even if it might be false, and I decide not to let go of it.

Maya: 'Really? I don't have any special skills. My English is very basic.'

Linda Nor: 'Your English is really messy!'

Maya: 'So mean!'

Linda Nor: 'LOL. Don't worry, you'll be fine. Hmm …
    how about working as a waitress again? You have
    experience, and I think you're good at it.'
Maya: 'Yes, that actually makes sense. I'll try to find some
    job postings on the internet.'

I'm about to end the conversation, assuming it to be just a
pipedream and not something I should get too hopeful about.

Linda Nor: 'Such jobs won't be posted online!'
Maya: 'So?'
Linda Nor: 'You have to come here and see for yourself.
    Bar job vacancies are typically posted at the front
    doors. They won't bother with work contracts or
    Skype interviews.'

See what I mean? It's true. It's all an illusion.

Linda Nor: 'I'll take care of everything. I'll provide you
    with an employment contract.'
Maya: 'What do you mean?'
Linda Nor: 'I'll ask my boyfriend to arrange a work
    contract for you. I told you, I'm dating a guy who
    owns a bar.'
Maya: 'Yes, but …'
Linda Nor: 'Don't say any more. Let's change the subject.'

40

Linda always has interesting stories to share with me. If nothing eventful happens to her one day, she recounts wild experiences from her past. They aren't all about her sexual escapades but also about encounters with famous people. However, a few days after our last chat she surprises me with something entirely different:

Linda Nor: 'My boyfriend agreed to provide you with a contract.'

An hour later, she sends the employment paperwork, complete with a guarantee letter, his passport copy, signature, and all the necessary details.

I'm in disbelief.

Linda Nor: 'Now there's no reason for you not to come.
To break free from your vanilla life, hahaha.'

I can't believe it. I download all the documents Linda sent me and read them meticulously. I print the papers to convince myself they're real. Oh, God!

* * *

It takes about two months to handle everything until my visa is finally issued.

> Linda Nor: 'Don't worry. I'll take care of everything. I know you've never lived abroad. Sure, you've worked on a ship, but this is a different experience. I've been there, you know?'
>
> Maya: 'Yes, you told me. But, I mean, will I be able to make a living?'
>
> Linda Nor: 'You can work at my boyfriend's bar, and you'll be paid as per the contract. If not, there are plenty of job vacancies here. I'll help you.'

That's what I want to hear. I don't want to go to London and be homeless. Given the city's standards, my savings are like a handful of peanuts.

> Linda Nor: 'Don't worry, you can trust me.'

Later that night, I tell my mom about my plans: I'm going to London because I have a work contract and have already purchased plane tickets. As I anticipated, her response is: 'Whatever. Do as you please.'

41

To my mom, the idea of me working on land is as daunting as

working at sea. 'Where is London? England? Remember that we were once colonized by them,' she remarks, observing me as I stuff things into the large suitcase I've just purchased.

'The British only colonised us for five years,' I respond. 'It should have been longer, so we could become part of the Commonwealth and not have to deal with these super complicated visa issues.'

'So, you're going there to get yourself colonized again?'

'No lah, things have changed. The English are nice and funny; just look at Mr Bean.'

'How long will you be in the UK?' asks my brother.

'Maybe a year ...'

'Shit, that's long.'

'Remember, your sister is working hard to save for your university tuition,' I retort, feeling irritable.

'I don't want to go to university,' he argues, then walks away.

'What are you going to do in the UK?' my mom enquires, in a tone that's hard to decipher.

I hand her a photocopy of my employment contract, so she knows where I'll be living and working, what I'll be doing and how much I'll be earning. I understand she's worried, but there's nothing she can do. After all, this is my life, and I am the one living it.

'I want to see more of the world,' I say. 'My soul is not confined to one place. I'm an international woman.' I'd also like to add: 'I want to break free from the expectations and opinions of others' but I hold back on that.

'The man is in London?' my mom asks.

'Uh, no.' She must think I'm going there to meet Maroje. 'We don't even talk anymore …' I feel a pang of sadness as I say that. To ease my mom's anxiety, I tell her about Linda Nor, how we met on the ship, and how kind she's been, providing me with references, job opportunities and even a place to stay for a while.

'She's a stranger,' Mom points out.

'Yes, she is. But everyone starts as strangers before becoming friends, right?' I shove my underwear into the suitcase, setting aside the worn-out ones. I'm going to London, so there's no room for shabby underwear.

'If I don't like it, I can just come back home. I still have enough savings for the return trip,' I try to lighten the mood.

My mom remains silent.

'I'll be fine,' I add, without turning to look at her. I'm excited about starting this new job in the UK. It's my first time going there, and I'm looking forward to it. There's no need for her to worry. I survived life at sea, and I've travelled through various European countries. I won't be a confused duckling. Plus, I won't be alone.

What if something happens? Jakarta to London isn't a short journey. Maybe that's what's running through my mom's mind, or perhaps it's just my own fears trying to sabotage me. But we have technology. We can communicate every day through WhatsApp. I refuse to let my feet falter on this path just because of uncertainty. It's an unworthy and uncharacteristic way for me to think. I genuinely want to embrace this new adventure, so I won't let negativity cloud my mind. Even though my mom tries to anchor me with her extreme and peculiar methods, like suggesting

I watch James Bond movies and making comments like: 'Look, it's scary, there's a lot of crime in London.' We both know it's just a movie. How could something like that really happen, right?

42

My mom waves her hand perfunctorily as I take an Uber to the airport. My brother is nowhere to be seen. It's only when I'm on the plane that I realize I'm headed to London! Just the thought of all those classy people with their British accents makes me a little nervous. But, ready or not, I'm already on my way. It's always been like that, ready or not, we have to start walking. Like Oleksii said, you have to dip your toe in.

After layovers in Kuala Lumpur and Amsterdam, I finally arrive in London. At Heathrow, I yawn; my neck is sore. Even so, I feel incredibly liberated. Here I am becoming someone new once more, sitting in Arrivals, much like in Tallinn when I was about to sail for the first time. My heart is pounding.

Linda arrives to pick me up twenty minutes later. She doesn't dress up. We hug.

'How are you?' she asks.

'More than tired,' I reply. 'Relieved too.'

'Excellent. Let's go,' she smiles.

Linda Nor gives me an Oyster card, a top-up card to pay for subway and bus fares. She also hands me the receipt: £20. I take some money out of my wallet, and she accepts it without hesitation. Linda corrects me on how to call the subway. 'It's called the Tube,' she says. We chat about boys for about an hour on the Tube before we get off at her station.

'I live in zone two, it's crazy expensive in zone one,' she tells me. 'We take a bus, then walk a little. Just a little, don't worry. Are you all right with that suitcase?'

I nod. My suitcase has wheels, so I can just drag it. I still don't understand what she means by these zones, though, but I don't press for an explanation. We arrive at her flat, located above a large workshop. 'At night, this garage is used for parties,' she says. Her place isn't bad, but it's not what you'd call nice. It reminds me of a room I once rented in Jakarta. The difference is that mine was tidier and less dusty. The good thing is she has a sofa and a small kitchen.

'Take a seat. What do you want to drink? I can make you a gin and tonic. I have whisky and wine, just name it.'

I shake my head. 'No thanks ...' It's only three in the afternoon, and all I want is to lie down or eat something.

'Do you want to spend the night here?' she asks.

I do a double take. What does she mean by that? I thought she brought me here because she invited me to stay at her place for a while. However, I don't want to show surprise. Maybe this is the British way.

'If possible,' I reply. 'I can sleep on the couch.'

'Oh, of course it's possible ... don't be stupid,' she says, then lets out a slightly awkward chuckle.

Linda Nor then tells me she has to go out for a bit to see her friends. I can come if I want. However, I can see that is just a polite offer. And even if she does mean it, I really don't want to go out. I just want to rest. She smiles and tells me to help myself to anything in the fridge if I'm hungry. She advises me not to open the door for anyone, even if they're banging on it. And she tells me not to ask why. 'Don't ask for the reason. Just don't open it.' I nod and nod. I guess, considering it's in zone two, as she said, there are probably a lot of odd people around here.

After Linda leaves, I quickly take out my laptop and connect to the Wi-Fi. I text my brother that I've arrived in London safely. He replies with an 'Oh', but I know he will pass the message on to my mom. The second thing I do is log into Expedia and Traveloka, two travel sites. I don't want to use Airbnb. It's too risky. I don't even know where I am now. I figure I better stay in a hostel for a while. In less than half an hour, I find a cheap hostel room in Hammersmith. I don't know where it is, but I book it for four days.

I'm starving, exhausted and jet-lagged. These three things make me unable to think clearly, so I decide to sleep.

I'm awakened by banging on the door. It's eight o'clock in the evening. The banging doesn't stop for several minutes. This must be what Linda Nor meant.

'I know you're inside!' a man screams.

My heart is pounding. I want to scream, 'No, she's not here!' so that the guy will stop banging and leave, but I know that would be foolish. I just curl up on the couch like an abandoned puppy, hoping the door doesn't break. Finally, after ten scary minutes, the banging stops. I'm so relieved. I hope whoever was outside has gone.

Once the fear subsides, all that's left is hunger. However, I don't get up to look for food in the fridge. I just want to get out of this place. I don't know exactly what time Linda gets home, but she certainly doesn't worry about making a racket when she fixes herself a drink, even though she knows I'm sleeping on the couch not far from her.

***

By nine the next morning I've downloaded Citymapper, a map app so I won't get lost in London. Linda doesn't wake up until noon, so I have to wait for her, even though I've showered and I'm ready to go. When she finally wakes up, she lazily says good morning and asks what my plans are.

'I'll buy a SIM card for my phone,' I reply.

'Brilliant,' she says, sipping her gin, then scratching something on her elbow. 'You know how to survive,' she continues. Perhaps she's offering a compliment. She then asks me to tell her about Maroje. Honestly, I don't want to talk about him anymore. I've almost forgotten him. But, because I will feel bad if I don't answer, I tell her just a bit. I think in the end, we both know that the conversation is just small talk.

She walks me to the door and points me to a kiosk where I can buy a SIM card.

'Do you have pounds sterling?' she asks.

'Yes, I exchanged some in Indonesia.'

She smiles. 'I'm sorry I can't give you a proper London tour. I'm busy this week. But I promise we'll hang out this weekend, okay?'

'Yeah, no problem.' I'm actually hoping she will make time for me. I mean, if she really has a job, I hope she will take some time off and introduce me to London. I don't expect her to take me to loads of places, but just to give me instructions on dos and don'ts. But of course, I can't ask her for that. Besides, I'm a big girl, and I have to be able to take care of myself.

'But, what about the job in the restaurant ...'

'Oh yeah, I almost forgot. You really want it?'

'Yes, of course,' I gasp.

'Oh, I thought that was just your excuse. I didn't know you were serious.'

My heart skips a few beats. What does she mean by that? I spent half my savings on a visa and plane tickets to come here. How could I not seriously want to work in London?

'Linda, I mean it ...'

'I will ask my boyfriend. That should be very easy. Don't worry, I'll take care of it. I'll get back to you soon, okay? Let me know your new phone number later.'

I nod.

'Don't be so nervous,' she says, then lets out a laugh. I respond with an awkward chuckle.

Before she closes the door, she tells me to be careful and to send her news after checking in to the hostel. Only when I walk away from her residence do I realize that I've just been thrown into a completely foreign realm. What have I done?

43

After dragging my suitcase, which luckily is not too heavy, I finally arrive in Hammersmith. It isn't long before I find my hostel, which looks like a typical British red brick building. I check in and get allocated a dorm room for four people. I'm used to living in a cabin with four people, so it doesn't really matter. It's just that my roommates in the hostel are two men ... and a woman who snores.

I spend my afternoon as a tourist: hunting for food and strolling through the pretty cool Hammersmith area (certainly cooler than Linda's neighbourhood in zone two). There are many second-hand clothing stores and familiar fast-food restaurants. Oh my God, I find KFC, and it feels like a blessing. After munching on some fried chicken, I return to the hostel because the weather is freezing. I know it's September, but I didn't think it would be this cold. If only I had the windproof jacket that I used to wear on the ship ... thinking of it makes me reminisce about nights on fire patrol and I remember Maroje too. Oh damn. It immediately puts me in a bad mood. I crumple on my bed until my roommates finally arrive.

'Hey, where are you from?' asks a black man who sleeps on the other bottom bunk. He has a thick British accent.

'Indonesia,' I squeak.

'How are you?'

'Fine,' I reply. 'Don't talk so fast. I don't understand,' I plead.

He laughs and starts talking slower. He asks if I'm a tourist, and I say I'm here because I want to work. He says we're on the same page. Then another roommate arrives, an older man. He introduces himself in a friendly manner. He is from Italy and works here. The Italian, whose English is broken but I understand him better, says he has lived in this hostel for three months, and some people have stayed more than a year. He says that living in a hostel in London is cheaper than renting your own room or flat. I don't know how my mom would react if she found out I'm sharing a room with two grown men, but they seem like nice people.

'You have to register yourself with an employment agency.'

'Oh, I've got a work contract already. I'm just waiting for the call,' I answer.

'Then good for you.'

Since the three of us work in a restaurant, the conversation flows without any awkward pauses even though they are in the kitchen. We chat about how exciting and stressful it is to work in the hospitality business. We talk until we finally exhaust ourselves and decide to sleep. Around midnight, another roommate arrives, a woman who appears to be a tourist. She immediately climbs into her bed above me then snores loudly.

The next day I tell Linda about my whereabouts. She asks if I am eating well, how the environment is, whether I like London, etc. She is pretty sweet, but she doesn't mention my employment at all. I want to ask her about it, but I don't want to sound too pushy. 'Oh, have some fun first,' she says finally, as if reading my mind. 'You just got here, relax.'

I'm already bored to death. Not that I'm not excited about being in London, but I'm not here for sightseeing. I don't want to waste my time idling. If so, what's the difference between me just staying at home? Two of my roommates have already left for work while I'm still yawning, and the snoring woman wakes up a little late. She says she is from Canada and is travelling around the world. Wow, what a nice life.

'When exactly are you going to start working?' she asks.

'I don't know exactly when,' I reply. 'They haven't told me. I hope soon.'

She nods. 'Then what are you going to do while you wait?'

I shrug, 'I don't know.'

'You mean you're not going to do anything?'

'Maybe sleep, eat, and explore around here.'

She lets out a voice that sounds like a 'hmm'. 'Sounds nice but why don't you take a tour of London first?' She gives a smile that implies that I'm wasting my time and not doing anything meaningful. After tidying up her clothes and packing her backpack, the woman leaves the hostel without even taking a shower.

In the afternoon, I eat at KFC again. I sit there for quite a while updating my Facebook status with a location check-in: I am in London, and it's a lovely sunny day like a dream come true. I take a selfie with some white people in the background just to make it convincing. The photo gets many reactions, and most of them are nasty comments like, 'So rich, always travelling' and so on. All those comments I reply to with a smiley emoji, implying that I'm a polite person, but honestly I don't care.

Linda Nor still does not call me for the next two days. On the third day, I decide to follow the snoring woman's advice, going out to explore London like a tourist. I intend to see the famous River Thames and then ride the London Eye, a giant wheel that has become one of the city's icons.

I'll tell you, the River Thames is brown in colour, and the London Eye is pretty expensive: over £20 per ride. So I tell myself I can ride that another time when I have more in my pocket. Then it starts to drizzle in the late afternoon, and like a hermit crab being touched I hurry back to Hammersmith to curl up on my single bed at the hostel. London is not very cool. Nothing's great here; I just want to work.

44

'Where are you now?' asks Linda.

'I changed my hostel.' I tell her the new address.

After four days, I will move to a hostel in Edgware Road because I can't extend my stay; it's fully booked.

'Okay, we'll meet there, shall we?'

I take the Tube and arrive in Edgware Road not long afterwards. As usual, I drag my suitcase along as I get to know the street. Many shops offer halal food. Linda has evidently arrived before me. She doesn't ask why I am changing hostels. Her expression looks worried and she seems in a hurry. She stands next to me, watching as I check in. As I get my room key, Linda hurriedly invites me to sit on the hostel couch, which is shabby but comfortable.

'I already told my boyfriend. He said you can start to work in a few days,' she begins.

She has no idea how relieved I am to hear the news. I feel like hugging her. But it looks like she hasn't showered and she's a little dishevelled. Her hair isn't as beautiful as Farah Fawcett's anymore.

'Thank you,' I say sincerely as I take her hand. She smiles, then gives an expression like 'ah, you don't have to say that'.

'I need your help,' she says.

'Yes, of course. Anything, as long as I can.'

'Good.'

Then without further ado, she tells me that she is in a lot of trouble. Her son, who usually sends her money, got angry with her and withheld his transfer this month. I didn't even know she had a child.

'I have to pay the rent today. It was due a few days ago. The thing is, I'm new in London so I can't ask anyone for help. You are my only hope. Actually, I almost never ask for help like this, I feel so ashamed. But I really have to.'

I give the request some thought. It's fine, she has helped me a lot, and it looks like she's in real trouble. Apart from taking pity on her, I will also feel bad if I don't help her.

'How much do you need?'

'Seven hundred pounds. You have it, right?'

I nod. I tell her I only have thirty million rupiah left in my savings, about sixteen hundred pounds. She look a little surprised when she hears about my savings.

'But I don't have cash. I have to take it from the ATM.'

'Are you sure it's okay to lend me the money?' she asks.

'Of course, you need it. But you will return it, right?'

'Yes! If necessary, we will make an agreement, with a signature.'

'No need, I trust you.'

She has gone through all the hassle of completing my visa requirements, picking me up from the airport, and she is about to give me a job. How could I not believe her? I mean, she's done a lot more for me than the other way around. When I arrived, I only brought her Dji Sam Soe clove cigarettes and a packet of Javanese coffee.

We walk over to the cash machine, and without hesitation I hand her the money.

'I will return it next month on the second.'

I can sense that Linda is a little nervous when she says that. Her voice wobbles, and she seems on edge. She must feel really embarrassed.

I agree to lend her the money for a month. I still have £900 in my savings, and this week I will start work, so I am not worried about running out of money. It means I probably won't be able to rent an apartment this month, but like other workers I can stay in hostels.

'You're really a good person, you know that?' she says, as she slips the money into her handbag.

'What are you talking about? Quite the opposite.'

She walks me back to the hostel and tells me she will contact her boyfriend for the job details. There is no better news than that. We hug tightly before finally parting ways.

45

My new hostel is crammed with backpackers. There's an age limit. You can't stay here if you're over forty years old. I don't have to worry. I can stay in this hostel for nine more years. The downside is I get to stay in a dorm room with ten other people. The bunk beds are arranged three tiers high. My room is full, but I don't know where my roommates are because the room is always dark. When someone comes back to the room at night, they have to sneak around or get ready to be yelled at. 'Damn it, people are trying to sleep here!'

In this neighbourhood, people swarm to the bars at the end of the working day. They stand under awnings, holding pints of beer or glasses of wine while chatting and smoking cigarettes. I just want to eat something normal and cheap.

I find Tesco, a large and well-stocked supermarket. They sell cheap frozen fast food. I can get a packet of rice for a pound and a boiled egg or seasoned chicken for two pounds. They just need to be reheated. With three pounds, I can eat a proper meal. I smile to myself for discovering a trick to survive in London, one of the most expensive cities in the world. Since working on the ship, I am no longer a picky eater. I will put anything in my tummy as long as it makes me full.

But I end up buying a large packet of crisps, a bunch of green grapes, a few bars of chocolate and other sweets, and a (rather expensive) portion of Thai food. I spend more money than eating at KFC. It's okay if I am a little extravagant. Soon I will start working, and the salary will be paid weekly.

While eating Thai food in the TV room at the hostel (they also have a lively bar), I double-check my contract and find out that I will be working in an area called Soho for £7 an hour. I open the map I got from the reception desk and start studying London districts.

Hostels are filled with travellers from all over the world. I am tempted to offers hellos but I'm afraid they might think I'm a weirdo. Instead, I stand and watch them from afar, like a statue in Prambanan temple.

Two days later, Linda asks if I have heard from her boyfriend, whose name is Matthew.

'No one called me, my phone is always on,' I reply.

'Maybe he forgot or is busy; I'll remind him,' she says.

However, I receive no news for another two days.

I go to the TV room to drop my butt in the corner of the long sofa. I try to contact Linda again through WhatsApp, but it turns out to be inactive. I give it a few hours then work up the courage to call her. I have even put together the words I want to say. Unfortunately, the call goes to voicemail.

Her phone is unreachable for the whole day.

My brows are permanently furrowed as a result of giving this too much thought. I don't want to give in to these negative thoughts, thoughts that may have crossed your mind too. I am just trying to be positive, which is kind of futile because I honestly feel really uncomfortable about this.

Night brings temporary peace, but when I wake up the next morning, I find all my messages to Linda have been delivered ... and there is still no reply.

I decide to send her some messages via Messenger. The messages are read, but again, no replies. My messages are nothing serious, just casual like: 'Hi Linda ...', 'Linda, how are you?', 'Are you okay?', 'Hello ...'.

Then I decide to call her number, but it is immediately rejected. She ends up texting me via SMS. That surprises me a bit.

'Who is this?'

'It's me, Maya ...'

It isn't long before I get a reply: 'I don't know you.'

I am astonished. Could it be that her phone's been stolen? Is she in trouble?

'Are you Linda?' The message is ignored for a few minutes until I send another one. 'Hey, answer!'

'I don't know you!'

I get the same message.

'You thief! Return this phone!' I jump to the most probable conclusion. Of course, the message is not answered. What kind of thief answers messages?

I turn to Facebook and chat with Linda on Messenger again.

'Linda, are you okay? Has someone stolen your phone?'

Two seconds later, there is a notification that I can no longer text Linda Nor on Messenger. And her profile disappears. I just got blocked? I try WhatsApp once more, but it turns out I am blocked there as well. So now I accept where this drama is heading.

In desperation, I send her an SMS text. About why she did those things. What about the job she promised and the money I lent her? Shortly afterwards I receive a text in reply:

'Stop terrorizing me and sending me rude texts. I don't know you and don't understand what you're talking about. About work or money. I don't owe anyone any money! I'll report you to the police if you keep doing this!'

Mf! Such a Satan! No sane person would assume anything positive at this point. You didn't have to be a genius to understand what Linda was playing at. But what I didn't understand were her reasons. While trying to calm myself down, I try to rationalize all of this. She's borrowed my money and doesn't want to pay it back; okay, I understand she might be having difficulties now, but pretending not to know me and just cutting ties? It's very psychotic.

Someone comes up to me and asks: 'Hey, are you alright?'

I am confused about how to answer. So I just move my lips. 'Maybe.'

'Hang in there,' he says. Perhaps he's sincere but that's not important. Okay, what should I do now?

I go to Tesco to buy two packs of M&M's. I need serotonin to boost my mood. Outside the shop I stand next to a homeless man. Reflecting. All the while eating a handful of chocolate buttons. I try to remember where Linda lives, then decide to go there.

It takes me two hours until I am finally in her neighbourhood again, in zone two, around Manor House. Eventually I find her flat, which is above a workshop. I knock on her door politely like a proper guest. No one opens the door. Maybe she doesn't hear me, or maybe she is in the bathroom.

I knock again. This time a little harder. Maybe she's not home? Then I start banging. I bang so hard that I want to break down the door. Am I stupid or what? She must be pretending she isn't home. And it reminds me of the time I spent the night here, and she told me not to open the door. 'Don't ask why!' she had warned me. I thought it was because there were so many criminals in zone two, but maybe they were just people who wanted their money back. Like I do. Ish!

I wait in front of the door for ten more minutes, banging until my hands grow callused. In reality, I'm not trying to force her to pay me back now. I'm just trying to get a handle on the situation. What should I do now? She promised me a job, and her boyfriend hasn't contacted me yet. I feel like I'm on the verge of a nervous breakdown.

I return to the hostel to wallow in self-pity and curse Linda. Why would she put me in this situation? Why has she abandoned me here? I'm all alone, and I'm overwhelmed with frustration, but I know shedding tears won't change anything. I need to think clearly and find a way to survive. In this moment of uncertainty, I'm reminded of the Little Mermaid statue in Copenhagen. Even though her head has been decapitated, and dildos plastered to her hands, she still sits by the sea. She may appear melancholic, but she endures.

46

I have a work contract, and it can't be fake, right? It has the restaurant's name and address on it. I figure I'll go to the restaurant, find Linda's boyfriend Matthew and sort things out with him. Despite my exhaustion, I can't stand having unfinished business, and I need answers as soon as possible.

I've never been to Soho before. I take the Tube and disembark at Piccadilly Circus station, immediately overwhelmed by the vibrant hustle and bustle on the street. The streetlamps shine brightly, and tourists swarm everywhere, snapping photos, laughing or studying their maps. As much as I'd love to play the tourist and explore, this isn't the time. My priority is finding a bar called Yard. I navigate the streets like a confused deer, relying on Google Maps to guide me.

Soho is a labyrinth of bars, cafés and restaurants, ranging from fast food to fine dining. It offers cuisines from Europe, Asia and fusion styles. The area is dotted with theatres, cinemas, bookstores, CD shops and other intriguing places. I locate Yard, tucked between a sushi restaurant and a closed-down shop. Yard is a modest, almost deserted bar that appears to specialize in fish and chips.

I enter the bar, and a disinterested-looking woman greets me with, 'Hi, how many people?'

I stammer, 'Oh no ... I just ... I want to see Matthew.'

She furrows her brow and disappears through the staff door.

I wait for what feels like an eternity until a burly man with fiery orange hair finally emerges. We exchange greetings almost simultaneously.

'Can I help you?' he asks.

I introduce myself and waste no time presenting my work contract, extracted from my ugly sling bag. He accepts the document without protest and reviews it. His expression hints at impending bad news.

'I'm sorry, I can't help you.'

'What do you mean? I'm supposed to work here, right? This contract is legitimate, isn't it? This is the restaurant, correct? And that's your signature, right?' I stumble over my words.

'Yes, yes, I remember creating this contract. But I sold this restaurant a few days ago, and we'll be closing down next week.'

'Huh? How did this happen?' I ask, although I already know the answer.

'I'm sorry. I wish I could help you.'

Though he sounds sincere, I must contemplate my circumstances. 'I have this work contract! You have to hire me. I came all the way from Indonesia for this job.'

He huffs. 'Oh, she mentioned you needed help getting here, but I never guaranteed a job.'

I don't want to give up easily. 'But Linda said you'd give me a job.'

'I wish I could help you. However, I don't own a restaurant anymore,' he sighs. 'I'm returning to my hometown in Ireland.'

'I can sue you, you know? I can hire a lawyer because you've violated our contract,' I threaten.

'Trust me, you don't want to do that. It will cost you a lot,' he looks at me with a hint of sympathy. 'You already have a work visa for a year. You can use it to find job elsewhere. There are many waitress vacancies around here. I heard you used to be a waitress on a cruise ship, so you must have a good CV.'

'Yes, of course, I do. But that's not the point, is it?'

He ponders for a moment, 'How about this: I'll call a friend who owns a bar, and you can work there.'

I express my frustration, 'How about you give me some money for my fare home?'

'I can't do that,' he replies, before continuing, 'Do you want to go home?'

I fall silent, wrestling with my predicament.

'I heard you came here because you wanted to add some flavour to your life, but if you go back now, you'll still be the same old vanilla,' Matthew states, before scribbling something on a piece of paper. 'Trust me, this is the best option for you,' he says, handing me the paper.

'What about Linda?' I ask, refusing to accept the paper.

He looks puzzled, 'What's with her? I haven't been in touch with her for two weeks.'

'She borrowed my money.' Matthew narrows his eyes, and I continue, 'And now she's unreachable.'

He sighs, as though this is not the first time he's heard this story. 'I can't help you with that. That's between you and her,' he replies, looking uncomfortable.

'I don't have much money left. That's all I have,' I admit, a feeling of desolation washing over me. Matthew looks at me with even more sympathy before pushing the crumpled paper back into my hand.

'Please help … I don't know what to do,' I plead, kneading the paper into a wrinkled mess. Matthew leaves me and disappears through the staff door.

The skinny waitress returns, her expression unchanged. 'Welcome to London,' she mutters, returning to her post behind the counter. I exit the restaurant with a heavy heart and a deflated spirit.

I decide to take a detour to Shaftesbury Memorial Fountain, featuring a statue of a flying angel at its peak. Many people are gathered around, enjoying the street performers. I join them, not for the music, but to sit and cry like a fragile little girl. Nobody pays me any mind. 'I broke your purple dildo, you b****!' I cry out.

47

Life in London is not as wonderful as I had imagined. Many people might think that living and working here is glamorous – and that's true if you have a lot of money. However, for those in the working class, especially in migrant limbo like me, living in this city is much like living in any other big city. Everything is ridiculously expensive. Even with the remainder of my savings, which would have made me comfortable back in Indonesia, I find it hard to make ends meet in London.

I contemplate returning to Indonesia. But what would I tell everyone? That I spent the rest of my savings on a ten-day holiday in London, mostly holed up in a hostel room? Venturing out only to the banks of the Thames and Soho, where I ended up being scammed? What a waste. If Kanompang finds out, she'd probably laugh at me. Matthew is right; I can't go home now. Not until I find something here. At least until there's a little more excitement in my otherwise mundane existence.

Oh, God Almighty, guide me, please. Though, of course, I don't receive any divine leads in the end! Duh.

What I do next is spend two consecutive days in the hostel's TV room, munching on Doritos. The relentless rain keeps me indoors. I keep telling myself that I should start looking for work, walking door to door with my CV in hand, like the main character in *Orange Is the New Black*. Who knows, maybe I'll encounter a rebellious girl who turns out to be a criminal, and I'll end up in jail. Life in prison might be more manageable – no need to worry about work or the future. Food and shelter are guaranteed. It might even be better than this aimless existence. Maybe I should become a criminal first? But if anyone deserves jail time, it's Linda, the one who got me into this mess. I can tell she has ringworm on her knees; she wouldn't stop scratching them even when we were on the Tube. Ugh. I hope her life becomes miserable. However, I also hope she lives long enough for the earth to reject her upon burial, so her rotting corpse ends up in the gutter!

Thinking of her angers me, and I unconsciously grab a pillow from the sofa and scream into it.

'Is everything okay?' the receptionist asks, relaxing at her desk. Besides handling check-ins and check-outs, she tends the bar and must be quite skilled at making drinks.

'It's not okay,' I roar. There are no other guests in the TV room, they're out exploring London. 'I need to find a job.'

'What kind of job are you looking for?'

'I'm a waiter.'

'Unfortunately, we don't have any openings right now.'

I cover my face again with the pillow and let out a second scream.

'Maybe you should go outside for a bit. You've been sitting here for two days. I thought you were heartbroken ...'

Then I think of Maroje, and I grow even sadder.

'Hey, don't cry. I have an umbrella if you want to go outside.'

Why an umbrella? I'd prefer food.

With my weak body and teeth full of Doritos crumbs, I take the proffered umbrella and exit the hostel. I'll let my feet lead me wherever they please. My feet, tiny like chicken feet, clad only in flip-flops, take me on a stroll on a cold, rainy London day.

I'm not sure what triggers it, perhaps a clap of thunder, but I return to the hostel to put on my shoes, grab my Oyster card, CV and passport. I take the Tube to Piccadilly Circus and make my way to Soho. It's still pouring with rain, and I walk from bar to bar, mustering the courage to enter and enquire about job openings. After all, this is London, not Jakarta. It's intimidating. My English isn't fluent, and I have to communicate with people who speak British English. Many times all I can manage is a confused 'What?' or a meek 'Sorry, sorry' because I can't catch what they're saying. Finally, at a McDonald's, I whisper to one of the cashiers after ordering a Happy Meal, my voice trembling, 'Excuse me, are there any job openings here?'

She casually informs me that I need to apply online. 'Thanks,' I say, to which she responds with a friendly smile. It isn't as daunting as I thought. I can do this.

With three CVs in hand, I visit bar after bar. 'Sorry ...' 'Nothing available right now, but feel free to leave your CV.' 'You might want to try the club down the street; they often have openings.' 'We don't have a position for you at the moment ...' 'Sorry ...'

Where are these abundant vacancies I've heard about? I've walked so much that I've worn a permanent smile, and there are no openings! Exhausted, I return to the hostel.

'How did it go?' the receptionist asks.

'No job, no rice, no power,' I reply as I hand back the umbrella.

She chuckles. 'Good to see you have a sense of humour now.'

'Thanks,' I say, casting my last smile of the day, and head up to my room. At least today I made an effort to do something instead of wallowing in the corner of the couch.

48

The next day I decide to return to Soho with a bit more enthusiasm. Soho is just as bustling as the day before. Tourists swarm like bees, seeking out cafés and theatres. Some are busy taking photos with the iconic red double-decker buses driving by. Wealthier tourists roam Oxford and Regent Street, indulging in branded shopping sprees. Luckily the sky is a little clearer today, so my light makeup looks very natural, giving the impression that I am a very lively and upbeat jobseeker from Indonesia.

However, just five minutes later, the rain begins to fall. I'm caught unprepared, and my hair gets drenched as I seek shelter. How classy, London. How could I forget to bring a comb and face powder for such an emergency? But that won't stop me from my mission to find a job. Despite looking like a drowned kitten, I keep on going in and out of bars, restaurants and clubs to try my luck. By three o'clock in the afternoon, I manage to leave my CV at two different restaurants.

I notice a vacancy sign in a restaurant window and approach. 'Is the position still available?'

'Can you cook?' It's an Asian-European fusion restaurant.

'Sadly, no. But I can work as a waiter,' I say as I'm about to hand over my CV. Without even glancing at it, the person shakes his head and walks off. 'We don't need servers,' he remarks before disappearing.

I decide to have a late lunch at Nando's and enjoy grilled chicken with a selection of hot sauces. I feel guilty afterwards for indulging in something so pricey when I should have been more frugal. Following the guilty but delicious meal, I force myself to explore more places, including the Chinatown area. Whenever I step into a fine-dining restaurant, I feel out of place and unworthy. With my appearance and less-than-perfect English, I doubt I could ever fit into such an upscale environment.

As evening descends, the Piccadilly Circus, Soho and Oxford

Street areas come alive with sparkling lights. Bars that were previously closed now welcome customers. My legs ache from walking, and my mind is clouded with negative thoughts. I just want to go home. Finding myself in a dimly lit corner of a street, I crouch down and let out a sigh of self-pity.

But nothing miraculous happens. I don't expect any miracles. In the real world, there are no fairy godmothers to come to your rescue. Everything we desire has to be earned through hard work.

Even though I know the night is still young in Soho, and the area will really come to life after dark, I decide to head back to the hostel.

*   *   *

When I arrive, I immediately seek out the receptionist. I want to chat for a while, to vent. I know she's a stranger, but she's the closest thing to a friend I have right now. Unfortunately, only a man with dreadlocks is behind the desk. It appears it's not her shift tonight. I have to suppress everything I want to say. So, I decide to curl up in the corner of the couch and watch television while other backpackers come and go, either checking in or having drinks at the bar.

'Are you all right, darling?' a man with a rather flamboyant voice asks.

I'm slightly taken aback by his question. 'I'm okay,' I reply.

He sits down next to me without an invitation. 'Are you sure? You look dreadful.'

Do I look that bad? I finally sit up straight to show that I'm not in terrible shape, just somewhat drained.

After some more casual conversation, I finally spill the details of what has happened to me. I tell him that I'm searching for a job and that I'm almost starving. I'm not sure why I did that – perhaps it's a desperate attempt to save myself. Sharing my sorrows makes them feel a bit lighter.

'You poor thing,' he says sympathetically. 'Let's explore Soho together. How about tomorrow?'

'Are you also looking for work?' I ask.

'What? Of course not, darling. I'm such a fabulous person that jobs are looking for me.'

49

The following day, Erick doesn't seem all that motivated to help me find a job. We head to Soho around three in the afternoon, and he tells me he's from Manchester, a rainy city in England. 'I know a great, affordable place to eat called Zedel, and that's where we're having lunch. Afterwards, we'll get coffee at Caffè Nero. And when night falls, we'll visit a gay bar. There are plenty of them in this area. You haven't truly experienced London until you've been to a gay bar.'

'But, Erick, I need to find a job, and I'm not gay,' I protest.

'Of course we're looking for work. That's why we're going to these places. And don't be sad if you're not gay.'

At Zedel, he flirts with the waiter, and I feel out of place in this elegant restaurant with its predominantly red decor and professional-looking staff.

'I don't want to work in a place like this,' I whisper, feeling intimidated by the patrons.

'We can look for another place, but let's have lunch here first.'

The menu at Zedel is in French, so I opt for something familiar, the quiche Lorraine, while Erick orders something that sounds like celery remoulade. After our late lunch, we head to Caffè Nero for a flat white.

'So, when are we going to start looking for work?' I ask.

'Don't worry, it's still early. Work usually comes when the sun goes down,' Erick casually replies.

I give him a disapproving look, even though I'm secretly enjoying the day so far. Sipping coffee while seated at a Soho street-side café and observing British people passing by makes me feel somewhat sophisticated. I ask Erick for a selfie and post it on Facebook to show everyone that I'm living a fun and cool life, making international friends.

'You don't want to work here, do you?' he asks.

'In this café? No, it's very crowded. I can't handle it, and I don't know much about coffee,' I say as I take a sip of my flat white.

'You're quite picky, aren't you?'

'That's my life motto: stay snobbish even if you're poor.'

Erick chuckles.

'I just want a normal job, not too busy or too stressful,' I add.

'Picky,' he repeats.

Erick then opens up about his dreams, which I find quite entertaining. He aspires to be an artist and have his own stage. What surprises me is that he's only nineteen years old. It's impressive that he has a dream he's passionate about and genuinely enjoys. As for me, what am I? A discarded piece of trash in the world's gutter.

But Erick isn't overly self-absorbed. He seems to respect me and asks about life in Indonesia and how I can afford to travel the world like this. He's never left England and only visits London once a month to hang out at gay bars in Soho. I don't really want to share all the details of my life; I'm afraid he'll figure out how old I am. So, I try to change the topic, talking about the British boys passing by us.

'Oh, he's too skinny for you. You need a strapping English guy, or a Scottish man in a kilt,' he says. We laugh until the sun sets.

'Let's go somewhere more fun,' Erick suggests.

We leave the café, ignoring the chilly autumn weather that's starting to make me uncomfortable. Erick shows me around a bit, asking if I'd like to work in a Mexican restaurant or an Italian one. I explain that I've already applied to many places, but they're looking for chefs not waiters.

'Come with me to this special store, I need to buy something,' he says, dragging me into a peculiar shop with an extensive collection of underwear, from cotton to latex and leather. On the shelves, I spot DVDs, same-sex adult films, different types of condoms and lubricants, as well as knick-knacks with a rainbow theme, like keychains and coasters. As we walk further into the store, I see an even more exotic assortment: sex toys. It's a gay sex shop, and Erick is clearly amused by my wide-eyed astonishment.

'You don't have anything like this in Indonesia?' he asks.

'No, not that I know of,' I reply with eyes still wide. I can see row upon row of dildos of all sizes and colours.

'I want to buy Tenga and some sounding needles,' he says. 'For gifts.'

'Huh?'

'You don't want to know what they are.' He goes to the cashier to ask about the items he's after. Meanwhile, I pretend to examine a highly elastic egg-like object while sneakily checking out the handsome cashier. There are no women in the shop, only two shy-looking young Indian boys. I've seen a sex shop before in Saint Petersburg when the cruise ship docked there, but I didn't go inside. Just seeing the shop from the outside had made me uncomfortable enough. Now, here I am, inside a gay one, which somehow feels even more intimidating. There's a life-sized poster of a man wearing a black leather hat, and a rather explicit object dangles from his crotch.

'Erick, you do realize I'm a girl, right?' I puff out my chest to emphasize my femininity.

Erick covers his mouth, 'Oh my God … really? I thought you were a young boy, like Oliver Twist.'

'Seriously, the cashier has been staring at me the entire time.'

'He's hot,' says Erick.

'Seriously!'

'I told him you're looking for a job, but you're like the Virgin Mary …'

'I am not the Virgin Mary ... I'm a badass girl!'

Erick nearly chokes on hearing that.

'I can see that you're on the verge of having your eyeballs pop out just by looking at these things. You don't even know what 99% of them are ...' he remarks.

'Yes, but that's because it's a gay sex shop!'

'I couldn't agree more,' he rolls his eyes.

The cashier comes back from the storeroom and shows us some items, which Erick then approves. He pays for everything quickly. The cashier glances at me. I can see his nametag: Josh. His hair is blonde.

'Hey, you need a job?' he asks me in a crisp voice.

'Yes, of course. I can work as anything, don't be fooled by my small and weak appearance. I'm not a good girl. I can do anything for pounds.' I don't know why I spout like that.

'Yes, gurl, she is really a badass,' says Erick, nodding.

Josh smiles. 'Wait a minute,' then he takes out his mobile and make a call. I try to listen to the conversation, but he speaks too fast. After a minute or two, he hangs up and tells me if I really can do anything, he can help me. I feel a little nervous, but I try to be cool.

50

'Um, is this even legit?' I probe, quirking an eyebrow.

'I'm not sure,' Erick shrugs. 'It might be a bit of a grey area.'

'I'm not signing up for any sort of … night services, am I? Prostitution isn't on my career wish list,' I quip.

Erick, giving me a teasing smirk, says, 'Oh, so you're a little spitfire but not that adventurous, huh?'

Rolling my eyes, I agree, 'Exactly.'

'There's a connection, but it's not what you're thinking,' Josh interjects with a knowing smile.

Handing me an address that's close to our current location, he instructs, 'Knock and just tell them I sent you.' I nod gratefully, shooting Erick a glance which clearly screams 'let's bolt'.

Once we're outside, Erick, with his ever-present flair, says, 'If you're afraid, we don't have to do it.'

'What kind of job is it? I'm dying to find out.'

Erick humorously prods, 'So, what's the plan?'

'Let's find out. If I don't like it, I can always decline it. It's that simple.'

Erick, however, adds a touch of playful paranoia, 'But I am a bit concerned about us getting chopped up or something.'

I shake my head, half-amused and half-startled, 'Erick, you scare me.'

He grins mischievously. 'I'm just kidding. You don't have to worry, you're safe with me. I don't know karate, but I know ka-razy.'

We make our way through the streets, taking in the shops, bars and restaurants until we reach our destination. It's a dimly lit Greek restaurant tucked away on a quiet corner. According to Josh, this is the place, and we begin our search for the side entrance and stairs leading to a basement.

Erick knocks on the door, and a man with a thick moustache answers, squinting at us in curiosity.

'Josh sent us,' I explain, as Erick appears to freeze for a moment.

The man's squint transforms into a friendlier expression, and he invites us into the basement, where there's a modest counter. We're instructed to sit on some sofas nearby. Two blonde women with slightly heavy makeup are already seated on the sofas, and one of them is smoking. The moustachioed man asks for my name.

'Xena,' I respond, choosing a pseudonym. The name just came to me, inspired by the warrior princess. Later I tell them my real name, but Xena has already stuck.

The man introduces himself as Geoff, offering a handshake after a brief moment of surprise. Erick, on the other hand, declines the handshake and plays along with the scenario.

Geoff sizes me up, 'You've got spunk. But I'm guessing you're not here to join the ladies? We're always short on Asians.'

'Uh, definitely not,' I laugh nervously.

'You ever done marketing?'

'Kind of. I sold internet plans for a bit,' I respond, a little perplexed at the question.

'Not too different,' he says, 'But you'll be marketing ... well ... these ladies.'

'To businesses?' My voice sounds incredulously high-pitched.

Erick breaks into a fit of giggles, 'No, darling. Street marketing.'

Rolling my eyes, I ask Geoff, 'Is this the offer?'

Geoff nods with a mischievous smile. 'The pay's decent.

Especially if you bring in clients.'

'I've never done anything like this before,' I say.

'It's easy, I'll teach you,' says Erick.

'You'll work here too?'

'Oh no, I don't want to steal your job. I just want to show how it's done. I've done it a few times.'

I'm unsure about this unconventional job offer.

Geoff outlines the details of the job. He offers £3 per hour for six hours every night, with an extra £5 for each customer I bring in. It's not a lot of money, but it will cover my hostel rent.

He suggests I return the next night to start working at eleven, if I'm still interested, and we're soon shown the door. Erick, however, takes it upon himself to commit me to returning the following night.

***

I'm not entirely sure what I've gotten myself into, but it's a way to earn money. I leave the dimly lit basement with a mixture of uncertainty and curiosity.

Outside, I express my doubts to Erick as we walk back to the busier part of the street. 'I don't know how to do this.'

'Watch me.'

Erick approaches a passer-by, a man. Then, with a campy style, he engages in a brief conversation and eventually asks if the man is interested in 'a lady tonight'. The passer-by declines and walks on.

Erick returns to me, raising an eyebrow. 'See, easy as pie.'

My heart is racing. 'Erick, is this even legal?'

Erick dismisses my concerns, 'Forget about the law, we're in Soho.'

My next memory is of Erick taking me to a bustling gay bar, where he forces me to enjoy a raspberry mojito and sit on the sofa while he mingles with other gay guys. I quickly lose track of time and reality.

Erick pokes me from my tipsy nap, 'I'm not heading back to the hostel tonight. Is it okay for you to go home alone?'

I look at my phone and see it's already one in the morning.

'Why aren't you going back to the hostel too?' I ask, a little confused at first. Then I notice an older man in a flannel shirt standing next to Erick, and it suddenly clicks. I give a short 'oh', then grumble an 'okay' as I shuffle off the couch.

'Hey, you don't have to go now. If you like, you can stay longer … or sleep some more.'

'No, I'm going now.'

'Bye?' asks Eric.

We share a brief hug, and I thank him for the day. My head throbs slightly, perhaps a result of the raspberry mojito.

51

It's still a mystery how I manage to get back to the hostel. One raspberry mojito and I'm down for the count. I can't quite live up to the Xena name, it seems. Thankfully, I don't get lost or end up joining the ranks of those who regrettably christen street corners in Soho.

My eyes flutter open in the afternoon, fully clothed in yesterday's outfit. Fumbled recollections of yesterday's clothes, check. I can't locate Erick anywhere in the hostel.

'I'd like to extend my stay, perhaps another month?' I ask at reception, where a pigtailed girl greets me. She's the same one who lent me her umbrella a couple of days ago. She informs me that the maximum stay at the hostel is two weeks, and I've got just one week left. Desperation or not, I take what I can get. I hand over some cash, brushing off her concerns about carrying too much money. It's just a hassle to visit the ATM, after all.

'Be careful,' she says as she pockets the cash, inputting something into the computer. She asks about my experience here.

'It's quite noisy, but affordable,' I reply honestly.

'How's everything else?' she finally asks. I'm relieved she hasn't forgotten about me.

'I got a job offer, but it's a bit outside my comfort zone,' I say.

'Thrilling,' she replies, handing me the change.

'Indeed. And, well, one can't predict every twist and turn in life,' I remark, tucking the change away.

'Have you seen Erick? The one who was in Room 12.'

She shakes her head.

* * *

I head over to Tesco to pick up lunch, which also doubles as my breakfast. Anticipating my own laziness, I snag dinner as well.

After savouring a £3 linguini pasta, I plonk myself down on the couch and watch TV until dusk. I eat reheated biryani rice at 6 pm, thinking about the risks that this evening's job might pose. By 7 pm, I'm back on the Tube, my wallet groaning because of exorbitant fares.

I traipse the small streets of Soho. An Indonesian restaurant catches my eye and I peek inside. My fellow countrymen are having dinner, but I can't muster the courage to introduce myself.

It strikes me that were it not for my time spent aboard ship, I would be totally out of my depth here, alone in a foreign country. It's astounding to think how a year can transform a person, taking them from bustling Jakarta to the back alleys of London in search of work. A weary smile graces my lips; it's a quiet but genuine acknowledgement of my journey. I've come so far, crossing oceans and battling uncertainty to find myself in a place I couldn't have fathomed before.

The gay sex shop catches my eye, and I spot Josh behind the counter. The place is heaving, and I feign interest in stickers and mugs sporting racy slogans like 'I Love Dick' while I secretly gather the courage to speak with customers.

Josh breaks the silence. 'Hey, why are you hiding there? Want to shoplift or something?'

I venture closer, confessing, 'I just didn't want to make the customers uncomfortable …'

Josh chuckles. 'This is a sex shop. If they're not comfortable, they won't walk in. It's a safe space.'

He's got a point.

'By the way I got "that" job,' I say.

'Congratulations, I know you have the talent.'

'Thank you,' I reply very sincerely, even though he is being sarcastic. 'I can hang out here for a bit, okay?'

I'm waiting for my work shift to start at eleven o'clock.

'Make yourself at home,' he says, then goes back to serving customers.

Home, Josh said. My mom will go crazy if she finds out that my home is filled with sex toys.

***

At around ten thirty I leave the shop and walk to the grey door Number 28. I knock, and a tall man opens it.

'Yes?' he asks.

'I'm meeting Geoff. I'm working today,' I say, and he lets me in. I spot Geoff on the couch, surrounded by a few slim women in miniskirts, tight pants and high heels.

'You actually came,' he says, disbelief in his eyes.

'Surprise,' I deadpan back.

He motions for me to sit beside him. 'First, you need to get to know these lovely ladies,' he says, nodding in the direction of the women on the couch.

There are six girls in total, chatting, sipping wine or smoking cigarettes. The place is far from fancy, just a dimly lit basement with low jazz in the background. There's a corridor leading to rooms I'd rather not explore. Most of the girls ignore me, but two nod and one offers a handshake. They seem to be from Central Europe and the Baltic countries, their makeup a bit heavy.

'Do you also give massage services? In case someone asks me,' I ask, remembering a popular service back in my home country.

One of the girls bluntly retorts, 'Honey, this isn't your typical Asian massage parlour.'

Her friend interjects accusingly, 'You're being racist. She's Asian, and you can see that.'

'I'm not racist,' the first girl asserts.

'You should avoid using "Asian" in front of Asians, that's just insensitive.'

'Okay, enough,' the first girl concedes. 'I don't offer massages, just so you know.'

Geoff steps in. 'Your only job is to bring in potential customers. Be careful not to attract the attention of law enforcement,' he advises, sensing my shock. 'You'll recognize them easily, so don't worry about it.'

* * *

My first night working as a promoter for escorts feels like a show. It's both exciting and scary, making me wonder if what I'm doing is illegal. Even though I'm not directly involved, I'm indirectly selling sex. The problem is, I have no idea how to go about it. So, for the first hour, I stand in front of the gay sex shop like a lost mannequin.

Josh, who works at the shop, comes out for a smoke break. He wonders why I'm still there.

'I'm nervous,' I admit.

He chuckles. 'Relax. This is London, where people do all

sorts of unusual things. Look at us, right in front of a sex shop.'

His words make sense. I've journeyed from judgmental Jakarta to this haven of London open-mindedness. I've got to free myself from my old mindset, worrying that every deviation from societal norms will result in mass persecution. London is not Jakarta.

I decide to approach the job like a sales promoter for cigarettes. I have experience knocking on doors to sell internet services, so I should be able to handle this as well. With that thought, I muster the courage to approach people walking past the sex shop.

At first, I'm unsure. Should I approach groups or individuals? Youngsters or older folks? Will people laugh at me? Do I need to shake hands, introduce myself, offer greetings? It's overwhelming. I tell myself to recall Oleksii's advice to 'dip your toe in'. I need to stop overthinking this.

As Xena, not Maya, I begin my work. I approach a man bundled up in warm clothing, thinking he looks harmless. I ask, 'Excuse me, are you looking for a woman?' His reply? 'I don't know what you're talking about. I'm not looking for anyone.' He walks away.

Josh, witnessing this, can't help but burst out laughing. I return to the sex shop, patting my chest.

'I did it!' I exclaim, proud of my small victory.

Josh teases me, saying my question is quite strange. Despite that, he decides to coach me. He has been in my shoes before taking charge of the sex shop. He advises me to view this job as a stepping stone, not a long-term career. Once things improve, I can find another job.

I head back to the hostel at four in the morning, taking a night bus. I have apologized to Geoff for not bringing in a single customer, but at least I have tried. I have offered women to four people over six hours. Geoff understands and, instead of firing me, he pays me £18 for the night's work, encouraging me to return the next evening. I vow to work even harder.

52

On my second night, I make more attempts to approach people, but still I can't convince anyone to come in. I feel even guiltier than before. At the end of my shift, I ask Geoff for my pay. Although his smile suggests it's alright, I don't want to get too comfortable with not succeeding.

The third night brings rain, which drives some people under the shelter of the sex shop's awning. Not far from me stands a short man who looks lost while gazing at the rain-slicked street.

'Are you okay, sir?' I ask. He nods, looking quite lonely. 'Perhaps you could use some warmth,' I suggest in a friendly tone.

He seems to take notice of me and regards me with interest. Then, he surprises me by asking, 'How much do you cost?'

I'm taken aback. 'Not me, but the others ... I mean, my friends are much more attractive.'

'You're attractive,' he insists.

'They have nice curves,' I say, gesturing to my flat chest.

He grins, revealing his small teeth. It's clear he's interested in women with larger busts. He looks rather cute and tiny, like a toddler with a wrinkly face.

Tonight, at last, I manage to bring Geoff a customer, and as I'm leaving he teases me, saying, 'Congratulations, you've managed to bring a minor.' He hands me an extra £5 as an incentive, and I can't help but smirk, knowing that the man I brought in was in fact older than a Galapagos tortoise.

The following night, I come prepared for work. I wear extra layers of clothing, bring an umbrella for the expected rain and have a can of ready-to-drink Nescafé instant coffee from Tesco.

The job no longer feels as daunting as it first did. I've shed my guilt and awkwardness, and now it feels almost routine ... fun even. I've discovered newfound persuasive phrases that I never thought I had in me. No more 'Are you looking for a woman?' I've moved on to lines like 'Fancy a pretty woman, sir?' or 'Looking for something fun tonight?' and sometimes a simple 'Ladies, sir?' with a seductive tone. I often follow up with 'Not me, but my sister ...' or 'It's my wife' or 'My girlfriend would love to see you in nothing.' Most of the time, they shake their heads, say no or just walk away, suspecting I might be joking.

Some folks make fun of me, such as a group of young people (likely short on cash), but I brush off their laughter. There's no fixed pattern to follow, and I never know who might be seeking a sexual encounter. So, I offer my services to almost everyone, even a married couple or a group of seemingly gay men (you never really know what's on someone's mind). The only ones I avoid are those who carry truncheons and wear neon-coloured vests –

obvious signs of the police. On average, I get four or five clients every night, earning an extra £20–25 each time. I can make up to £60 a night, which isn't too shabby.

'You're doing great,' Josh tells me, after I guide another client into the grey door Number 28.

'I've got a great teacher,' I reply, poking Josh in the chest.

'That's not true,' Josh laughs. 'I only tried it for three nights and didn't get any clients. They suspected I was a gay guy trying to trap them into something.'

'Really?' I want to ask if he's gay, but I decide it's unimportant and disrespectful.

53

I bid farewell to Tricia, the pigtailed receptionist at the Edgware Road hostel, who has enlightened me in many ways.

'Can't I stay another week?' I ask with hope in my voice.

She shakes her head. 'Maybe you could find another place to stay for a while and then return here,' she suggests. I give her a hug before leaving the hostel. My hopes of seeing Erick again have faded away. When he didn't return after that night, I can only wonder about his fate. Regardless, I'm grateful to him for helping me land that job. I hope he's doing well.

Leaving Edgware Road, I take the Tube to a hostel in Earl's Court, located in west London's zone one. I'm curious to see why this area is sometimes referred to as 'Little Australia'.

Without hesitation, I pay for a bed for two weeks in a six-person dorm at £12 per night. It's a slightly higher price compared to the previous hostel, but I'm relieved not to be crammed into a dimly lit room with nine other people. Earl's Court is a decent area, and in my opinion it's cooler than Edgware Road. While Tesco is a bit further away from my new hostel, I discover two other convenience stores close by: CO-OP and M&S Food. There's also a Chinese takeaway and a KFC nearby, which feels like heaven.

My room isn't too run down, although I struggle to drag my suitcase to the third floor. This hostel occupies an old building from the 19th or 20th century, built in the Georgian Revival style. There's no elevator, and I can even spot some ceiling leaks. The hostel isn't packed with lively backpackers like the previous one; instead, it reminds me of the one in Hammersmith. Most of the occupants seem to be jobseekers, and some of them are older than me.

I'm sharing a room with several people who appear to be Turkish, Lebanese or possibly Arab. Three tall men with lots of body hair and small luggage are already there when I arrive. There's also a woman with vibrant orange hair who seems to vanish at night and sleep through the day. Of course, I only learn this later. What surprises me most is the casual attitude towards undressing. Sometimes, I wake up to find one of the Turkish men undressing as if I'm not even in the room. He then climbs into his bed and covers himself with a blanket. I can clearly see his Turkish trumpet. It's shocking, and I want to scream like a character from a TV drama. However, I remind myself that this is a risk I accepted when I chose a mixed-dorm hostel.

I could have selected a female-only room, but it's a bit more expensive. After all, it's just a naked man going to bed, which pales in comparison to my job. In London, I need to leave behind my innocent, vanilla girl mentality.

* * *

As September draws to a close, the weather grows colder, with gusty winds and sporadic rain. While it's sometimes enjoyable to see the sun in the morning, I spend most of my afternoons at the hostel, watching television or browsing the internet using the free Wi-Fi. Occasionally, I sit in the hostel's dining room, equipped with a microwave, coffee maker, television and shared refrigerator. I observe the other residents, slowly getting to know their faces and guessing their daily routines.

One black girl, dressed in rather tatty office clothes, leaves in the morning and returns after five in the evening. Each time she spots me, she offers the microwave: 'You wanna use this microwave?' Even when I'm sitting far from it. I usually smile and decline, wondering why I would need to use the microwave when I'm munching on crisps. I genuinely like her; she's friendly. I can tell she's searching for an administrative job, but it's been a week and she doesn't seem to have found one yet.

At lunchtime, I sometimes run into my other hostel mates at KFC. They have paint or dirt on their overalls, indicating they are construction workers. We exchange brief greetings, out of politeness to a familiar face. I've eavesdropped and learned that they're from Ireland. Moreover, the hostel has a few elderly men, and I'm tempted to offer them ladies since they appear lonely.

When my mom finally calls me on WhatsApp, I tell her I've already found a job.

'What do you mean "already"? Weren't you supposed to have a job right when you arrived there?'

I'm caught off guard. 'Well, the job I had yesterday didn't suit me.'

'So, what's your job now?'

'It's a better and more enjoyable one.'

'Is it halal?' she asks.

'I'm just trying to make a living here,' I reply, annoyed. She used to lecture me about how working in a bar or pub is a sinful job because I'd be offering alcoholic drinks, which are considered *haram* in Islamic teachings. If she knew what I'm doing, she'd probably curse me into a bronze statue.

'So, do you have a lot of money now? Are you able to buy a house there?'

'Mom, I've only been working for two weeks. I can barely afford the hostels.'

'What? You're living in a hostel?'

'Uh, yes, because it's closer to my workplace,' I lie.

'Why don't you just rent a cheap room?'

'It's not Jakarta! There are no cheap rental rooms here,' I reply, explaining that living in a hostel is more affordable than renting a flat.

'It's winter there. How many layers are you wearing?'

'It's still autumn, and I've bought a lot of jackets from Oxfam.'

'What's Oxfam?'

'It's a very expensive and classy boutique.'

'Oh, so snobbish already.'

I end the conversation by apologizing for not being able to send money home. Essentially, I'm just a poor immigrant worker trying to make a living.

54

I don't get to see Josh every night due to his changing shifts. We're not exactly close, but we engage in small talk when we can. Josh is from Sydney and has no intention of settling here. He's actively looking for another job, and he continually suggests I do the same. I'm not sure why he insists on this. I actually quite like my current job. It allows me to save money, and it's not monotonous. Sure, standing outside in sub-ten-degree weather can be chilly, but it beats offering internet services on a dusty, scorching street or being Utpal's punching bag.

'Remember, it's just a job, not a career,' Josh reminds me.

'Of course!' I reply, to show that I'm already considering my next move.

I've been at this job for three weeks now, and I'm starting to gain some recognition on this block. Truth be told, I'm not sure what I'd do if I were to quit. I mean, perhaps I could look for something else while marketing Geoff's girls, but, honestly, I'm not too interested in that.

* * *

I decide to extend my bed rental at Earl's Court for another two weeks. I've grown too lazy to search for another hostel and drag my suitcase around again, even if I'm faced with the same 'Turkish dish' every night. Josh is right – I shouldn't grow too comfortable with this job, but what can I do?

In mid-October, Josh says his goodbyes. His friend in America has reached out with a work opportunity, so he's headed there. The next worker at the gay sex shop is a tall, quiet man. I'm not sure how to strike up a conversation with him, so I decide to stop going to the store after Josh's departure.

Instead, I spend my evenings standing outside the shop and occasionally contacting Josh via WhatsApp to check on how he's doing. Before he leaves, I take a photo with him and post it on Facebook, tagging him. 'Bye-bye, Josh, c u later.' As usual, the post gets plenty of likes, but one comment makes me frown: 'You keep changing men … are you now a whore in a foreign country?' Jealousy, I suppose. I don't even know this woman, but somehow she's on my friend list. I don't block her, though. I'll let her watch my life and grow even more envious.

During the week I refrain from complaining about anything. Even though I have to wake up at ungodly hours every night, I manage to get a quiet and sufficient amount of rest during the day. Geoff doesn't seem to have any complaints about my work either. On one occasion, I bring him an elderly married couple looking for an 'adventure'. It turns out they are the parents of one of Geoff's women and this leads to some dramatic scenes in the basement. How could I have known, right? Don't blame me. It's quite entertaining to watch.

55

It's my birthday, marking twenty-seven years for the fourth time. Last year, I celebrated it in Copenhagen in front of the bronze statue of the Little Mermaid. This year, I'm by the side of a street, enjoying pistachios and offering them to a passing hot daddy. 'Hi, sir ... fancy some nuts? Or do you fancy something else?'

However, the third week of October isn't so great for business. Not because the weather is getting colder, but because Geoff's girls are vanishing one by one.

'Try to find out where they are,' Geoff pleads one night.

'I ain't no Sherlock Holmes ... blimey,' I reply, shaking my head.

Geoff snorts loudly. 'You've been working here for three months.'

'Two months,' I reply.

'You must have realized we're not the only ones who run this kind of business.'

Aware that Soho has a history of prostitution, I already know other establishments offer similar services to Geoff's. I've even accidentally bumped into other marketers, like the girl with eccentric-coloured hair, thick makeup and a cigarette in hand. She scolds me, 'Hey, you're in my territory.'

'Excuse me?' I don't understand what she means.

She explains that the spot I am working is where she finds potential customers. I apologize profusely for not knowing there are similar businesses, and that I have strayed into her territory. She then points out other territories to ensure I don't make the same mistake again. 'You're lucky I'm a polite and forgiving person,' she says, hinting that had I encountered someone else, my fate might have been different. 'You're very generous,' is my response as I retreat to my zone.

So, the point is Geoff wants me to investigate other brothels and find out if our women have gone there.

'If I do that, I won't have time to bring in clients, and I won't get a bonus,' I tell Geoff.

'I'll give you a bonus. For three people,' he says.

'Four,' I say.

He snorts but agrees.

So, I return to the eccentric girl's area. She immediately approaches me in an aggressive manner. 'I told you, didn't I?'

'I'm not here looking for clients,' I say.

'Then what? To spy on me?'

'Oh, golly, why would I do that?'

'Learning my techniques,' her eyes widen.

'No.' I want to tell her that my technique is fine without having to copy hers, but that may upset her. So, I say, 'I need information ...'

'What information? You can find out about the weather online, there's something called Google.'

'Not that, but something else ...'

'Spill it, cut the crap, you're a distraction.'

'Have you got my girls?'

She looks at me for a moment. 'No. We lost some too. Because of this, I've had to help them sometimes, you know what I mean? I'm still in high demand ... I'm a hot commodity, you know?'

Then it's my turn to widen my eyes. I'm glad I don't have to help Geoff's girls.

'Okay, thanks,' I say, fleeing the scene.

I visit other territories to meet people in the same profession. I approach a very nervous guy, who seems new to this and I ask the same question I asked the girl. He says he's been on the job for a week but hasn't seen any new girls in the business. I visit three more territories and get similar answers.

I report all of this to Geoff, and his reaction is an unpleasant snarl, saying they must have been lying. So, what should I do if it turns out they are lying? Blow up the brothels? Pretend to be a customer?

'You won't need to work for a while,' Geoff finally says.

'What?'

He gives me the salary for the night and the bonus he'd promised. He tells me to go home early, even before my shift has ended.

'We only have a few girls left. I'll call you again if we get more girls.'

'No,' I say in disbelief.

'Sorry.' Geoff doesn't want to talk anymore. He leaves me.

I exit the basement into a dark, bustling Soho. I've been laid off just like that? How frustrating!

56

The question resurfaces in my head: what should I do next? I'm not as anxious as I used to be, I still have some savings and have already secured my accommodation for two weeks. I'm not entirely unfamiliar with London anymore. I can navigate the streets without relying on my phone. I know the Tube lines and where they go, and my English ... I think it's improving, though I'm certain I'll never quite master the solid British accent. At least I know what 'nippy' means, and it's a rather posh word. I've learned how to use it to lure potential clients: 'It's a little bit nippy, isn't it? Fancy a cup of tea with a pretty lady, sir?'

Anyway, I return to Earl's Court and view my temporary dismissal as a relaxing holiday. For over a month, I didn't request a day off because my job felt like a vacation. Despite enduring the cold and taking cover when the police were around, I genuinely enjoyed it. It was something Xena would do. It was thrilling.

Now in Earl's Court there's nothing fun to do. I've been lazing around in a hostel bed for a week, feeling like an unemployed rich girl. Sometimes I visit charity shops to browse for good jackets or sit in Pret a Manger for a coffee and a hoisin duck wrap.

Since I haven't heard from Geoff for a week, I decide to visit Soho. I pretend to have a coffee even though my real intention is to check out the grey door Number 28.

When I reach the T-junction where the gay sex shop with the bright neon lights is located, I spot the eccentric girl standing there, seemingly looking for clients.

'Hey, this isn't your area?' I ask immediately.

She turns to me without a smile. 'It is now.' Then she goes up to a group of men to engage in a flirtatious conversation with them.

What does this mean? I observe the girl for a while, but she's taking her sweet time chatting with potential clients. So, I decide to visit Geoff. I enter the grey door as nonchalantly as I can, but I find the room is bursting with new girls. I raise my eyebrows at Geoff, seeking an explanation.

'We merged,' he says.

'Why didn't you call me?'

'Someone has replaced you, no offense.'

'That weird girl?'

'She works just as well as you.'

'I don't believe it!'

'If she quits, I'll call you right away.'

'THANK YOU!' I exclaim as I walk out and slam the door behind me.

57

Josh is right. I should have started looking for another job weeks ago. Moreover, I've wasted the past week doing nothing but feel sorry for myself.

Though I'm pretty upset, there's no more time to dwell on it.

I'm allowed to be angry, yes, but only for a moment. Now I need to do something. I have to survive. This is the price of being me. I can't wallow in emotions for too long, whether it's grief or anger. I need to pick myself up and get back to work.

The next day I begin my job search with a newfound determination, fuelled by Red Bull. I roam the familiar streets of Soho, checking every restaurant front for job opportunities. It's ironic that when I had a job as a marketer I saw many vacancies, and now they've all vanished. It's always like that, isn't it?

Before long, I find a job opening at a Mexican restaurant. However, the restaurant is small and the prospect of working there seems uninspiring.

'Are you from Malaysia?' the restaurant owner asks.

'The neighbour, Indonesia,' I reply indifferently. He realizes I'm not very keen on working there or with him. He could have just asked me where I'm from instead of making guesses.

'By the way, there are some Indonesian restaurants around the corner,' he mentions, implying that he's not particularly interested in hiring me either.

'I don't know,' I shrug. 'Maybe.' This place has not impressed me and I walk out. 'Thanks, though.'

I've never really thought about working in an Indonesian or Malaysian restaurant. I've never even eaten at those places. Their dishes seem pricier than the frozen food I buy from Tesco. Speaking of Indonesian restaurants, I've occasionally spotted groups of Indonesians and Malaysians hanging around Soho. Still, I've actively avoided interacting with them as much as possible. I don't want to run into anyone I know and have them ask about my job. I don't want to spoil their vacation with my pitiful story. They might also be friends of friends (not that I have any). The thought of them revealing my profession to people I know is not something I want.

* * *

Today is not my lucky day. I return to the hostel empty handed and with knees about to give way. I've walked around Soho for three days and have come up empty. I've even tried looking for another brothel job since it's the only work I have experience in, but every position is already filled. I start to simplify my eating habits and seek more economical alternatives. I discover a Filipino grocery store near Earl's Court and realize they sell various flavours of Indomie. That makes me shout with joy. It's been almost two months since I last had anything Indonesian. Indomie, with its low price (£1 for three packs), feels like it understands me. The hostel in Earl's Court doesn't have a proper kitchen, but they do have a microwave. So, I toss an Indomie into a bowl of water and zap it for five minutes. It tastes like home.

58

I reach into my jacket pocket and retrieve a crumpled piece of paper with the name of a pub in the Chelsea area written on it. This is the paper that Matthew gave me. It reads 'Phoenix Pub'. I hadn't visited it earlier because I didn't fully trust Matthew, and I wanted to avoid anything to do with Linda, as irrational as that sounds. I also suspected Matthew might have invented the place just to get rid of me. However, after confirming its existence through Google, I've decided it's time to give it a try.

An eighteen-minute Tube ride from Earl's Court takes me to Sloane Square underground station. And from there it's only a short walk to the pub. It's not as bustling an area as Soho, but the front of the pub is charming. There are hanging flowers in hues of orange and red, which I initially mistake for plastic flowers. They're real though and it's a delightful autumnal sight.

I enter the pub, my eyes scanning my surroundings like a curious goose.

'Hello …' I greet the bartender.

'Sorry, we're still closed.' A young man emerges from behind the rectangular bar in the centre of the room.

'Yes, I can see the sign,' I mumble. 'But I'm here looking for a job.'

'Sorry, we don't have any vacancies,' he replies, picking up glasses and starting to polish them. I can't help but feel drawn to the sight of those polished glasses.

'Please. Matthew recommended I come here.'

'Which Matthew?' he asks.

'Matthew Matthew,' I reply, as I don't know his last name.

The boy calls to his dad and his father appears from a backroom.

'Matthew sent someone,' says the boy, before returning to his work wiping glasses.

Daddy looks at me standing awkwardly at the bar counter.

'Matthew owned the bar in Soho,' I begin. 'I don't know his full name.'

Daddy seems to recall him. 'Oh, I see. Are you that girl from Malaysia?'

'Indonesia, Bali. Bali is in Indonesia, but I'm not from Bali. But you must know Bali. Indonesia and Malaysia are two different things.'

He pays little heed to my ramblings.

'You should've come last month.'

'Well, that ...' I don't know what to say.

'There are no more vacancies for you. We've already hired someone else.'

I start to feel despondent, and I hope he can see it. 'I can do any job. Anything,' I insist.

He remains silent.

'Please ...' I beg. 'I could be a garbage man or a gardener tending the flowers. I like the look of this pub, I'll do anything.' The pub isn't very large; it's the stereotypical pub you see on television. The interior is a deep, antique brown. There's a rectangular bar in the centre of the room with rows of beer taps for pulling different draught beers, and circular bar stools surround it. Wooden tables and chairs are arranged haphazardly in the centre of the room while in the corner are several leather armchairs and a large table for eight or ten people. There are no chairs on the opposite side of the room, only a shelf attached to the wall for drinkers to rest their glasses on while standing.

'I have no job, no money to eat and I don't want to beg on the street,' I say pitifully.

He sighs. 'All right … but I won't give you a contract. You'll only work part-time, and you'll come in only when needed. You won't be paid the minimum wage.'

'What's the minimum wage?' I ask curiously.

He doesn't answer my silly question. 'You'll get £4 an hour, paid weekly.'

'Do I get free meals?" I ask.

He nods. 'One meal per day.'

'Okay,' I extend my hand, and he shakes it, then pulls it away hastily. 'Do I work today?' I enquire.

'Tomorrow,' he says and then turns to his son, the glass cleaner, 'Paul, show her around and explain what she has to do.'

Paul casts aside the rag and grumbles. 'We've got to stop hiring people out of pity, we're not a charity.'

I don't have the energy to be offended. I need the money to live, so I let Paul say what he wants to say.

Paul isn't all that bad when I get to know him. He is about to start university and is helping his dad in the meantime. His father is also named Paul. Paul Senior and Paul Junior. Paul Jr explains the tasks I'll need to perform every day. These include sweeping and mopping the floor before and after the pub opens and closes, clearing tables and taking food from the kitchen to serve to customers when the head waiter is overwhelmed.

'It's not a super busy pub, so we can only accommodate thirty people at a time, unless there's a party,' Paul Jr says, showing me an attached events room that can accommodate up to seventy more people.

Since I'm a busboy, I won't be taking bar orders for beer or wine. That's Paul's responsibility. I'll be taking customer orders only when it gets too busy, as a way for me to gain experience. 'I'll study the menu,' I reply enthusiastically, even though he seems unimpressed. I can relax a bit because I'm only a busboy and there's a head waiter who's paid minimum wage and has a contract.

59

Despite my newfound earnings, my weekly pay cheque from the pub is a long way from matching the salary I earned in my previous job. Obviously I can't save much, but it's far better than being unemployed in a foreign country. I'm determined not to resort to begging on the street or eating pebbles.

The job itself isn't particularly interesting. Every afternoon, my routine remains the same: clearing tables, washing glasses and plates, drying them with a rag, and endlessly mopping and sweeping the floor. Sometimes, when the head waiter is swamped, I help with taking orders. The work leaves me feeling exhausted, like a pestle and mortar seller trudging around villages in Indonesia.

I stop taking the Tube to save money and start using the bus even though it takes quite a time to reach the pub. The weather is getting colder by the day; people are walking faster with scarves choking their necks. My roommates at the Earl's Court hostel come and go, some have found jobs in different parts of town while others have returned home now that the holidays are over. Gone are the Turkish trumpets and microwave girl.

There is one new resident though: a dashing guy who looks like a rugby player and he is quite friendly. His stature and smile remind me of Maroje, and it makes me a little melancholic. We haven't talked yet. I just look at him longingly, thinking of my ex.

I've been working at the pub for a week now, and nothing significant has happened. I'm beginning to think about finding another job. Often, after the pub closes at midnight and we finish our tasks, Paul Sr offers me a chance to sample the different beers and ales, so I can better understand the distinctions. However, I decline the offer because I don't want to drink and risk falling asleep on the bus home.

***

Around five o'clock one afternoon the pub suddenly fills with customers and they're not regulars. They enter in groups, reserve tables and fill the room with laughter. More follow and soon the pub is crowded. And there is a table of Indonesians! Even though they're speaking fluent English, I can recognize my fellow countrymen.

Paul Jr approaches and whispers, 'Don't you want to say hi?'

I do, but I feel hesitant. I take plates of food to their table, but I don't dare to make eye contact, and they don't seem particularly interested in me either.

I listen in to their conversation. They discuss a show they'll be watching at Cadogan Hall, which isn't far from the pub. Occasionally they switch to Indonesian, and hearing my mother tongue spoken in London warms my heart. I smile to myself, feeling less alone.

As more people join them, I decide to muster up the courage and say hello. I approach their table with more plates of food. However, the longer I'm around them, the less inclined I feel to greet them. They're dressed smartly in semi-formal attire, and the boys look quite polished. They discuss the places they've visited, events they've attended, academic lectures and political issues like Brexit.

I decide against saying hello and start washing and polishing dishes. Paul Jr comes over and raises his eyebrows. 'I'm busy,' I say, gesturing to the pile of plates. He leaves, taking a stack of beer glasses I've dried.

Honestly, I feel that these Indonesians are quite different to me. I hope they leave for their concert at Cadogan Hall soon.

Paul Jr returns to the washing station, and I pretend to be busy wiping dishes. He seems to realize this and only says, 'They've left.' Perhaps he knows I'm avoiding them.

'Yeah, I'll be out in a minute to clean up,' I reply.

I wipe my hands and step out of from my safe space. On my way to the bar, I pass one of the men from the Indonesian group. 'Sorry,' I say, feeling like I've interrupted his visit to the restroom.

At first he ignores me like most people do with waitstaff. But my 'sorry' catches his attention, and he asks, '*Dari Indonesia*?' in Indonesian, enquiring if I'm from Indonesia.

I'm caught off guard, and a moment of panic triggers

something I hadn't planned. '*Khob khun kha*, I'm from Thailand, sir …' I say while placing my hands together in a gesture of respect. I'm trying to mimic a Thai accent. I hope I'm convincing, but the man looks a bit surprised.

'Excuse me,' I continue, preparing to leave.

'I'm Tan,' he introduces himself.

I grimace.

'I'm Kanompang, sir, Pang-pang … *khop khun kha*. I'm working now, busy, sir.' My heart feels like it's about to burst, and I hurry to the bar to clear the dirty dishes. Why did that person greet me that way?

60

Two days later, the man named Tan returns to the pub and he's not alone. He arrives with a group of friends and reserves the same large table. They engage in conversations about topics I can't quite grasp. So I return to my role as an unassuming busboy, efficiently clearing tables and delivering orders without making eye contact. It's time to utilize the blinkered donkey label Utpal gave me to my advantage, even if Utpal had me down as a blindfolded donkey.

'What's wrong?' Paul Sr asks when he spots me trying to hide in the back.

'I'm feeling tired, not well,' I mumble, making an excuse. 'I'll work here in the back, assisting the cooks.'

'No can do. Quickly serve the food,' he orders.

I avoid the Indonesian table as much as I can, although it's nearly impossible since they're seated at the largest table and demand the most attention.

'Help me take the orders at the big table,' requests the waiter, who I haven't mentioned until now because she rarely interacts with me. She's all right; a girl whose background I don't know, perhaps from Latin America.

'What? I can't,' I protest.

'Yes, you can. I've seen you do it. Hurry up. They're calling.' She takes plates of food to another table and leaves me with no choice.

I approach the large table. Without uttering a word, I stand to one side with order pad and pen at the ready. They don't notice me until Tan looks up then informs the others.

'You've got to say something,' he instructs me. I remain silent, fearing that my fake Thai accent will be exposed.

'Orderrr?' I whisper, using my practiced Thai intonation.

They proceed to order while I take quick notes. Fortunately, no one seems to notice my awkward behaviour except for Tan who regards me with absolute suspicion.

In the end, I am forced to shuttle back and forth to their table to deliver their food since I'm the only one who knows who's ordered what.

Once they finish their meal they finally leave, and I feel immense relief.

'What's with you today?' Paul Sr asks at the end of the day.

'I'm okay,' I reply.

'She's been avoiding those Malaysians,' Paul Jr interjects.

'Indonesians,' I correct.

'You can't avoid them. There's an Asian cultural festival going on at Cadogan Hall for a month,' Paul Sr explains.

'What?!'

'Anyway, why are you avoiding them?' he asks again.

'She's a fugitive back home in her own country,' Paul Jr teases.

'I'm not!' Then they both laugh. 'I just don't want them to know that I'm Indonesian.'

'And that's because?' asks Paul Sr.

'Because the sky is blue, that's why I feel sad,' I conclude, not wanting to continue the conversation.

61

Before heading home, Paul Sr hands me this week's salary, which I stash in my wallet without counting. Everything seems fine tonight. I leave the pub around one in the morning and wait for the bus at the usual stop. The weather is quite cold, and I can see my breath in the frosty air. A man approaches the bus stop looking somewhat confused. He comes up to me shyly and asks for an address. Feeling sorry for him, I pull out my phone, open the map app and show it to him. He thanks me politely and walks away. Not twenty seconds later, two formidable-looking men in police uniform approach me.

One of them flashes his warrant card. 'We're sorry, but we have to search you, ma'am,' he says, in what sounds to me like an Italian accent.

'But why?' I ask, my anxiety surging. I've never had to deal with the police before, not even in Indonesia. I've never broken any laws. Numerous thoughts race through my mind. I'm in deep trouble. They're going to arrest and deport me for working without a contract and for flouting all Britain's immigration issues.

'There's been a lot of drug trafficking in this area, and we suspect you might be involved,' the policeman explains.

'Oh, you mean the guy from earlier? I didn't buy anything; he was just asking for directions,' I hastily clarify, feeling somewhat relieved.

'Nevertheless, we still have to search you,' he insists. His imposing presence making me nervous.

Reluctantly, I agree, knowing that I shouldn't challenge the police. Anyway, I didn't buy any drugs from the man earlier so I hand over my ugly tote bag.

'Purse?' he asks.

'It's in there.'

One of the policemen holds my bag, while the other starts to inspect its contents. There's nothing unusual about my belongings – only a scarf I bought at a charity shop, a cheap umbrella, baby powder, a comb and Chapstick. They take everything out and then put it back in. Next, they open my wallet, remove the cards and all my money, display them to me briefly and swiftly return them to my wallet. Throughout the process my heart pounds despite my best efforts to appear calm.

'You're clean,' the intimidating Italian officer declares, returning my bag. They quickly bid their goodbyes and get into an unmarked car, which drives away. I breathe a sigh of relief that the ordeal is over. But the reprieve is short-lived.

Only when my bus arrives and I open my wallet to retrieve my Oyster card do I realize my wallet has been emptied. This includes my two ATM cards, my Oyster card and my salary.

Frozen in front of the bus door like a statue, I watch it close and the bus drive away. The realization hits me like a tonne of bricks – I've been robbed!

My throat feels parched, and the urge to scream builds up inside, but what escapes is an intense, shuddering panic. I can't stop repeating 'Oh my God' for five full minutes, pacing around the bus shelter, waving my hands and tugging at my hair. What should I do now? Report it to the police? But I was robbed by the police! Of course they were imposters; they even left in a normal car without any flashing blue lights. How could I have been so naive? But I clearly saw them place my money and cards back in my wallet. So, how did it all suddenly disappear? Am I so blind?

After enduring a barrage of self-recrimination, berating myself for being foolish and careless, and shedding a few tears over the loss of everything I had, I begin the process of addressing this shit. First off, I couldn't report it to the police. What if they asked about the reason for my stay in London, my work contract, visa and other stuff? I don't know, they might put me in jail! So, I decide not to file a report. Plus, I can't call anyone because I have no friends in London. I'm left with no choice but to walk back to the hostel, and I don't have cash because all my ATM cards have been taken!

Cursing my misfortune, I trudge through the cold Chelsea

night on foot for an hour, occasionally crying and hoping for a kind stranger to rescue me and provide a ride home. In the real world that just doesn't happen. By the time I reach the hostel my feet are sore and I'm chilled to the bone. Completely worn out, I collapse onto my bed and quickly fall asleep, carrying my tears into my dreams.

62

My first thoughts when I wake the next morning are that the events of the previous night were a hallucination. Unfortunately, the reality of my situation quickly sets in. My body aches, and my stomach churns. I text Paul Sr, telling him I am sick and can't work today. He doesn't enquire further, he just agrees. I have worked there for three weeks without a day off and haven't complained once (except for avoiding Indonesians, of course). I like working.

I want to eat, but I don't have a penny to my name. It reminds me that I have to do something about my stolen ATM cards. Using my laptop, I check my account then instruct my bank in Indonesia to block the cards. Thank God the money is still there. Not that I have a lot of savings, but I have enough to buy a plane ticket to Jakarta. Even though I can't ask for a new card – my Indonesian bank won't send a new card to London – at least my savings are secure.

There's nothing else I can do for now. I lose myself in reverie, lamenting the fate that has befallen me. But the melancholy doesn't last long because soon I start feeling very dizzy from hunger. I rummage through every pocket of my clothes and bag and miraculously find a £10 note in my unwashed pants. I treat it as a divine gift.

I get out of bed as if I have arthritis. I am planning to go to KFC. Just as I'm about to leave the building, the hostel receptionist greets me. He reminds me to extend my stay otherwise, I will have to leave. I slap my forehead and pretend that I've accidentally forgotten about it. I explain to him that I was robbed the previous night. So, could he just give me a little time to solve life's problems? He shakes his head. I get annoyed and want to curse him but I don't.

After dining at KFC – tasty but not as good as the Indonesian version – I return to my room to do the last thing available to me: I take my crappy laptop and sell it at a second-hand electronics store. The laptop is worth £100. I pay for four more days in the hostel and save the rest for bus fares and meals. I am going to borrow some money from Paul. I can do that.

***

The next day I go to work as usual. I bite my tongue to prevent myself from saying anything about the other night because I don't want people in the pub to pity me. But that's the wrong approach because in the end I say nothing to Paul Sr about borrowing money. I'm worried that he won't lend me any. He might say, 'Oh, sorry, I can't lend you money because I can't trust you yet. You haven't even worked here for a month. No offense, okay?'

Then I would smile and say, 'Oh, that's okay,' even though it would hurt a little. The atmosphere would become very awkward after that. They would see me as a girl trying to borrow money, and I would see myself as a pathetic person who, in the end, didn't dare to hold her head up for fear of being talked about by others. So I abandon my plan to borrow money. Is it wise or foolish? It feels more foolish. Out of pride and a fear of judgment, I end up having to face the consequences: living on only £40 for the whole week until my next pay cheque. Maybe I can do it.

First, I will stop using the bus and start walking to work. It's only a fifty-minute walk, and I can do that. Second, I will start eating Indomie and cheap instant rice every morning and afternoon even though it might damage my intestines.

I am grateful that neither Tan nor the other Indonesians come to the pub today. After my shift ends, I plug in my earphones and walk back to the hostel. I suddenly start thinking about my mom. If she knew about this whole mess, she would no doubt call me incredibly stupid. Ha ha. Then it starts to drizzle lazily, so I reluctantly dig through my bag for an umbrella. I can't find it. Did I leave it somewhere? Super stupid, but I'm happy, ha ha ha. Fortunately, it's only drizzling, not a full-on storm. It's okay to let myself get a little bit wet. Very naturist. I am embodying the rain. I'll take a long, warm shower later in the hostel. Anyway, what do I expect? It's London. The weather changes as it pleases. People who don't live here say that London rain is romantic. Romantic my ass.

After five minutes of walking in the drizzle, my hair begins to droop, and my head is spinning. I pull my scarf from my neck and use it as a veil. A car horn sounds from behind, so I turn my head. Who is it? I am not an easy target, you know? I'm not someone you can honk at whenever you want. I continue walking. The car starts to catch up and moves slowly beside me.

'Get in, let me drive you home,' says a very dodgy-looking man from behind the wheel.

'Oh, no, thank you,' I reply.

'It's raining, and you're soaking wet,' he insists.

'Yeah, I know.'

This person obviously has bad intentions. It's getting creepy. I walk faster. The car continues to follow me at an eerily slow pace. Suddenly I hear a bell ringing from behind. It sounds like a bicycle bell. I don't want to turn around, afraid of encountering another pervert. The car is still following me, and now there's a bike following me too. The bell rings again. Who the hell is riding a bike at one in the morning in the suburbs of London in the rain? I pick up the pace and head towards somewhere with more people around, but then I hear the bell right behind me. Oh crap! What now?

I finally turn around. I have psyched myself up to explode and tell the pervert to leave me alone. But all I see on the bike is Tan, and he is smiling with his teeth showing. I am torn between relief and fear, but I decide to approach him because I can see the creepy car is still following me.

'Hello, sir ...' I greet him politely like an obedient servant. Out of the corner of my eye, I see the curb crawler finally drive off. I breathe a sigh of relief.

'Hello,' says Tan.

'Thank you, sir,' I say, as I leave him. LOL. I don't want to make things worse.

He rings the bell again and continues to follow me.

'Yes, what, sir?' I pause out of respect. After all, he has saved me.

'Why are you walking, Pang-pang?'

'Exercise is good, sir,' I reply with a smile and give him a thumbs-up gesture.

'But it's raining, no?'

I smirk as I look away. 'I'm showering at the same time ... saving water, sir.'

'Why don't you take the bus?' He catches up and cycles slowly beside me.

'My wallet is at home, sir,' I reply, my polite Thai girl accent drifting.

'Where do you live?'

'At the hostel, sir.' I feel like running. With each new line, I'm sounding less and less Thai.

'Which hostel, huh?'

I don't want to answer him, but I am worried that he will keep following me.

'Earl's Court, sir ...'

'But that's quite a distance,' he says. Then he takes out his wallet and hands me his Oyster card.

I don't take it. I just smile and politely decline. 'Thank you, sir, but no thank you.'

'Well, in that case, I'll have to follow you home.'

I turn to him and emit a loud 'What!' which sounds absolutely nothing like a demure Thai girl. His mouth opens, and he looks a little surprised to see me change like that.

'I just want to make sure that you get home … safe.'

'I appreciate it, sir. But no need, sir. I am fine,' I smile again as I brush wet bangs off my forehead and wipe the water dripping down my face. I set off again and walk faster than before, almost half running, and now the rain is really starting to chuck it down. I don't want to look back because I know that stubborn Tan is still following me. How long is he going to do that? He doesn't get the word No, does he? I really don't want to deal with him, or to me more precise I don't want him to find out that I am Indonesian. I can hear his bicycle chain rattling behind me like that of the ghost in *The Shining*. And, finally, I lose my patience.

I stop and turn to him. 'Give me the card, sir … I'll take the bus, okay …' Smiling in annoyance.

63

I catch a fever the next day and barely have the strength to get out of bed, so I don't go to work. I feel incredibly nauseous but can't rely on anyone, so I end up going to the pharmacy and buying a pack of paracetamol by myself. I take three pills at once for a speedier recovery. Then I eat my rice and Indomie while sitting in the hostel's living room watching TV with some elderly people.

An old man approaches me and strikes up a conversation.

He mentions that his eighteen-year-old daughter in Thailand 'looks like me'. He thinks I am eighteen. 'What should I do?' he asks after confiding that he was kicked out of Thailand for being unemployed.

First, I am happy to be considered as an eighteen-year-old. Second, I can't help him because I don't want to think about other people's problems. I am struggling myself. I think all problems are boring until they become my problems. So, for the moment, his problem is just boring.

I return to my room to rest and find my roommate, a handsome guy from Spain, spraying Lynx on his neck. He works as a bouncer in a club and is excited about returning to Barcelona after two years of work. He keeps calling me 'man' as if I am a boy. I tell him to be quiet because I want to sleep. Even though he's taken aback, I don't think he's offended. There's something about people. When I am sick, they seem to unload more information about their lives on me. Is it because I look vulnerable that they feel safe sharing their stories?

The next day I go back to work. Paul Jr mentions that a man from Indonesia was looking for someone from Thailand named Pang the previous day. Paul Jr eyes me with suspicion.

'He must be mistaken,' I reply, shoving my hand into my pocket to make sure I still have the Oyster card, which I've used a few times now for Tube rides.

'Is he coming today?' I ask. Paul shrugs.

Tan finally arrives as evening falls. He sits down for a beer alone. I approach him and hand back his Oyster card with both hands, as if presenting a flag to the president. 'Thank you, sir. I used it a couple of times, sir. I will pay you later.'

'No need,' he says. 'You've found your wallet?'

'Yes, sir ...' I quickly dash back into the kitchen and pretend to wipe plates and glasses, but there's nothing much to clean so I just hide until he's gone.

Tan leaves the pub ten minutes later.

I ask Paul Sr for an early dinner because I am hungry.

'I think he likes you,' says Paul Jr suddenly, referring to Tan.

'Oh no, yesterday I borrowed his Oyster card,' I say.

'Why?'

'Mine is gone, man ...' Paul Jr immediately walks away when I call him 'man'. Ha ha.

I am not sure that Tan likes me though – not that I am an expert at this. Look at my history: a love story that ran aground in the middle of the ocean. I am very clueless. I think Tan is just suspicious and wants to prove something. Nothing more than that.

64

I find myself at the end of my rope. It's clear to me that I should return to Indonesia now. I have no more money, and my hostel rent is due today. I'm pretty certain the Middle Eastern receptionist won't accept an offer to 'pay later'. However, I only have eleven pounds left.

Surprisingly I don't experience any panic attacks. Normally I would be lying on the floor gasping, or screaming into pillows in the corner of a couch … my usual rituals when unable to face the misery that life has handed me. But this time, something different is happening. I deliberately skip work today without telling Paul anything. Instead, I decide to go for a walk to Hyde Park because I've always wanted to visit.

Maybe it's because so much has happened that I've reached a point where I don't really care much about anything anymore.

In the park, people are strolling around despite the autumn weather. A chilly breeze bites at my skin. According to the weather forecast, the sun is supposed to shine for half the day. I observe the geese and ducks in the lake as people feed them breadcrumbs. I even chat with one of the geese and laugh to myself. 'Where I come from you're considered a menace, you know? We avoid your random pecking. Here they take your picture as if you're a celebrity.' The goose doesn't respond, but I keep talking to her about life all the same. Then even she has had enough of my pitiful tale and waddles off, and I feel very alone.

As darkness descends I am tempted to type a WhatsApp message to my mom: 'Mom, please send me some money via Western Union.' Of course, she would immediately ask 'How much?' and she wouldn't enquire further because she'd understand that her daughter was in trouble. I rarely ask her for money.

With a part-time job helping out her friend's catering business and the income she receives from Dad's monthly pension, Mom probably doesn't have as much money as I need. But she can always find a way (such as selling her gold earrings or bracelet). She has invested her money wisely.

In the end, I refrain from sending the message because I'm not ready for that yet. Instead, I continue to sit by the lake, deep in thought, resembling the Little Mermaid in Copenhagen, gazing forlornly at the swans. Oh, fate, what have you dealt me?

You know what's even more annoying than my current predicament? Nothing. I think this is the lowest point in my life. But then I remember someone once said: 'Life is like a ball. First, we need to hit the bottom before we can bounce to a higher place.' Perhaps I am at the bottom right now.

One positive is that I no longer need to think about what I want from life. That's because I don't have time to think about such trivial things. Right now, I'm just trying to survive. As a big confused ball, I'm simply waiting for my momentum to bounce. Something good is bound to happen to me soon. I believe it. So, I wait by the lake.

But nothing happens.

In fact, the situation only gets worse. I lose my last eleven pounds! I only realize it's gone when I get to Kensington Gardens. Somewhere between Hyde Park and Kensington Gardens my money has disappeared like autumn leaves in the wind or it has found its way into someone else's pocket or maybe it's been eaten by a goose. Perhaps the money slipped out of my pocket when I reclined by the lake, striking a Little Mermaid pose. Damn.

Bouncing ball my ass. I'm a cannonball that hit the ground and, instead of bouncing back up higher, just exploded into a million pieces. Now, what am I supposed to do? To hell with Mother Nature – it's her fault I lost my precious eleven pounds. Alright, it's not her fault, but I really need to blame someone other than myself. I can't be too hard on this soon-to-be-homeless skinny girl, right? Okay, then, perhaps I should send that WhatsApp message to my mom. It has to be done.

So, I walk back to Earl's Court composing the new message. 'Mom, please send me money via Western Union. Please. Urgent.'

Half an hour passes and I still haven't sent the message. I could sell my phone as a last resort. It's just that if I do, I'd become wholly disconnected from the world. No can do. I can be homeless but not phoneless. So, my mobile is the last treasure that I hug tightly.

65

My stomach rumbles like the percussion section of an orchestra as I pass by KFC. I dig around my trouser pocket and find £1.25 in loose change. Maybe that's enough for a small portion of fries. I'm starving. KFC isn't that crowded when I walk in and I glance up at the digital menu board above the cashier's head.

'Can I help you, ma'am?' the cashier asks multiple times. I don't respond because I'm still looking for a meal that costs less than £1.25. I'm annoyed because I can't find one. I believe the price of four nuggets or a small portion of French fries should only be £1. Unfortunately, I can't find the pictures of these two items. Maybe the promotion is over?

Eventually someone cuts in front of me and places an order. I don't mind. I don't have the money anyway. I'm about to leave the fast-food joint to buy instant rice for 70p at Tesco when someone calls out to me. I turn and see Tan standing in front of the cashier. He's the one who cut in line just now. I hadn't realized it, I was too focused on the ever-changing digital menu display.

'Oh, hey,' I reply, my voice squeaking with hunger. Ouch, damn it, I totally forgot my Thai accent.

'You want something? It's on me,' he says.

'Oh, no, thank you, sir, I'm just looking.'

'Come on, it's my birthday. At least sit with me. Nobody celebrates my birthday. Please?'

Really? His birthday? In KFC? I cast a disbelieving look, but Tan's face is full of pleading. Feeling bad for him, I finally nod. We choose a table against the wall to avoid endless people passing by. Soon his order is ready and he collects his fried chicken. I wait and sit in my chair. He returns to the table with two large portions of crisp-looking French fries, two jumbo Diet Cokes and a bucket of fried chicken.

'Eat,' he says, spreading the fries on the tray and starting to eat them.

'No, thank you, sir.' I smile and look down. My stomach begins to object, and I may actually be drooling. I pretend to myself that I'm fasting and this whole KFC meal in front of my face is an endurance ordeal. I close my eyes.

'I won't be able to finish all of this. Eat with me, this is my birthday party.'

I don't budge, just silently swallowing my saliva.

'Please?' he continues.

I give in and pick up a solitary French fry, my hand shaking from hunger. I'm thankful that Tan ignores it, otherwise I would be really embarrassed. He takes a bite of his fried chicken. 'I need some ketchup,' he says, getting up. And when he goes to the counter to ask for ketchup, I grab more fries and stuff them in my mouth. I chew quickly.

'Have the chicken,' he offers casually when he returns. I nod.

'Is that for me?' I ask, pointing to one of the paper cups.

He nods. 'Have a drink, it's for you.'

I lift a chicken drumstick to my mouth and bite into it. Oh my God, it's the best fried chicken I've ever had in my entire life. I think my hand is still shaking a little when I strip the chicken bone with my teeth, but I really don't care anymore.

'Have some more,' says Tan.

I eat the next one.

'Race me,' he challenges, and we end up racing to eat the rest of the fried chicken.

'It's good?' he asks.

'It's good, sir,' I say. 'Really good,' I whisper again to myself.

He laughs. Did I say that out loud? Jeez, I realize I have just finished four pieces of chicken and a large order of fries with a half-gallon of Coca Cola. Tan must think that I'm a glutton. To redeem myself, I try to wipe my mouth with a napkin as daintily as possible. Unfortunately, it doesn't work because I've just eaten like a caveman.

'Let me walk you back to your hostel,' he says.

'No, sir, thank you, sir, no need.'

He's about to say something more so I get up from my chair, wish him 'Heppy besdey, sir' and run out of the restaurant.

66

I get kicked out of my hostel despite insisting I have forgotten today is the last day of my stay. As predicted, they don't understand. They even tell me I'll be charged for late checkout. It's almost eight o'clock in the evening, and I haven't shoved my dirty clothes and toiletries back into the suitcase. 'I have no money! I can't pay the surcharge!' I roar. Don't they have a heart? I've lived here for a month.

At 10 pm, I drag my suitcase out of the hostel. 'You guys are evil!' I shout at the front door as I pass some new arrivals. 'Don't stay here. The room is full of bats!' Instead of leaving, they look excited.

Outside the hostel, my face is red hot. I cover my mouth with both hands and scream. I walk for a while and then sit on the pavement, covering my mouth again to scream in anger. Okay, enough. It's really time to ask my mom for help.

I pull out my phone but instead of sending a text I decide to call her. It's around 5 am in Jakarta.

'Hello?' She answers my call right away.

'Mom, you're Subuh praying, right?'

'How is it possible to pray and pick up the phone!'

Okay, that makes sense.

'I'm in the hospital,' she continues.

'What? What are you doing at the hospital? What happened?' I ask in shock.

'Your brother had surgery last night,' she answers simply.

'What? What kind of surgery?!'

'Don't scream, okay?'

'Yes, okay,' I say. But I am panicking, so a scream is appropriate. 'Why did he have surgery? Why didn't you tell me?'

'It's done. He's stable. Don't panic, I don't want to hear you scream. Noisy, you know? You can't scream in the hospital ...'

'Yeah, but I'm not there, Mom!'

My mom then tells me that my brother had acute pain in his tummy since the afternoon, which turned out to be appendicitis. She gave my brother a Vicks massage because she thought the pain came from wind trapped in his body. I want to get mad at my mom for being careless. However, that doesn't matter anymore. I am grateful she took him to the hospital. My mom has always had strange ideas, but in the end she will always do the right thing. Then, after I calm down, I ask how much the hospital fee is? She says she's using national health insurance – I have been paying the premiums for the family. And she will top-up the fees with her savings if needed (they definitely would be). My mouth goes dry after that.

'Mom,' I groan. 'I'm sorry.'

'What for?' she asks.

'Because I can't send money home,' I almost cry when I say that.

'Don't think about it. We're not in trouble either.'

How could she say that when she's about to dip into her savings?

'How are you there?' she changes the subject.

'I'm okay.'

'You want to come home?'

I am hesitant to answer. 'Mom, my phone's running low on battery; I'll call you later, okay ...'

'Gosh, this kid,' then she hangs up.

I cover my face with both hands, this time not because I want to scream but to sob. I am so helpless. I need to borrow money from my mom. I am sure she will wonder and correctly guess that my days here have been showered with calamities and misery to the extent that I have no money. Although it is true, and even though I am not a very good daughter to her, I don't want to add to her worries. She must be so anxious about my brother.

Maybe I can survive for another day or two? Until things get better at home, only then I'll reach out to her again. I believe this is the right decision. So, I get up from the pavement, brush the moss off my butt and walk towards Earl's Court underground station.

* * *

I cover myself with three outer layers, wrap my head in a scarf and put my hands in my pockets. I crouch beside my suitcase, watching the passers-by. I do all of this in front of Earl's Court Tube station. There is a homeless person sitting on cardboard not far from me. No one gives him a penny. Even so, perhaps there is a sense of freedom not being attached to anything but the thought of eating, and for that he could beg. He must have gotten used to it. Should I start begging? I mean, I am literally homeless now. I once saw a girl wriggling her sleeping bag all over London. She used the sleeping bag as a blanket when she was not sleeping. It was icy, and she was filthy. What I remember the most is her sinister face, as if saying 'fuck off' to those who looked at her. Maybe I should start doing that? Well, I'm already dragging my suitcase. In a minute, I'll sleep on top of it then wear it as a blanket tomorrow morning. Pardon me, I don't know what I am talking about. Probably, all I have said is wrong and ignorant. If we don't know and never experience how other people really feel, maybe we should just shut up.

Midnight has finally come, and the trains have stopped operating. No more passengers exit the station. Only occasionally does a night bus pass on the street.

'Ma'am, do you need to go somewhere?' asks a station officer who suddenly appears, looking like his shift is over and he is going home. I have been sitting in front of the station for two hours, and my tears have dried. Even though my eyes are red and my face is frosty, I don't budge from my spot.

I shake my head in response to his question.

'You can't sleep here,' the man continues.

'I ...' I pause for a reasonable excuse, 'I am waiting for someone.'

The officer frowns.

'We made an appointment to meet here,' I add, trying to reassure him but he is getting more alarmed.

'Oh, so you've contacted them? Do you need a phone?' He looks sincere.

'We made an appointment to meet here,' I squeak, now with

a quiver of sadness in my voice.

'Perhaps—'

'I'll wait here until he comes.' Then I cover my face and pretend to sob. 'He's coming,' I say, continuing the fake sobs and intending to just stay here until the kind officer is gone.

However, he doesn't leave. I peek through my fingers, and he seems to be watching my face. He knows that I'm faking it. So, I start sobbing louder to convince him. I peek again, and he is still watching me. Oh damn. Doesn't he know that I don't have a place to go? I don't want to move from the station because this place has very decent lighting. There is a twenty-four-hour souvenir and snack shop next door. So, I am not too worried about ill-intentioned people as it is bright and there's always someone around. Such as the homeless guy next to me. Doesn't this officer understand what I am doing? I am just trying to protect myself and survive.

I keep covering my face and pretending to cry until I actually do cry.

'Ma'am,' says the officer. I don't answer him because I get really carried away. I can hear him snort his nose. 'What can I do for you?'

I keep my mouth shut.

Then I hear someone talking to the officer. 'She's with me,' he says, enabling the officer to finally leave. I am still crying for the next thirty seconds because I am suddenly caught up in the emotions that I have released. Then, I peek out from between my fingers again. My eyes are wet and my sight is blurry. I expect a prince has come to save me, but instead I see Tan on his bicycle.

He waits until my sobs recede.

'Why are you here?' he asks.

'I'm going to go, sir,' I reply, confused. 'Waiting for a train.' I kick my suitcase to show him that I am about to travel.

'Where do you want to go? All lines have stopped operating.'

I look around the dirty floor for an excuse. Luckily, he doesn't probe further. He takes out his phone.

'For tonight you can stay at my place, tomorrow you can go.'

I want to say 'No need, sir, thank you' but I don't. My dignity has gone along with the last gust of wind. I don't have the privilege of playing hard to get.

'It's almost winter, it'll only get colder,' he says. He knows that he should give me a logical reason so I can save face and not look too easy. My eyes dart here and there, starting to look for excuses again. I half-heartedly want to decline the invitation. But I don't want to freeze to death outside. I have experienced staying up all night when I was working as a marketer for prostitutes. But back then I didn't have to sleep on a cold pavement.

'I've booked you an Uber,' he says, putting his phone back in the pocket of his windbreaker. 'Get out in front of the flat and wait for me. I'll be there soon on the bike.'

I shake my head. But my ears and fingers feel like they are not in place anymore. It isn't long before the Uber he ordered arrives, and Tan helps me load my suitcase into the boot. He opens the passenger door and lets me in. After making sure the driver knows the address, he gets on his bike and races along behind the car.

I arrive at his flat in the Paddington area. It is only ten minutes from Earl's Court. I get off in front of a three-storey white building that looks identical to the buildings on either side. After waiting for ten minutes, I finally see Tan's nose. He is panting and his forehead sweating.

'Burning calories, great,' he says, as he dismounts and pulls a key from his pants. I look at his slightly bulging tummy. The door is open, and he tells me to come in. 'Bring your suitcase, too.'

'Oh yesss, forgottt,' I thought he was going to carry it for me. Turns out he has a hard time getting his bike into the room too.

Bikes are left on the ground floor. He helps me carry my suitcase up to the second floor. There's no lift.

67

We enter his flat, and it takes me by surprise. There is a king-sized bed, a wardrobe and a media console with a plasma TV on it. Next to the TV is a mini fridge, and next to that is a mini kitchen with an electric stove and a sink. There is a coat stand and a small desk and chair under the window with a stack of books on it. In the corner is a small bathroom. It's a studio apartment.

'Don't worry, I won't do anything,' he says when he registers the shock in my eyes. My hands curl into fists as Tan locks the apartment door, just in case.

'Where do I sleep, sir?' I ask.

'On the bed.'

'Where do you sleep, sir?'

'On the bed.'

'Me. You. Same bed?'

'Yeah, there's only one bed.'

Shit.

'Don't worry,' he says. 'Or would you prefer to sleep on the floor?'

'I don't know, sir,' I say.

The floor may be cold, but certainly warmer than the pavement. I had no idea Tan's place would be this small. I thought at least he would have a sofa to crash on.

Tan undresses down to his boxer shorts, then goes to the bathroom to brush his teeth. I still haven't sat down or done anything when he comes out and wipes his face with a towel. Even so, he doesn't say anything. Maybe he thinks I am challenged.

'I understand it is not a mansion, but please turn off the light when you're done standing,' he says, as he climbs into bed and takes the side next to the wall. He pulls the blanket over his almost naked body. 'Good night,' he adds, hugging the bolster. I was hoping for some more conversation before lying by his side and saying good night. But he must be really tired from speeding on his bike.

I stay rooted to the spot for the next five minutes like a Madame Tussauds' waxwork. But my body is tired. My eyes are tired. Finally, I peel off two layers of jackets and remove my boots.

He won't rape me. No, he wouldn't dare. Even if he tries it, I will scream. I have seen other apartments in the building. There must be other residents. As I strip off my clothes, I keep telling myself that Tan isn't a bad person.

It's not that I have never shared a room with a man. For the past two months I have been sleeping in a room with dozens of men I didn't know, and some of them were undressing right in front of me. However, I am still scared. Maybe my suspicions are due to the news I read. But humans are good creatures. Tan must be a nice person. He lent me an Oyster card and has let me crash in his room. I don't know what his motive is ... maybe he wants something from me. Whatever. I have to stop being such an innocent little girl and resurrect Xena.

After washing my face and brushing my teeth, I climb into bed, slip under the bed covers and turn off the light. Mom will disown me if she knows I am sleeping on the same bed with a man, but I am worn out and can't think much anymore. Oh, the mattress and blanket are so warm and comfortable ...

* * *

I wake up just before midday, with no Tan next to me. I hurriedly check my body and find there is nothing wrong. I must stop having negative thoughts like this. He's a good person ... who might have motives.

On the table I find a small note: 'Got to go, use the Oyster, the cash is for meals.' He's left twenty pounds along with a key and an Oyster card. There's also his mobile number on it. I don't touch the money until I finally finish my shower and can think straight. I leave the flat at three in the afternoon and make my way to Chelsea, to the pub.

'Oh, you're back,' says Paul Jr when he sees me. He then shouts, 'Dad, she's back!'

Paul Sr comes out of his room and greets me. He looks like he wants to say something.

'Hey, yeah, how are you?' he asks.

'What is it?' I know something is up. He is silent at first. 'Am I fired? Oh, God, don't tell me I'm fired. Is it because yesterday I didn't come in and I didn't tell you? I was not feeling very well. I am sorry for that. I should have just texted you but bad things happened.'

'Oh, no, no, you're not fired. It's just that since you're a part-timer we thought it would be good if you don't come in every day.'

I honestly don't want to understand what he's saying.

While wiping a beer glass, Paul Jr chimes in, 'Dad just picked up a new foster kid, so he has to divide his time equally between the two of you.'

Then I see a skinny boy, who looks to be from India, struggling to lift a box of wine to carry it to the storage room. Not only do I not get the minimum wage, now I have to reduce my working hours too?

'He just arrived from Bangladesh and he didn't even have shoes on,' Paul tells me, trying to explain something unnecessary, which is probably an exaggeration anyway. I mean, this is his pub. He can do whatever he likes. I really appreciate his gesture, though, so I understand this situation. I want to confess that I don't even have 10 pence on me and that I am staying at a stranger's place out of his pity, but I restrain from pouring it all out because I can't bear to see that skinny kid. I am skinny too.

'Oh, well,' I finally say, as if it is no big deal.

'Good,' Paul looks relieved, 'so you'll come three times a week, you can ask Junior for the shifts.' After telling me that, Paul Sr goes back to his office.

'Tomorrow and the day after you don't have to come in,' Paul Jr says.

I nod. 'Right, okay.'

'Anyway, there'll be an event at Cadogan Hall the day after tomorrow, the closing night of something. If you want, I can ask a friend to put you on the catering wait staff.'

'Yes, of course, please, yes, I do want that,' I say, a little too excitedly.

'Are you sure?'

'Why not?' I was once part of a catering team for events during my internship at a hotel, and I worked on big events on the ship. For example, I was movie-night-popcorn-boss, wine-bottle-opener-person and, on VIP night, fast-lady-who-walks-around-the-room-carrying-trays-of-hors-d'oeuvres. I handle big events well. Even after delivering my extensive catering CV, I see that Paul Jr is still far from convinced. Maybe he has something else on his mind. He probably thinks I am a big fat liar. But he says he will give my phone number to his friend.

* * *

It is only five o'clock in the afternoon when I leave the pub. I decide to go back to Paddington to Tan's flat. There are Malaysian restaurants in the area, and a profusion of Paddington Bears in gift shop windows. How lovely, I say. I stop by a convenience store and spend the £20 Tan left for food. I buy a dozen eggs, a kilo of rice, a portion of minced beef, a bag of mixed vegetables and two bottles of instant Chinese food seasoning. I also take a bag of dried chilli flakes and a bottle of chilli sauce. And I spend the rest of the money on a pint of milk and a half-kilo of grapes. I must admit I am very good at choosing cheap things. I think perhaps I have turned into that kind of lady who compares prices at the supermarket. My mom. I am in no position to judge. If you know what a penny means, you'll understand.

Back in the flat, I open the window and start cooking rice while watching TV and checking out Tan's things. In the corner of the room is a pile of dirty clothes and the sneakers he usually uses for cycling. There's no suitcase, just a large backpack, which is perhaps where his clothes are. In the bathroom are simple toiletries and a small bottle of ZARA cologne.

After the rice is ready, I warm the pan, add the margarine, half of the beef, crack some eggs, then add a pinch of salt. I put in the vegetables, some spoons of the Chinese seasoning, add the spicy chilli flakes and a spoonful of hot chilli sauce. I stir it absently. I don't really know what I am doing. It vaguely resembles a stir-fried dish. It looks fine as hell. Delicious, even. Probably because I am hungry.

At about half past seven I close the window because it is getting colder. I switch on the heating and transfer the food onto a plate I find in the cupboard. The bedroom door swings open and in walks Tan. He looks surprised to see me standing in the mini kitchen.

'Hi,' I say, then add, 'sir' in the Thai accent I keep forgetting to use.

'You're not working?' He takes off his jacket and looks smart in his shirt, cardigan and leather shoes.

'I'm free today, sir. Part-time only.'

'Ah, I see,' he nods. 'You're cooking?' He looks at the plate and sees the rice and messy stir-fry.

'Yes, sir, with the money you left. You want, sir?'

He nods.

'Rice?' I offer.

'No rice, I'm on a diet,' he replies. On a diet, but he drinks gallons of beer. I scoop the stir-fry onto a plate and hand it over respectfully.

'No rice, no power, sir …' I say.

He laughs. Then I sit on the floor and Tan sits at the end of the bed. I scoop a mouthful of rice and beef and enjoy the food solemnly. Oh my God, my cooking is really delicious. Thank God for the instant Chinese seasoning.

I watch as Tan puts a spoonful of food in his mouth. He chews for three seconds, pauses then slowly opens his mouth and spits the half-chewed stir-fried beef back onto the plate. Then he grabs a glass.

'FUCKING HOT!' he shouts after chugging a full glass of tap water.

'Me, sir? Thang-kyu …' I try not to laugh. But I can't bear to see his face turning red and his eyes watering. It's actually not very spicy. Tan reaches for a second glass.

'There's some milk in the fridge,' I inform him. He opens the fridge and spots the grapes. He grabs a bunch and starts to devour them.

'You tryin' to kill me?' he says.

'No, sir, no, but I thought you like spicy, sir, you're Chinese ...'

'Hey, you're racially profiling me.'

I quickly finish my meal. I am used to eating at speed like someone in a guerrilla war. On the ship, we are only given fifteen minutes for lunch or breakfast. Only then do I apologize to him for the Chinese comment. For thinking that he is Chinese in the first place. And while it might seem true that he is, still I am the one in the wrong.

He then says that it is fine, he knows I am kidding. He also tells me that he is from Semarang in Central Java, Indonesia, and his family is of Chinese descent.

'*Saya tinggal di Amerika selama dua puluh tahun,*' he explains in Indonesian. He says that he has lived in the USA for twenty years, to explain why he does not like spicy food.

It shocks me to hear him talking in Indonesian, but of course I should act like I don't understand it.

'Come on, stop pretending,' he continues, still in Indonesian.

I keep quiet for a while. 'No understand, sir,' trying to dodge the issue while waving my hand at him.

'You're from Jakarta, right? Your name is Maya.' With slightly narrowed eyes he breaks through my defence.

The only word that comes out of my mouth is 'Ugh!' – like seeing a wriggling eel.

68

Naturally I deny it. Giving up easily isn't really my style.

'Say something in Thai then.'

'Cannot, sir … I cannot. I grew up in the Philippines,' I say, trying to escape by digging a new hole.

'Tagalog then.'

I sigh. '*Babalu, ayde-ayde, bomboclat, chakabumba … chiki-chiki paisano …*'

Tan bursts out laughing. 'What the hell are you saying?'

'Swear words I learnt on the ship.' I answer him in fluent Indonesian.

He smiles at my admission. I don't know what to say next, so I get up and wash the dishes.

'How long have you known I'm Indonesian?' I ask. From that point, we start to talk in our mother tongue.

'Since the day we met, I asked the bar owner.'

'Paul and his blabber mouth,' I say.

'Not his fault.'

'Why have you been playing along with me?' I finish washing the dishes and snatch the bag of grapes from his hands.

'You must have had your reasons, right?'

'And you're curious,' I conclude.

I get into bed and change the television channel. Something about baking.

'I've been thinking. I'm going to stay here for a while, in your place, until payday if that's okay.' Even though I feel bad about it, I don't actually have many other choices, and by now I am convinced that Tan is harmless. He is just trying to help me; he's known I'm Indonesian all along.

'Okay,' he says, as if it was not a big deal at all.

I say my thank yous.

'So, what happened? Why were you stranded?' he asks.

'I wonder if your name is really Tan?' I ask back, changing the subject.

'Jonathan,' he answers. 'But I prefer to be called Tan. Less mainstream.'

I purse my lips. It seems he really wants to be different.

'So?' he asks for my answer.

I sigh. I am not sure if I want to tell him my life story.

'So, what are you doing in London?' I ask him, trying to run away again.

'I don't live in London. I live in Norwich. It's two hours from here. It's where I study. I'm only here for the arts and culture festival and a little research at the University of London.'

So that explains the modest flat. He's renting it.

'And you?' he asks back.

'Oh, I'm just working – being a migrant worker like most people,' I say, in a tone that might be a little too cynical while waving my hand.

'You're saying that I am a spoiled rich kid, huh?'

'I didn't say that.' I put on a very innocent look and shake my head in exaggerated fashion.

'Don't judge me,' he says.

'Sorry, I already did.'

Instead of being offended, he just laughs.

'So, because you know I'm Indonesian, that's why you're being kind?' I ask.

He looks at me. 'I'm not that sort of person, I would help anyone in your position.'

I am embarrassed because I thought ill of him. But instead of apologising, I deflect by saying, 'Ah, you're lying for sure.'

'But what about you? You're willing to stay here because you trust me, right? Because we are both Indonesian, even though I am a stranger.'

Maybe he has a point. When I am abroad, on the ship for example, I find it easier to trust fellow countrymen. But, still, I don't want to admit it. 'Uh, no. It is only because I was so tired and cold. I would have gone home with anyone. After all, you're not Indonesian, you said you've lived in America for twenty years.'

He doesn't react to my nonsensical and annoying remark. He knows I am lying to myself. Instead, he asks me to tell him what really happened for me to end up like an abandoned puppy. First, I have to correct him: 'I'm not an abandoned puppy, but a stranded mermaid.' And then, in a colourless tone devoid of emotion, I finally tell him everything. Starting from my job on the ship, about Maroje who broke my heart (minus holding the Oleksii totem), Linda who stole my money, my strange and magical job in Soho and the incident of being scammed one night by a couple of fake Italian policemen and losing all my money.

'I had £11 left and I lost it in Hyde Park when I posed elegantly like a mermaid by the lake. You know? Staring at the swans? It's a cruel world!'

I can see how Tan wants to laugh so bad, but he holds it in.

'It's very tragic,' he says. 'But also a little funny.'

'Nothing funny here, move on.' I change the TV channel again.

'Poor you.'

'Eh, I don't want to be pitied. I'm a warrior of life, like Xena the warrior princess.'

Finally Tan laughs out loud.

'What are you laughing at?'

Before he can answer, he quickly gets up from the bed and runs to the bathroom.

'Stomach ache, it must be because of your cooking,' he says.

'Hey!'

He closes the door and shouts, telling me to turn up the television volume if I don't want to hear strange noises.

'We've got to do something about this Linda woman who stole your money,' he says through the door, in between sighs. The toilet is basically in the same room with me, so I can hear everything.

'When I go back to Indonesia, I'll go to a shaman to send her some voodoo,' I say it in my nasal voice because I am pinching my nose. He laughs again.

69

The next day, Jonathan takes me to the Royal Albert Hall, a gigantic concert hall renowned for its acoustics and for hosting philharmonic and other musical performances. My phone rings just as we're on the street admiring the building – it's a call from the caterer telling me to come to Cadogan Hall tomorrow at two o'clock in the afternoon. I should wear a white shirt and black pants or a skirt.

'What are we going to see?' I ask Tan, before putting the phone in my tote bag and entering the building. This morning's activity is his idea as he realized neither of us had anything to do all day.

'A classical music performance,' he replies.

'Oh, like Beethoven or Pavarotti?'

'We're going to enjoy Mahler's Symphony No. 1 in D major.'

'Wow,' I respond, even though I don't entirely understand what he is saying.

The problem with walk-in tickets is that we can't get a seat, so we stand in the gallery with hundreds of other people. Just like at a pop concert, only we're watching a full orchestra and we're not expected to make a sound, including tiny coughs or sneezes.

The event lasts for one hour and forty minutes with a fifteen-minute interval. I try hard to enjoy the classical music even though my legs are starting to cramp from standing, and I don't quite grasp the beauty of this arrangement. I prefer music like Green

Day or Westlife where we can all shout or sing together, or at least dance. Finally, everyone claps loudly, and they don't stop clapping for a few minutes, encouraging the orchestra to play one more piece. I am stupefied.

'You enjoyed it,' Jonathan says as we walk home. Not asking but telling me.

'Oh, did I?' I reply, somewhat evasively. I wasn't sure if I really enjoyed it.

'You had such a big smile when you clapped.'

'Oh, right ... yes ... it was good music. Plus, everyone was clapping so I just went with the flow. I feel happy when other people are happy.' I was actually glad when the show had ended. Don't get me wrong, I don't hate this kind of thing at all. At least I could say to myself that I've seen something like this in my life. But going to this kind of thing again? I'm not really sure. I'd rather watch Celine Dion in Las Vegas.

'Oh, you got carried away,' he says.

'How about you? You seemed very serious back then.' He must really enjoy events like this. He is educated and comes from a classy background.

'My feet were tingling,' he replies.

My eyes widen.

'I held in a fart for an hour and a half,' he continues.

My eyes nearly pop out. Then I laugh.

'But don't worry, I let it pass, just now.'

'Oh Lord.' I walk away from him, then laugh some more.

Jonathan takes me to lunch at Wasabi for some not-so-expensive sushi. 'I'll pay you back after payday,' I say. He answers with an offhand okay and doesn't seem to care.

After lunch, we walk to the Victoria and Albert Museum, which is not too far from us. He asks me if I like museums, and I shake my head honestly. I don't understand anything about history or things from the past. However, he still invites me in. We go on a free tour, and it turns out that the museum isn't so bad when we have someone explain it to us. We visit the Muslim history section, and I see a robe embroidered with Arabic scripture. Underneath it is captioned 'Enchanted Robe', worn to ward off black magic and the like.

'Amazing, right?' he says. 'Some people feel connected to the past through historical objects. It's like finding a missing part of themselves.'

'Hmm. Amazing, yes, because these things last longer than the owner. The owner died a hundred years ago,' I say.

'You don't like the past, do you?'

'What for? It's already happened. Thinking about the future gives me a headache already.'

'But you're not enjoying your present either.'

I turn to look at him. Mr Smarty-pants!

70

After we finish at the museum, the air is colder and it starts to rain as usual. We run back home. As soon as we arrive at the flat, we immediately set the heating to the highest level. I take off my shoes, get into bed and wrap myself in a blanket while turning on the television.

'TV is life,' says Jonathan. He sits down at his small desk, turns on his laptop and starts typing quickly.

'Laptop is life,' I say.

'I've got some emails to reply to.'

I let him do his thing.

From under my blanket, I look at Jonathan, hunched over, very serious and focused. Jonathan does not have a towering stature. In fact, he's a bit short and stocky, not much taller than me. His skin is fair and he is well-groomed, his hair cut short. His eyes are a bit slanted, and he seems to be trying to maintain a moustache and beard, uneven and a little unsightly. Why am I describing him in my head?

Twenty minutes later, he closes his laptop and climbs into bed.

'What are you watching?' he asks.

Out of respect, I had the volume down when he was working. 'A cooking show,' I reply.

'British Bake Off.'

'If you want to do your work, I can go out for a while,' I offer, turning up the volume of the TV.

'It's done,' he replies.

'Don't you need to go to your university or something?'

'You're trying to kick me out of my own room?'

'No! I was just asking. Why so sensitive ...'

For a while we just watch TV without saying anything.

'Why are you doing this?' I finally ask. I've had this nagging question since last night. Even though he says he would do this for anyone, I don't really buy that.

'It's nice to have company,' he replies, without looking at me at all.

I try to process the answer. 'But I'm a stranger.'

'Same goes for you. I'm a stranger to you, right?'

He's right.

'But I was in a position of needing help. A person in need should use all the resources they can get.'

'And I was in the position of needing a friend.'

'You have a lot of friends, don't you?' I say again, hoping for an honest answer.

He doesn't answer.

'Do we still have grapes?' he asks instead.

I know he's changing the subject. 'You've finished them.'

He complains about buying more grapes.

I ask him to tell me more about himself. I expect him to avoid such a personal question but he surprises me by challenging me to ask anything I want to know.

'Age?'

'Thirty-four.'

I want to call him 'Uncle' to make fun of him but, considering I am thirty-one and still acting like a toddler, I decide against it.

'The youngest of three siblings, and my parents–'

I interrupt: 'They have their own company?'

He nods. He studied in the United States since the second grade of high school and continued to live there, only returning occasionally to Indonesia for holidays. It's very typical. I don't ask about his education because he is pursuing a PhD, which I certainly wouldn't understand. I think it has something to do with journalism and research. He is a Taurian and doesn't like spicy food. His favourite vacation spot is the Maldives.

'My favourite vacation spot is the T-junction not far from my house where the chicken satay hawker is. Besides that, you already know everything about me,' I say as I get out of bed and start washing rice for dinner. 'I want to cook something.' I mean if he wants to eat out alone, then he can go ahead.

'Don't make it spicy,' he says, which means he wants to eat in with me.

I put the rice on then start to wash the vegetables and meat. I explain to him that my brother has just had surgery, nothing serious, just appendicitis, so he doesn't have to put on a worried look. That's why I couldn't just borrow money from my mom to go home. What's more, I don't have any friends or relatives I can turn to for help. I tell Tan that as well for context.

'You want to go home?' he asks.

I purse my lips. I'm not sure about that.

'London is getting colder,' I reply. Not literally, I mean it's cold metaphorically. But he misinterprets this.

'It will be even colder when it comes to mid-December, then January. It can be very depressing.'

'I don't mind the cold or the snow.' Like most Southeast Asians, I have never seen snow. And living in a hot climate all my life or during monsoon season with its mosquitoes, winter is something new and exciting.

'Are you a winter person?' he asks.

I shrug. 'It's great. I can wear thick jackets and cool boots.' Even though I only bought the second-hand ones from Oxfam.

He smiles. 'What about London? Do you like it?'

While delicately placing the meat in a pan on the stove, I try to think. 'London is very different from what I imagined. I thought there would be a lot of people who look like Mr Bean or Sherlock Holmes. People in dapper clothes with classy British accents. But all I see are tourists.'

He laughs. 'You watched too much television.'

I look at him sarcastically.

'You worked in Soho. Of course all you saw were tourists. After all, London is the city with the most nationalities in the world. People from all different countries come here to work.'

'I know,' I have stayed in various hostels and seen it with my own eyes.

'So, do you like it here?' he circles back to his original question.

'I've lived here for almost three months, but I haven't felt anything special.'

'Maybe because you take everything for granted? You don't enjoy what you have now.'

'Not really, it's just different when you go somewhere on vacation rather than for work. I haven't had much time to soak up the atmosphere. I came here with the goal of making money. I've worked on a ship, don't forget, so I've seen other European countries. They're all the same.' I add vegetables to the pan and stir vigorously.

'No chilli, please,' he says, when he sees me about to sprinkle in chilli flakes. I almost forgot about it.

We start eating around six o'clock. Jonathan doesn't eat much rice as he is trying to reduce the size of his stomach. Outside, it starts to rain heavily, and suddenly the smoke alarm goes off. We go out into the corridor to check and find a young couple in the next apartment frantically waving away smoke from their door. Don't they know it's prohibited to smoke in the building?

We take turns showering, and I am rummaging through my suitcase for clean clothes with a towel wrapped around me when Jonathan asks if I trust him.

I answer with a brief and firm 'no.' Of course, he shouldn't take it personally because it's hard for me to trust anyone anymore. The only reason I am here with him is because I don't have another choice.

'That's fair enough,' he says, showing understanding.

71

Jonathan has been missing from the room since nine o'clock in the morning, and the winter sky is still dark. I don't know where he's gone, but he's left another £20 note on the TV console. There's a note next to it: 'You snore.' I frown. I don't snore.

At two o'clock, I leave for Cadogan Hall. I text the number of the caterer, saying that I am on my way. 'Just come in,' they reply. The first thing the caterer asks is whether I brought the clothes she asked for. I nod. Luckily I have the white shirt and black pants that I used to wear when I was a waitress on the ship. The owner of the catering outfit is a Russian woman. She's big and has an accent. I don't know what kind of friendship exists between her and Paul Jr, but perhaps it's a unique one. She introduces me to the other three waiters: two black men and a girl called Laura with a nose piercing.

'There will be four to five hundred guests, but they won't all come here. Most will leave after the event is over. You guys,' the Russian lady points at the two men, 'are responsible for the snacks, cleaning up the leftovers, and making sure the food trays are never empty.' Both of them look very grateful that they don't have to serve hors d'oeuvres around the room.

'You two,' she points at Laura and me, 'are in charge of drinks. There's only red and white wine, and some juice. Everything is free, but don't be too generous. Also, don't offer new glasses. And if you're too busy, just play a little deaf. Don't overexert yourselves.'

The after-party will take place in a room that can only fit two or three hundred people, so it's going to be cramped. The tables have been laid out according to the plan. Laura and I are preparing the glasses and opening bottles of red wine. Bottles of white wine are stored in containers filled with ice to keep them cold. Everything is ready by the time the show finishes at eight o'clock. We stand behind a long table that functions as a bar. I don't know what was going on in the theatre – what they screened and all that – but the long wait has made both Laura and me stale and drained.

'Finally,' says Laura, as guests start to enter the room. I

put on my usual big smile, just like when I greeted the boarding passengers. But my smile immediately disappears when I see the people who enter the room. 'I'm dead,' I say to my co-worker. She ignores me and stands still, already starting to pretend to be deaf.

What the hell, why am I being so big-headed like this? I need to get over myself. I mean, will they even pay me any attention? Of course, these people – many of whom turn out to be Indonesians – are celebrating something. Whatever the show was in the theatre, it must have been successful as all people who enter the after-party are smiling happily. They're radiating happiness. Why would they look twice at me?

Several men in suits come over and ask what drinks we serve. 'Wine and juices, also sodas,' I say. For the first few minutes our bar isn't that crowded, but we soon start to become overwhelmed. 'Wine, wine, wine, apple juice, wine, Coke, no, Diet Coke, wine, uh, who asked for red wine earlier? Sorry, can't change the glass, okay? No beer or sparkling wine.' They don't care about me, they care about their drinks.

'No. No beer, sir.' The more Indonesians who flock to the table, the more I struggle to catch my breath. Only when the first wave of drinks orders subsides does everything calm down.

Groups of sophisticated-looking Indonesians in smart clothes congregate around drinks tables. Wine glasses in hand, they talk in fluent English about the arthouse show they have just watched. The men wear suits and ties, while the high-heeled women are in dresses and *kebayas*, many of them made from batik declaring pride in their culture. It seems these are Indonesians living in London. Some of them are wealthy people, others are intellectuals who must be very smart because they have received scholarships from the state. Me ... I am a restaurant waitress with a threadbare white shirt.

'Your people?' Laura asks me.

My people indeed, but I pretend I don't hear the question. 'I'm going to clear up,' I say instead. Lots of glasses have been left on tables. With a tray, I start walking around collecting them. These people with their fancy clothes and money and education are too lazy to return their glasses.

I spot the group of Indonesians who drank in the Phoenix pub in Chelsea. They look very classy and fit perfectly into this centuries-old building. The women have neatly styled hair, bracelets and lipstick, and light shines from their eyes. The men wear shirts, jackets and cologne, and speak in confident voices. I am about to make a fast U-turn when Jonathan notices me.

'Hey, Maya,' he shouts. His friends turn to look at me. As I'm holding a tray of glasses, I can't make any sudden moves. I offer them a smile that I hope covers my extreme awkwardness.

'Sorry, sir, I'm not Maya. I'm Kanompang, sir.' I leave the scene immediately.

'You know her?' I can hear one of Jonathan's friends ask him.

Jonathan says nothing and continues the conversation as if nothing happened.

My heart is pounding and I nearly drop my tray. 'Your turn to clear up,' I say to Laura. She pretends not to hear it.

72

I return to Paddington at ten o'clock after everything is done. The glasses have been arranged on their racks for washing, the empty wine bottles have been separated, the tablecloths have been folded. Laura hid a bottle of red wine to take home, and the caterer gave us £70 each. With mixed feelings, including tiredness, happiness to have money again, and a little worry, I walk into the flat and find Jonathan in his t-shirt and boxers on the edge of the bed watching television.

'Hi, Pang-pang!'

'Hi, Tan-tan,' I reply.

I take a bottle of wine from my bag. Laura is not the only one who can do that. But I didn't do it because I like drinking. It's an attempt to bribe Jonathan. I don't know how he feels about my lie earlier, but I hope the bottle of stolen red wine will thaw any possible chill in the air.

'Merlot?' I offer.

He takes two glasses from the shelf. Although I am reluctant to drink, I take a glass. I don't really like alcohol. It makes me sleepy.

'I'm tired,' I say after finishing the first glass and while pouring the second. My body feels warmer, and I relax a bit.

'Pang-pang is tired, sir.' Jonathan imitates my accent.

'Oh, shut up, Tan-tan,' I laugh.

To my surprise, Jonathan doesn't say anything about what

happened that evening, and that makes me feel even more guilty.

'What was the event? There were so many Indonesians.' I decide to start the conversation.

'A Javanese gamelan performance synchronized with a silent movie. The actors were there, as well as the Indonesian ambassador to the UK, as you may have noticed. And also in attendance was Pang-pang, right? But not Maya.'

I pour my third glass of red wine and climb into bed, still in my crumpled black and white clothes.

'What's the matter with you and the Indonesians?' he asks.

I shake my head. 'Nothing. I am Indonesian.'

'But you don't want to be an Indonesian when you meet another Indonesian?'

I lie down and look up at the ceiling.

'I feel small,' I say. 'I feel insignificant. You know that, don't you? Maybe you don't? I feel like a wet rag compared to these people. Only educated people attend arty shows. Lower-class people don't go to the theatre, they don't have time. These are the beautiful people … all polished and shiny. They're smart and good at conversation. I feel ashamed to be around them. I mean, look at my dirty, shabby clothes. Plus, I didn't want to embarrass you. What would they say if they knew you knew me?'

'I have no problem with that,' he says.

To suggest that we are all the same humans and that humanity is equal is a cliché. The reality is not like that. Put yourself in my position – it is completely different. When you're just a waitress while everyone else is a cool guest, and you're out of your league, out of your class, then you'll know. You wouldn't understand the feeling of seeing your fellow Indonesians in London studying or vacationing and having fun while your job is to clean their tables. Maybe you think I am overreacting, but honestly that is how I feel.

I wanted to greet them once, then I realized my place. What a stupid idea. I know they wouldn't be snobbish. They would chat to me for a while with genuine friendliness and interest. 'Oh, you're from Indonesia, which province? How long have you been here? Where do you live?' Then what? I wouldn't understand what they're talking about, and we wouldn't have any topics in common beyond that basic introduction. The atmosphere would become awkward because they would feel bad about my job, and I would tell them I had to go to another table to clear plates. And because they were regular customers, we would pass each other often, and the awkwardness would repeat over and over. It might just be me, but I don't want to take the risk. It's better not to know each other in the first place. And you know what? Not many people turn their heads twice to a waiter. Even if they smile it's just a formality.

I see Jonathan nod.

'Eh, why did you do that?' I am surprised by his nodding.

'I see what you mean,' he says.

'Huh? I didn't say anything.'

'Oh, I heard everything.'

I thought I was only thinking out loud in my mind. It must be the wine talking.

73

The night doesn't end there. After pouring out what has been swirling around my head all this time, I suddenly become really drowsy, both from alcohol and relief.

'Sleep next to me,' Tan says. Is that a suggestion or a request for permission?

'Don't I do that every night?' I ask.

'A little closer,' he continues in a muffled voice, perhaps worried that I might be offended or reject him.

I slide over closer to him without thinking.

'Can I hug you?' he asks politely. 'Not in a sexual way,' he adds. 'Just a simple spooning. I'll be the big spoon.'

'Yeah, sure.' That is definitely the wine talking.

I turn my back on him and he wraps his arms around me. I am not a total newcomer to cuddling. I have done it before in bed with Maroje – even if only for a few minutes on a rocking ship. But I have never really been spooned in a warm, stationary bed. Jonathan's right arm is around my waist while his left is on my neck. His slightly chubby belly bumps into my skinny back. All night.

'Don't feel small,' he whispers.

74

I am pretty sure that I don't snore, but Jonathan keeps on teasing me. He even threatens to record me the next night. I tell him it's him who snores like a pig. Well, anyway, I go to work, and when my shift ends, Paul Sr gives me this week's pay cheque. Now I actually have enough to live on my own until my next payday. However, there's nothing wrong with pretending to be broke for a few more days so I can save some money, just as a precaution.

After work I stop by an Asian food shop and look for Indomie.

Jonathan is waiting in the room. He has just finished his shower. I see his cycling helmet laying on the floor next to a pile of dirty clothes.

'What's with riding the bicycle every night?' I say.

'So that I can get tired and sleep faster. Plus, the streets are quieter too.'

If you want to feel tired, maybe you should try working as a waiter, I think.

'How was your day?' he asks.

'Okay,' I reply, taking off my jacket and boots.

Then I take out two packs of Indomie and hold them up in front of him. 'Ta-daa,' I say, excitedly.

He doesn't budge.

'Ta-daa,' I repeat.

He is still unmoved.

'What? Instant noodles?' he asks, with no enthusiasm.

'This is Indomie!' I say impatiently.

'Oh, Indonesian products.'

'This is "the" Indomie. Aren't you excited?'

'Should I be?'

'This is food that knows no race, rank or social strata. Everyone enjoys it, from the motorcycle taxi drivers to the president. And it's everywhere, even in London. Amazing, right?'

'I've never eaten it.'

I shoot daggers at Jonathan.

'You have to! I'll make it for you.'

'Isn't it unhealthy?'

'Shut up!' I snap. I boil water in a pan and cook the Indomie with an egg. After the dish is ready, I blow the rising steam at Jonathan. Instead of being charmed by its irresistible smell, he covers his nose. I eat the Indomie.

'You don't want any?' I ask. He doesn't even look at me for a while, and it is only during the commercials on TV that he approaches the bowl. I give him my fork. He tries the noodle gingerly but after just a few mouthfuls his expression changes.

'It's good,' he says.

'Told you,' I grin.

Jonathan doesn't ask to hug me again tonight, probably because he isn't drunk. Not that I was looking forward to it. But I suddenly think of my brother and my mom. I hope they are well. I remember Maroje too. I miss him a bit.

'You okay?' Tan asks because I haven't uttered a word since my shower.

'Hug me for four minutes?' I ask.

He tells me to get closer to him. In his arms, I tell him that I miss my family. I tell him about my mom, her job, my stubborn brother and my late father. He holds me tighter.

'I have to shut my mouth,' I say.

'Don't say that. I enjoy listening to you.' Jonathan's voice is calming and non-judgmental.

I think I am actually starting to like Jonathan. Part of my heart is comparing him to Maroje, but we all know how Maroje has treated me. And Jonathan ... he's just the way he is.

'Hey, thank you,' I say.

'For?'

'Offering me a place to live, and pretending to have a birthday so you could buy me some chicken in KFC.'

'I wasn't pretending, it really was my birthday.'

I turn to see if he's kidding and I'm about to poke him in the stomach. But what I see is a pair of black button-like eyes, dark and honest. And before I can say anything, Jonathan puts his lips on mine. He kisses me for a long time.

75

I tell this to my mom. That I like someone, and I kissed him back. I have to tell her because I have no friends to confide in. Mom doesn't say anything annoying, she just asks if he is a foreigner? And she sounds a little relieved to know the facts about Jonathan.

Half an hour later, I get a message on WhatsApp. It's from my mom. She sends me a YouTube link. The link leads to an Islamic song by Haddad Alwi and Sulis. In the afternoon, before leaving for work, I receive another link – a spiritual song from the Bimbo group called Sajadah Panjang (Long Prayer Mat). When I've finished my shift, I open yet another message and get a link to a thirty-minute religious sermon by someone called K.H. Zainuddin M.Z.

OMG, what's wrong with my mom? I told her I kissed a man, and she urges me to repent my sins? What will she do if she finds out that I am actually sleeping next to Jonathan every night? She'll send me to a religious institution to whip out the demon in me.

I arrive back in Paddington and I'm hyped to tell Jonathan about my mom – which I honestly think is pretty funny – but it turns out that he is busy chatting to someone on the phone. I wait for him to stop talking. But the conversation goes on for another twenty minutes, so I decide to take a shower. Coming out of the bathroom while drying my hair, I ask him casually: 'Your girlfriend?'

He shrugs. 'Sort of.'

I pause a bit. 'You have a lover?'

'She's a very close friend. And she's sick,' he says.

'I don't get it,' I say, with a hint of annoyance in my voice as well as on my face. And Jonathan catches it.

'I didn't know you were the jealous type,' he says.

'What?' First, why does he think that I am jealous? Second, why does he think that I am not the jealous type?

Then Jonathan suddenly explains everything even when I

don't ask him to. That once, he had dated a girl for eleven years, which came to an end. Then he tells me about the monotony of relationships with the ridiculous and boring concept of monogamy. Then he talks about the chemical reactions in the brain which are triggered by dopamine. It's only fun and beautiful when you fall in love, but once the hormone wears off, the feeling goes away. And since then, he no longer believes in something called exclusivity or falling in love or having romantic relationships between two people. He says our brain is playing tricks on us. So, he is now in various relationships with different people, in different places. 'I have a big heart,' he says. 'I don't believe in falling in love anymore.'

I have no words.

'I want to be friends with as many people as possible,' he finishes.

It's possible that everything he has just said about himself is true, but maybe there's an underlying reason that has made him like this, something he hasn't revealed to me.

'So, the person you were talking to earlier …?'

'My close friend. She lives in America and we've been close for two years.'

'And you have other close friends?'

'There are several. Maybe seven,' he says.

I sigh. My chest hurts quite a bit, but I don't show it.

'But it's not all that important. Because they're not here. What matters is the person I'm with right now,' Jonathan says with certainty, as if that is what he really believes to be true – not just because he wants to cheer me up.

I hang up the towel, climb into bed and pull up the covers.

'Very tired, going to sleep now. Night.' Even though I know he wants to keep talking.

'Night,' he replies.

Turning my back on him, I cry. Not out of jealousy.

76

For a little while, before last night, I did think I might like Jonathan a lot. He looks so sincere, and I can imagine myself being his girlfriend. However, it seems that he has a completely different understanding of life from mine. Maybe it what he believes makes sense to him. But for me, it's too complicated. I want something simple like most people. Just an ordinary boyfriend. What am I thinking anyway? I am just a waiter. He is studying for his PhD.

As I am not working today, I am going to spend the whole day in the flat. It has been raining since morning and Jonathan has disappeared with his umbrella. I try to control my feelings and act normal by reminding myself that Jonathan is just a stranger … a platonic friend. However, when I see him coming back to the room with coffee from Pret a Manger my composure wobbles.

'Breakfast,' he says, handing me a plastic bag of croissants and hoisin duck wrap.

I try not to look him in the eye for fear that I might say something stupid. The rain is getting heavier. We look out the window and see the wet streets and people passing by under their umbrellas.

'You will understand,' he says suddenly. He gets into bed and invites me to join him. We watch TV. Then he starts to talk about how Hollywood has shaped our idea of romance. According to him, things like giving flowers and grand gestures are just concepts pushed by movies and books to make money. Feelings like jealousy, sadness or happiness are all dictated by society, he argues. It's all about perspective. 'Getting too attached isn't good,' he adds.

'Nothing is important to you?' I conclude.

'I have priorities,' he replies. 'My priority number one is myself, then my education, then my job.'

'Then the person you called last night?'

'Yes,' he answers. 'But the most important thing is now, here, me, you,' he says, then pulls me in and hugs me. And, stupidly, I let him.

I admit that Jonathan is very different compared to everyone I have ever met. He is smart, funny and candid. Sometimes I watch him silently as he reads a book, then he will look at me cutely and say: 'What? Say something.' And I will smile, and he will smile back. Or like when he comes out of the bathroom and suddenly says: 'Funny.' When I ask what's so funny, he says he forgot about it already. He remembered something funny when he pooped, he says. And most importantly, he is nice to me and seems to be genuine. He doesn't have an agenda.

'I think you're funny. I don't know why, but I think you're funny,' he says, hugging me. 'And cute.'

Oh my God, I am melting, and I have to do something about that. I just can't help myself when someone I like calls me cute.

77

I feel obliged to protect myself a little. From Jonathan as well as from myself. I just find how easily I fall into his arms. I wish I could control myself, but that's a difficult thing because I get carried away easily. It's not that I don't like being hugged. It's just, if the hug continues, I might just keep falling for him. Then what would my fate be?

The next day I sit on the floor with my clothes in a pile next to an open suitcase.

'What are you doing?' asks Jonathan.

'Folding clothes. What does it look like?' I say.

'Why?'

'Why not? To make it tidy-*lah*,' I reply, still folding the clothes and then putting them into the suitcase.

'But you're put them in the suitcase,' he says.

'Because it's a suitcase,' I reply. 'It's meant for folded clothes.'

'There's a cupboard, you can keep them there,' he says.

'That cupboard is for your clothes.'

'No problem. I like to share.'

It will never end. I know he knows what I am doing.

'You want to leave?' he asks.

I am silent for a while, looking for the right thing to say.

'You feel uncomfortable here?' he asks again.

'No,' I answer, then I correct it. 'Yes. I mean, I feel good, but last night, you know, hugs ...'

'You don't like that?'

'I like it,' I answer hurriedly, then lose track of where I was going with this.

'But?'

'No buts,' I lie.

'Then why do you want to go?'

I feel like burying my face in the pile of clothes and screaming.

'I like it, but I'm scared.'

Jonathan moves closer. He drops onto his tummy on the bed, his friendly face raised. He is looking at me.

'You don't want me to hug you again?' he asks.

'I want, but ...'

'Are you afraid of your own feelings?' he asks very gently. His question felt like he was stating a fact about me.

'I don't know,' I reply, surprised that I just realized this. 'You think so?'

'Every time something is bothering you, you decide to leave, rather than to talk about it or work it out,' he says.

'I'm not like that,' I say doubtfully.

'Then, what's with the suitcase?'

I stop folding my clothes. No one has ever read me that well other than Jonathan, even though he's someone I have only known for a few days. Maybe he's right. Maybe I do have a tendency to run away from problems. My own mind is my problem.

I feel like crying.

'Hey, look at me,' says Jonathan.

I hesitate to look up, tears already welling in my eyes.

'It's okay to be afraid. But you don't need to worry so much.' Jonathan shows me his smile. He has the smile of the Cheshire Cat from *Alice's Adventures in Wonderland*. Seeing it, I smile back.

'Let's go out, the weather is good outside,' he says.

* * *

The day unfolds wonderfully. I put aside my clothes-folding task, and we head to the Natural History Museum to explore dinosaurs, rocks and stuffed animals. We enjoy a can of lemon-flavoured San Pellegrino together. Afterwards, we find ourselves in Covent Garden. What once was a fruit and vegetable market has been transformed into a chic, upscale tourist attraction. Hand in hand, we blend in with the crowds, soaking up the warm glow of the autumn sun on our faces. We glance at each other and exchange a smile that is not only on the lips but also in the eyes.

'Take my picture,' I ask Jonathan. It is one of the happiest days and I want to keep this memory forever. So I upload the photo to Facebook. 'O, London, I fancy you,' I caption the picture.

We get home late and go straight to bed, exhausted. On the bed we face each other, and I say something that doesn't come easy to me.

'Hey, Tan-tan, Jonathan, whatever your name is ... I think ... I think I like you.'

He smiles. 'I know, Maya. I like you too.'

78

I believe Jonathan is quite sensitive to my feelings. Last night he hid his phone because he was worried that I would be jealous if his girlfriends called or texted him. This afternoon he teases me because I spray too much perfume on my body.

'Are you trying to make me like you more by smelling good?' he asks.

'Are you crazy or what?' I reply, laughing.

I leave for work in a good mood, singing to myself along the way, and I finally come to a conclusion about the purpose of my life. With Jonathan, I feel myself, complete, wanted. Maybe all this time, I have simply been looking for this kind of feeling? A warm feeling that I had only heard or read about before.

* * *

I do my shift in the pub, smiling despite the low pay and tiring work. As the shift comes to a close, I just want to be back in Jonathan's arms. I have an unread message on WhatsApp which must be from him and I can't wait to read it. When I have a spare minute to myself I quickly open WhatsApp … and I am stunned.

It is from Maroje.

The message reads: 'You're in London, right?'

I don't know what to do. My chest is bursting. Oh my God, Maroje has texted me after ignoring me for so long.

'Yeah, how did you know?' I type.

He replies immediately. It's eleven o'clock in London. Where can he be, it must be late for him?

Maroje: 'I saw your Facebook page.'
Me: 'Oh.'

It was the picture I posted yesterday in Covent Garden.

Maroje: 'I'm in London too.'

I am stunned ... again. I really don't know what to do ... again.

Maroje: 'Just arrived this afternoon.'
Me: 'Why are you in London?'
Maroje: 'To meet you. My contract just finished two days
      ago. I came here straight from Portugal.'

I can't reply.

Maroje: 'Are you okay?'
Me: 'Sorry, I'm at work.'

I am dazed and confused and in shock ... what am I supposed to do?

Maroje: 'When's your shift ending?'

Me: 'One more hour.'

Maroje: 'I will pick you up.'

Me: 'Okay.'

I have agreed to let him collect me. What's more, I have given him the address of the pub. Maroje is in London? The fact that he's texted me is already surprising. What's more, he says he's here because he wants to see me. Part of me suspects that Kanompang or someone else on the ship is playing a prank on me using his phone. But when I finish my work and exit the pub, that same tall guy is standing on the curb. I can't believe what I'm seeing.

'Hi?' I try, mostly to test myself, afraid that he might be a hallucination or just some random stranger who looks like Maroje.

He immediately approaches me and says hi in return. His voice is the same as I remember it. Deep and cold. I get ready for a hug, but he stays in his place, in silence, watching my face.

'You're here.' My voice has risen to a squeak again, normal for me when facing him.

'I am here,' he replies deadpan.

I touch his frozen cheek.

'But why are you here?' Even though I'm really flustered, I can't just surrender myself to him. I still remembered how desperate I was when he ignored me like I was some sort of meaningless pebble.

Maroje shows me his seaman's book. He shows me how he signed off from the ship two days ago. So, he isn't lying. But can it be it true that he has come to London just for me?

You're not going back to Croatia?' I ask as we walk towards the bus shelter.

At first, he doesn't answer. Then, very faintly, he whispers flatly: 'Because I'm missing you. I want to see you.'

Aw … the air is getting very warm. Winter in London is like summer in the Caribbean. He has never said anything like that before, and I can only imagine how hard it is for him to get those words out of his mouth.

'Lier,' I accuse him, in disbelief.

Maroje takes my hand. He doesn't say anything to reassure me. The grip of his hand implies that I should believe him. His enormous hand grips me hard. I feel like Thumbelina again.

'Where do you live?' he asked.

'Paddington,' I replied. 'With a friend.'

'I'm staying at a hotel in King's Cross.'

We walk in silence because I don't understand what he wants.

'Alright, I'll go home now,' I say when I see my bus coming.

'Don't,' he says. He keeps a firm hold of my hand until my bus has come and gone.

'So?' I ask, confused.

He doesn't answer. I still can't really digest what I am feeling right now. Anger? Annoyance? Or bliss? Mixed feelings. If Jonathan is to be believed, right now my brain is releasing a lot of dopamine.

'Come with me,' he pleads.

'No,' I answer quickly.

Maroje cups my cheeks with his palms. My face looking at his face. I remember his sharp eyes, his perfectly symmetrical nose and lips, and his cold and distant expression. I have missed him so much, and how happy am I that he is here.

I finally nod while slowly releasing an 'okay'. The corner of Maroje's lips rise, and my chest swishes.

I WhatsApp Jonathan, telling him I'm not coming home. Two seconds later, he calls me and asks me where I am and if I'm okay and whether I had been tricked again?

I tell him I am meeting a friend and will stay at their place. I can hear a curious tone in his voice. 'Friends? From?' All of a sudden, I am very hesitant to tell him that this friend is my ex-boyfriend. So, I distort the truth a bit.

'You don't have to worry; he's my friend from the ship.' Then an 'Ooh' from Jonathan that I can't decipher.

Maroje orders an Uber, and soon we are in King's Cross. I have never been to this area, and all I can think about is Harry Potter and Platform 9 ¾. I resist the temptation to take Maroje to King's Cross Station – it is one o'clock in the morning, and we'd better head straight to bed – ugh, this sentence sounds so wrong.

The hotel that Maroje is staying in isn't very luxurious. Just another budget hotel, but not the worst, and I didn't mind. I see some hotel guests drinking beer in the bar downstairs. They throw glances at us, but I can't imagine we're anything out of the ordinary. Only a tall and handsome white man with a skinny Asian girl entering a hotel together. Nothing suspicious at all.

And if you want to know what happens next, I really can't tell you anything. No, not because what happens is a secret or because I am too embarrassed to reveal it, but because nothing really happens. The long conversation I was hoping for (like his explanation for ghosting me all this time) doesn't happen. We just sleep side by side, in silence, all night long. And he doesn't snore.

79

Maroje wakes me up with a: 'Check out at twelve.'

I'm stuttering and hoping I didn't drool. I think Maroje was just a dream, but he is standing by the bed, tall and shirtless. And, oh my God, what a miraculous sight.

'Check out?' I ask, confused because I am hypnotized by his six-pack abs.

'I've booked an Airbnb,' he says without looking at me. 'For the two of us.' Maroje is a man with a million codes. However, do I want to stay with him? First, I need to confirm his feelings for me, so I grab his hand, and it makes him flinch in surprise.

'Maroje, how long will you be here?'

He thinks about the answer, then says something I didn't expect: 'As long as you are here.'

I look into his piercing eyes and give him a quick kiss on the cheek. His face blushes, and a smile that I have forgotten about for a long time is back on the corners of his lips. He makes me go, 'Aw, why are you so handsome?' Maroje shows me the place he has booked, and when I look at the map it is on the border of zones two and three. I have never been that far out before.

My phone rings. I glance briefly and see Jonathan's name. Maroje waits to see what I will do. Not wanting to seem suspicious,

I answer the call and speak in Indonesian. '*Aku baik-baik aja, nanti balik ke* Paddington,' I'm fine. I'll be back in Paddington soon, I say in a bit of a hurry and hang up.

'My friend from Indonesia, we share the same hostel room,' I explain to Maroje.

'You're gonna stay with me, right?' he asks after some time.

'I have to talk about this with my friend first ... I'll call you later, okay? You said we have to check out now? Okay, let's do that ... and then, then you go to the Airbnb, and I ... I want to meet my friend first.' It's hard to sound logical when you have to think so fast to lie. I hope my lie is convincing enough.

***

We part ways at King's Cross underground station. At Paddington, Jonathan is waiting for me in a relaxed posture which immediately calms me down. On the way over, I have been thinking through a lot of things and even before entering the flat I have made up my mind. It's not as if this is something complicated. After all, I do have to get out of Jonathan's room at some point, right? Even without Maroje's sudden appearance. So, I take this as one of the signs from the universe.

'Are you alright?' I ask, throwing my bag onto the bed.

'That question is supposed to be for you,' he says.

'I'm fine. It's just that I have something to say,' I say, trying to sound as casual as possible.

I'm trying not to get nervous, even though this is important. Jonathan pats his chest and mimics the rapid beat of an anxious heart with a 'bam bam bam'. I force myself not to laugh. He's trying to make this less difficult by breaking the ice, but on the other hand he's actually making it even more difficult for me. I mean, why is he so funny? How can I be apart from him?

'I think it's about time that I get out of here,' I say finally.

'You have a new place to live?'

'Well, for the time being. After all, my savings are enough to start living in hostels again. I can't keep bothering you ...'

'Where did you sleep last night?' he asks, instead of responding to my earlier statement.

'At a hotel in King's Cross.'

Jonathan frowns.

'With Maroje. He just got off the ship and came straight here from Portugal.'

Jonathan frowns even more. I can tell he is judging me. I guess he could say something like 'I thought you hated him because he was a jerk and ignored you, etc.' but he doesn't say anything, which is actually worse because it makes me curious.

'Okay,' he says. Nothing more.

Now it's my turn to frown. 'That's it?'

'Yup. If anything's up, you can always call me,' he adds very casually, and that pisses me off.

'I'm not a child. I know what I'm doing,' I gush, too defensively.

'Sure,' he answers. That makes me more annoyed.

My mood immediately changes, and the atmosphere in the room starts to feel uncomfortable for me. I feel like I am burning. With anger. Roasting. On the other hand, Jonathan still looks very relaxed and is occupied with his notebook. Feeling neglected, I start packing my things into the suitcase in silence. But I can't stay quiet for long.

'Can I take my "like" back?' I ask.

'What?'

'You know, when I said I liked you ... can I ask you to return my "like"? Because now Maroje is here. So, I feel bad that I still like you when I'm living with him.'

'Nope. I'm keeping the "like",' he replies.

'How so? You can't do that.'

'You can't unlike something just like that.'

'Of course I can. We can always "unlike" things, like on Facebook.'

'Not this one, you can't unlike me.' He looks serious. 'You like me. Forever.'

I feel really annoyed at being teased. 'Crazy or what!' I snap, but with a smile.

* * *

I kick my suitcase when I'm done, and although I feel a little reluctant to do so I have to say goodbye to Jonathan.

'Come here,' he says, spreading his arms. I then climb into bed, lie down beside him and let him hug me from behind.

'When must you return to Norwich?' I ask.

'Four days ago,' he replies. I think for a moment. And immediately feel bad again.

'You're staying here for me?'

'No, for me,' he replies.

'What?'

He responds with a smile while I try to process his statement with my peanut-sized brain.

'Mr Self-centred,' I say. 'I thought you stayed because you wanted to make me feel comfortable.' I snort. I thought he was staying here because he liked me or cared about me and didn't want to see me homeless, crawling on the side of the road.

'I WANT to make you comfortable. Precisely. Making you comfortable is number two, but fulfilling my own wish: "I WANT" is always number one. I want to make you happy, I want us to live together, I want you to feel the love I feel. Yada, yada … Do you get it? Actually, most people put themselves first, they just don't realize that.' Jonathan explains all of this to me patiently.

He's always like this. But I don't want to have to think about this kind of stuff. If he's right, does that mean that most people are basically selfish without realizing it? Is the motive for making other people happy basically for one's own happiness? If so, is that less sincere? Jonathan pisses me off because he forces me to think about things like this.

After some time, I get up and prepare to drag my suitcase away. 'I have to go,' I say.

'Hey,' he calls. I turn my head. 'Please take care.'

80

Maroje gives me the address of his Airbnb. It is in Honor Oak Park, in zone three. I have to change trains a few times, even transitioning from the underground to the overground to get there. After more than an hour, I arrive at the station, and Maroje is waiting outside. Zone three is entirely different from inner London, where I've been living.

I look around me and see rows of Victorian terraced houses. I remember a customer in the pub explaining that Londoners prefer old buildings to new apartments. Brick buildings have more character. And dust. Winter feels more pronounced here, probably because there aren't many shops and the pavements are deserted.

'Very ... quiet,' I say.

Maroje nods. It's probably why he chose this place. The ambiance reflects his character. Or maybe it's simply because of the cheaper price, I don't know. He wheels my heavy suitcase easily, like a gentleman is supposed to do. Walking ten minutes past endless rows of houses, we finally arrive at our street and house Number 59. There are several wheelie bins out front, different colours for different types of waste. The house looks old and a little cold. Maroje opens the door and leads me up to the first floor. On the ground floor is the kitchen and the dining room, as well as another tenant's room. We rent a room on the first floor with a shared bathroom. The room looks quite comfortable with a warm atmosphere, although not as clean as Jonathan's flat in Paddington. Inside the room there is only a large bed and a few cupboards. Unfortunately, there is no television.

***

I can't believe I am with Maroje right now. We sit on the bed without talking. I feel a little nervous. Maroje always gives me that vibe, like we are both schoolkids. Our hands almost touch, then Maroje does a really cute thing by moving his pinkie and tickling mine. What the hell is he waiting for? I want him to hug me or something. After being separated for so long, does he really only want it to be like this? All I can hear is his breathing. Maybe I should make the first move?

Just as I'm about to hug him, my phone vibrates and interrupts the moment. I grab it and read the text. 'Missing you already.' The message is from Jonathan. Why did he send me this? How irritating.

'You're smiling,' says Maroje, noticing the change in my facial expression.

'What? No I'm not,' I deny. He looks like he doesn't believe me. And because I don't want to look guilty, I dig myself a deeper hole by saying: 'There's nothing wrong with smiling after all. Smiling is a good and healthy thing.' Maroje looks even more distrustful of me. Of course he's not stupid. Just because he's silent doesn't mean he's stupid. But I am not done trying to show that I am a simple girl who has no secrets.

'Okay, I did smile. My friend sent me a very funny meme.

You don't have to be weird about it. I'm hungry. Lunch?'

Maroje stands up and pulls my hand. We head to some nearby shops and along the way he hugs me like he is cold and in need of my warmth. How romantic, I think. After a lunch of fish and chips, I pop into Sainsbury's and buy some grapes.

* * *

I haven't replied to Jonathan's message. And at one in the morning he sends me another one: 'Suddenly I'm craving Indomie.'

I glance at Maroje who is already asleep. He dozed off before ten, not long after our dinner. Most seamen who have just signed off from their ship are exhausted and spend their first week hibernating.

Maya: 'Go to the Pinoy store.'
Jonathan: 'I'm in Norwich already.'
Maya: 'Good.'

I stop the conversation. The conversation that makes me feel both happy and guilty. I turn to look at Maroje. After stroking his hair, which is very soft and beautiful by the way, I fall asleep like an untouched Snow White.

* * *

Maroje is still asleep when I go to work. I leave him a note saying where I've gone, just as Jonathan did (but I don't leave Maroje any money). My shift is pretty uneventful, but when it ends Maroje is there waiting for me outside the pub. I can see him yawning as he puts his hands in his jacket pockets. Ah, how romantic waiting for me. This is the dream, isn't it? Having a man waiting for you as you finish your job.

'Have you eaten?' he asks.

'Yes, you?'

He replies with a nod. Again he attaches himself to me as we walk to the Tube station. He seems very protective of me during the whole hour in the underground, even though the carriage is not so crowded. He's like a prince, and I am the cute princess Thumbelina.

By the time we get home, we are both very tired and fall asleep right away. Very boring, right? This routine continues for a whole week, and I am starting to feel overwhelmed by the distance I have to commute to work. Even though Maroje always picks me up, I feel so drained. I wonder whether to quit my job.

***

'Yes, that's best,' says Maroje, when I accidentally pour my heart out. I turn to him.

'But I don't know what I'm going to do next,' I say. I can't waste my time in London without making money, how am I going to buy food? Maroje has been paying for me recently, but still. And my visa is still valid for another eight months.

'Don't worry,' he says.

I guess I can't carry on working in a pub for such mediocre

pay either. So, I thank Paul Sr because he has been so nice to me, then I bid my goodbye to Paul Jr, who asks me to add him on Facebook.

* * *

A week has passed since Maroje's arrival. He seems to have regained his energy. I can see he is more alert and is starting to talk more than before.

'Let's go for a walk,' he suggests, on the day I quit work. Even though I have been in London for four months, I have never been to Tower Bridge, Trafalgar Square or even to Camden, which is said to be the hometown of hipsters. On my second day of being unemployed, I take Maroje to Buckingham Palace and we join a guided tour inside the palace. The stately rooms are very grand and they are full of huge, expensive oil paintings with ornate gilded frames. From the confusion showing in his eyes, I guess Maroje doesn't understand paintings. Neither do I. Jonathan would definitely have enjoyed them and could have explained them to me.

By this stage, I have stopped asking Maroje why he didn't contact me at all the last few months. I have asked him several times what happened, but the only answer I get is: 'I didn't cheat.' And that is the most important thing to him. I think he has a problem explaining what he means or how he really feels. Him cheating or not is just not enough – I need a meaningful response to my question. He can't expect me to be satisfied with his reply.

I tell him that I am upset with him, that I have been occupied by anger, and that he has made me seriously miserable.

He holds my hand tightly. 'I will never leave you again,' he says, without looking at me.

81

People have told me that winter is the most depressing time to be in London. There is no sun, and the nights come in faster. There is snow and slush and hail and cold winds, and people become more impatient, just like me.

Couped up with Maroje for days at a time is not something I would call an easy task. We spend hours in the room with nothing but hollow conversation. There's no television, and the only time I am vaguely happy is when I go shopping at Sainsbury's and cook a meal. Surprisingly, however, Maroje doesn't seem to mind being in the cage alone with me, even though he isn't doing anything either. Sometimes he just stares at me or looks out the window, watching snow fall.

'Are you going back to the ship?' I ask one time.

'Yes,' he answers simply.

He wants to make captain one day. He has to go back, and his vacation will end after two months. I think about spending two dark, cold and depressing winter months with someone who is also dark, cold and depressing.

'Don't you want to go back to Croatia to see your family? I mean, it's your vacation.'

'Will you be back on board?' he asks back.

'If I get the call.'

'So, you're going to stay in London?'

'I don't know.' I explain the validity period of my visa, how hard it was to acquire it and how I don't want to waste it. Plus, I want to save money for my family. (I don't tell him about the time I got scammed.) I just can't go back to Indonesia empty-handed.

Maroje goes silent for a while. 'Let's find a job,' he says suddenly.

***

We wander through Soho from place to place in the cold of winter, looking for job openings. I get an offer to work in large and eccentric-looking club. There is a vacancy as a janitor for the women's toilet. The pay is decent: £9 per hour, six hours a day. I have some knowledge of cleaning fluids and how to handle them from when I worked on ships. (According to American hygiene standards, it's called the three-bucket system – how to clean things to an approved sanitary standard – I won't explain it because it's too long.) I take the job right away. It's halal money, a halal job. What else do I need to worry about? It's tiring and dirty? Well, someone has to do it, right? I find some comfort in Maroje as well, as he, aside from being very stern, does not look down on any vocation.

'If I don't like it, I'll quit right away,' I tell Maroje, who questions my ability to mop the bathroom floor.

I will start working tomorrow at five. We wander around

Soho again, trying to find a job for Maroje, but there is none.

82

Working as a toilet attendant isn't as bad as you might think. At five o'clock in the afternoon, the bar opens. I start mopping what needs to be mopped, spraying and wiping the sink with disinfectant, replenishing toilet paper, taking out bags of toilet paper and tampons from the trash, etc. Hardly anyone comes to the bar until six or seven when people finish work. And the club only really gets buzzing with music and DJs or bands around eight o'clock.

I feel this is the best-paying job I can get. I earn £54 a night, the equivalent of one million rupiah. In a week I'll be able to afford a ticket home. That's also because I don't have to spend a dime on food and accommodation.

During my first three days of work, I am very grateful that no one forgets to flush the toilets. I am sure that the girls' toilets are cleaner than the boys' because they don't have to pee standing up, so the water doesn't splash everywhere. The club is a pretty fun place, and the patrons are just as cool. My toughest job so far has been cleaning up the vomit of a middle-aged woman who drank too much. She reminds me of Linda Nor.

When my shift ends at eleven, Maroje is always waiting for me outside the bar.

'You don't have to wait for me every day,' I say, as we walk to the Tube station.

'So, you can be free?' he asks.

I immediately frown. 'Of course not. I mean, it's cold.'

He doesn't answer and we remain silent the whole way home. It's not that we talk often anyway, but this time his silence is cold and maddening.

* * *

Over the next three days, Maroje's behaviour intensifies. His attentiveness is more pronounced than usual. Not only does he put his arm around me and hold my hand whenever we walk together, but he periodically checks on me via WhatsApp when I am working.

'Are you alright?' he texts.

The message is fine, it's harmless, but if I don't reply for some time, say twenty minutes, he will resend the same message. And the next text will be, like, 'hey … what are you doing?' Of course, I reply with something along the lines of: 'Cleaning up people's vomit', 'clearing broken glass' or 'refilling toilet paper'. After that he doesn't need to reply. He just wants to know how I am doing. I'm very lucky, knowing there's someone who is constantly watching over me.

I get my pay cheque after a week of work. Even though a part of me wants to hide this from Maroje, in the end I tell him.

'But I can't go home now,' I say when he reminds me I can now afford the flight home. 'I don't want to go home empty-handed.' Has he forgotten?

Even though Maroje doesn't say it, I feel that for whatever reason he wants me to return to Indonesia immediately. I want to tell him that I enjoy my new job. In Indonesia, I would have no interest in becoming a janitor. The salary there is crazy low. Perhaps I'd get £54 too ... per month. But quite apart from that, I can do anything I want to here and I don't have to worry about being judged. I don't know anyone in London.

***

Surprisingly, Maroje has never crossed the line in bed. Metaphorically or physically. He sleeps on his side of the bed and me on mine, side by side like two friends. He rarely even hugs me. He only embraces me once in a while, and even then for no more than two minutes.

Despite me feeling I am special to him, I feel like something is missing. We chat less and less. There is no stimulating conversation. I don't get that at all from Maroje. Our relationship feels like a cohabitation of two boring pensioners. I no longer feel any spark for him. But maybe I still love him.

***

I have been working at the club for over a week and I am enjoying it more and more. Every night the music is different, and on special nights female dancers perform on special stages in costume to add to the atmosphere. Sometimes I imagine one of the dancers spraining her ankle, and the manager looking for an emergency replacement. Then, I, busy mopping the dirty floor, will be summoned, and I will shyly agree to it. And although I may look as stiff as a broomstick, it turns out that I have a great talent for dancing. After that I am hailed as a dancing idol. LOL. What a delusion.

The truth is the manager tells me several times to switch shifts with other workers. But I have to refuse because I don't want to leave at four in the morning for fear there will be no more trains running to zone three.

***

One night I invite Maroje to join me at the club after my shift ends at eleven. I tell him there's a special event on with a famous DJ and the music will be really good. Maroje and I sit down and order a drink at the bar. I want to look like a normal girl, not a cleaner from Indonesia. The bartender already knows me so he gives me a free drink, which makes me happy.

Maroje sits beside me. I give him a cute smile, which he returns with a slight smirk at the corner of his lips. We haven't enjoyed any time together like this in ages. I can't read the expression on his face clearly, whether or not he likes the music. Maybe he's staying for me. I don't particularly like this kind of music either, I'm just enjoying not being inside our room.

Maroje says he needs the toilet. While he's gone, a man suddenly sits down beside me and orders a drink.

'The seat is taken,' I tell him politely.

He then looks left and right. 'I don't see anyone ...' he says, while giving me a charming look. I can't help but smile. He stays on the seat while waiting for his drink.

We engage in small talk, mostly about the weather, like how it's freezing cold outside and how dark it's getting. It seems such a long time since I last enjoyed small talk. However, not two seconds later, the man is suddenly yanked back by his collar and he falls off the chair. I see Maroje standing over him, his fist clenched and ready to fly. Everything happens so fast, and before I know it two bouncers are ejecting us from the club. I am so embarrassed.

I don't want to talk to Maroje at all after that. Not in the underground or when we switch to the overground, or when we walk back to our rental room in zone three. What was he thinking? Why did he do that?

'He was flirting with you,' Maroje says finally, noticing that I am holding a blazing firestorm in my chest. 'I don't like seeing you being teased by other people.'

He must have practiced this in his mind on the journey.

Some people might say his actions were somewhat hot. I am not part of that 'some'.

'He was just talking to me,' I say.

'It all starts from there.'

It's true what he says. It all starts with small talk, but I think he's gone too far. And what is even more outrageous is what he says next:

'You quit tomorrow.'

'What?'

'You don't have to work there anymore.'

That's what really pisses me off. I walk faster to distance

myself from him, but to no avail because he has long legs and wide strides.

'I don't like someone telling me what to do!' I say.

'You like cleaning toilets?'

'Not particularly! But the payoff is huge! I have to send my mom money for my brother who just had appendicitis surgery!' That's not exactly the reason, but I had to say something.

'I'm sorry,' he says. 'I was very jealous.'

Two seconds after he says that, the firestorm inside me immediately goes out. I have a hunch that Maroje is the type who is secretly jealous. And very reserved, keeping things close to his chest. So, him admitting it outright is a big surprise. He is being honest about his feelings. And there is nothing hotter than that.

'The pay is pretty good though,' I whine, still regretting that I have to give up the job.

'Tomorrow we'll find another job, okay?' he says in a very soft voice. He leans closer and embraces me, warming up cold London nights in zone 3.

83

I sulk all the next day, refusing to talk or eat anything. Maroje does ask me to look for work, but I don't even bother to turn my body towards him. He ends up going out alone all afternoon and only comes home in the evening, while I spend my time watching Shinchan cartoons on YouTube.

'I got a job for both of us,' he announces, when he arrives back at nine in the evening.

'Really?' I ask sarcastically.

'Yeah.' He takes off his thick jacket and climbs onto the bed.

'What kind of job?'

'You like cleaning bathrooms, so I got the same job.'

'At the club?'

'No, I'll show it to you tomorrow.'

I don't really believe what Maroje says.

***

The next day he wakes me up. After forbidding me to wear boots and makeup, he takes me to a barbershop.

'Your hair is still short,' I say.

'You're the one getting the haircut,' he replies.

Even though it is a unisex barbershop, I can tell it's more for men. The place looks very masculine. My hair is a little long, but not shampoo commercial long. Maroje wants me to have super short hair like when I was on the ship.

'Pixie cut,' I tell the barber, though I don't understand why Maroje wants me to have such short hair.

I feel fresher with short hair, even if it's a bit colder with my ears exposed to the air.

After that, Maroje takes me to the Vauxhall area, just south of the Thames. There, we visit a place I never imagined existed.

We enter a building and are greeted by a man. 'Is this your friend?' he asks Maroje but looking at me.

Maroje nods.

'Can you speak English?' the man asks me, to which I reply with a nod, still fascinated by the place we've entered.

'He can, but not very well,' Maroje continues. I don't know why he says that.

The man shows us to lockers where we can leave our jackets and bags. 'Follow me, I'll show you what you have to do.'

I already know what I have to do. It's just I'm wondering whether I can do it here. The man explains what our job entails, including picking up trash, maintaining inventory records, and other duties.

'Is there anything you want to ask?' he says, obviously not expecting a question. 'Fine, if there's nothing else, you guys can start work tomorrow. I'll arrange your shifts later but for tomorrow you can come together. Your name is Maroje, and you are Maya?'

I nod again. He looks at me for a long time.

'A slightly girly name ... but maybe that's a normal name for a man in Indonesia.' He gives me an insincere smile.

I frown immediately. Did he think I was a man all this time? Before I can say anything, Maroje grabs my arm and pulls me outside.

'Maroje, he thinks I'm a boy,' I say.

'Yes.'

What does 'yes' mean?

'You have to be a man; they don't accept female workers,' explains Maroje.

'Why?'

'Because it's a gay sauna.'

I glare at him. I can see it is a sauna, with two large bathrooms, a Jacuzzi, two sauna rooms, two steam rooms, a large room with a TV, and small rooms with beds. Even though I noticed a rainbow sign at the entrance, I didn't think that the sauna was gay-only.

'Why do you want me to work in a gay sauna?'

'So the men don't flirt with you.'

'That doesn't make any sense because you told me to disguise myself as a boy.' Surely I should look like a woman?

'That's why I'm going to ask for a shift with you, so I can continue to protect you.'

'That's ridiculous.'

Maroje flinches when I curse him.

'You know gay men are harmless ... they wouldn't rape you if they find out you are a woman.'

I glare at him again. 'No one ever wanted to rape me!'

'Just do what I tell you! Okay!'

I have never heard Maroje's voice rise that high. I'm shocked into silence and a little scared.

'What if he asks to see my passport? He will find out.'

'I told him you lost your passport, so you're being paid below the minimum wage.'

I try to act casual, even though I'm feeling more than a little uncomfortable with the aura that Maroje is giving off. I am annoyed that I've had to disguise myself as a man, but on the other hand I can't deny that I feel challenged – I want to know what a gay sauna is like. I'm no stranger to gay stuff.

***

The next day, we leave the house at four in the afternoon for a five o'clock shift. The sauna is still empty at this hour. Every now and then, the man we met yesterday gives us directions of what to do. I just have to mop and clean the toilet – easy peasy. Customers start arriving at seven, and nothing untoward happens. They shower and then head straight for the sauna. At nine o'clock, more customers pour in, and the music is cranked up. There is piped disco house music in the sauna. Although this is not the first time I have seen naked men, I must admit I start to get overwhelmed. I try not to open my eyes wide every time a guy takes off his towel, showers or walks starkers into the steam room.

Maroje forbids me to go into one dark room and another room with a big TV. Let him handle those rooms, he says. But, of course, out of curiosity, I peek into those rooms, pretending to check the trash can. My heart feels like it is about to explode watching something I won't repeat here.

'It's time for your first round,' says the manager, tapping my shoulder. I need to inspect all the mini-rooms nestled in the labyrinths with soft lighting. In each room is a thin foam mattress and a trash can. I have to collect the trash. What I don't know is that there are a lot of used tissues and condoms in the bins. My hands shake violently when I have to put them all in the large bin bag. Even though I'm wearing gloves, it is still challenging. This is no better than having to clean a clogged toilet. I do the job quickly.

My face turns deathly pale when I pass one of the rooms

and see a man showing his asshole as if serving it to passers-by. I almost let out a small scream (but, of course, I hold it in). I flee to the storeroom to catch my breath. I feel like crying. I have done some unusual jobs like marketing prostitutes and helping Josh tidy up sex toys in a gay sex shop, but this takes me way out of my comfort zone.

'Are you alright?' asks the supervisor.

'I saw an asshole,' I tell him.

'Plenty of assholes here.'

* * *

I spend a lot of time in the storeroom, pretending to take out rolls of tissue and I do some inventory. Only every now and then do I go to the toilet to clean it. Luckily, not much of interest happens in the toilet beyond number ones and number twos. I tidy up the lounge room with its large red leather sofas. There are vending machines and a television tuned to HBO. People chat casually and, in this room at least, they are quite modest. Nothing is exposed. I see Maroje being chatted up by an equally hot guy. This makes me giggle despite my stress.

I try to keep my wits about me until my workday is finally over. I tell myself that this is just a job, and it will end in an hour. But so much happens in that final hour that I can't describe it all here. Trust me, if I had asthma, it would have been triggered by this place.

* * *

At 11.30 pm, Maroje and I check out of the sauna. Our shift is done. After only a few steps, I turn to him and scream, 'I do not want to go back to that place! I do not want to pretend to be a man! Today I saw things I would not have seen if I was still a janitor at the club!'

Maroje only glances at me once, and his face is icy.

'Whatever,' he replies.

His frosty attitude makes me furious. Does he care about my feelings? Or me?

84

I spend the whole of the next day lying in bed with the heating set to high. I don't want to leave the room at all. It is December 20th and Christmas is everywhere. Lights flicker by the roadside and in the windows of houses, and the smell of the festive season wafts through the air. Out of boredom, I decided to call Paul Jr at the Chelsea pub.

'Hey, boy, you got any job info?' I asked.

'We're on vacation in the Maldives,' he replies. Then he pings me a photo of himself sunbathing on the beach. I am so jealous. 'Try calling the Russian mob. You take a vacation too; it's a holiday.'

'Holidays are only for people who don't have to work,' I reply.

I then text the Russian caterer whom I worked for at Cadogan

Hall. After a line of small talk, I ask her straight out if she has a job for me.

'£120 for a couple of hours, a birthday party, you want?' she replies.

'Yes, please, of course, I really want it,' I type, feeling excited.

'It's in Norwich. I won't cover your travel expenses.'

Norwich?! I'm thrilled. 'It's okay, I'll take it!'

'You have to be there tomorrow before 5 pm. I'll send you the venue address.'

I struggle to contain my joy.

'Why are you smiling? Who are you chatting with?' Maroje asks. He has suddenly appeared behind me. I hadn't realized he'd returned from the bathroom.

'I got a job, and I'm going to take it,' I say.

Maroje immediately checks where Norwich is.

'Two hours by train,' he tells me. 'How long is the party?'

'Just a few hours …'

'Okay, you can go. I'll buy you a ticket to leave at two in the afternoon tomorrow and return to London at nine the same day. I'll pick you up at the station.'

I fall silent. Why does he have to do that? Shouldn't I be able to decide for myself when I will leave and return?

'But …'

'No buts, I already bought the tickets,' he says, typing his credit card number into the phone.

I feel like crying.

85

We travel to Liverpool Street train station. Maroje doesn't take his eyes off me until I get into the train carriage. The journey from London to Norwich is so relaxing without Maroje's big body 'protecting' me.

'I'll take a nap,' I WhatsApp Maroje so he wouldn't kick up a fuss if I don't answer his messages.

'Yes,' is his response.

I'm not really going to sleep. I'm going to text Jonathan.

'Tan-tan, where are you?'

'Who's this?'

'Damn it, just forget it.' Maybe he deleted my number.

Two seconds later, my phone rings. 'I thought you had forgotten about me,' he says.

'Sorry if I didn't reply to your messages, okay? I didn't even get to read them. With Maroje hanging around me 24-7, I couldn't.'

I tell him I'm heading to Norwich to be a waiter at a birthday party. He tells me he is at his university. I say it's okay if he can't meet me because I don't have much time either and that I was told to go home right after the party finishes, I just wanted to tell him that I would be in the city where he lives. After he says a flat and noncommittal okay, we end the call. I look out of the window, allowing my eyes and mind to wander through the vast green fields of grass until I finally fall asleep.

Standing at the entrance to Norwich station, I am about to

enter the address of the catering gig into Google Maps when I hear someone shout 'Oi!' and there is Jonathan. My smile lights up instantly, and his eyes open wide as he returns the smile. I quickly run to him for a hug, and our bodies rock happily in a tight embrace.

'You said you're at university!'

'I skipped a lecture for you.'

'Aw, so sweet …' I pinch his cheeks and we laugh. I wrap my arms around his and hang there like a monkey. I don't know why I do it – perhaps because it is so cold, but mostly because with him I can be myself and have nothing to hide.

'You missed me?' he asks.

'You wish,' I scowl. 'Lead the way to the venue, I don't know the place …' The train station is in the city centre, and our destination is within walking distance. Jonathan asks me to tell him what's been going on in my life, and every now and then he tells me things about Norwich.

'He keeps you on a tight leash all the time?'

'Not like that. I think he loves me too much. He's very protective.'

'Are you sure it's love?'

I shrug. Everyone has their own way of loving.

***

Even though I really want to spend more time with Jonathan, I have to meet up with the Russian lady soon to prepare for the event. I hug Jonathan once more and tell him to go home.

'My train is at ten, right after the party finishes,' I say. 'Thank you for picking me up.'

'I'll try to come here again if I'm not sleeping,' he says with a laugh.

'It's so good to see you,' I said spontaneously, and he gives me his Cheshire Cat smile.

* * *

The birthday party lasts for two hours. A girl is celebrating her eighteenth. I stand behind a counter serving punch and snacks as well as protecting a large birthday cake and cutting slices for those who want it. A group of boys tries to add some spirits to the punch. After cleaning up the remnants of the party, the Russian lady hands me my salary. I thank her and ask her not to hesitate to contact me in the future for any jobs..

I glance at a bulletin board in the entrance to the venue and spot an interesting event scheduled for the next day: Dancing in December.

'Your boyfriend is waiting,' the Russian lady tells me.

A shiver runs down my spine. 'My boyfriend is in London,' I stutter. Turns out it isn't Maroje who's come to pick me up.

* * *

'I thought you were sleeping?'

'I woke up,' he yawns. How sweet of him to see me off. I put on several layers to walk back to the station to catch the ten o'clock train.

'Do you really want to go back tonight?' he asks.

'Maroje wants me to go back tonight.'

'What about your wants?'

'He's my boyfriend.'

'Your will is controlled by your boyfriend?'

I don't answer that. Jonathan likes to make me question things, and that's what I like about him, like getting slapped by logic.

Arriving at the station, I take a deep breath. 'Is Norwich good during the day?'

'It's a perfect little city,' he says.

'You have a couch where I can crash?'

Jonathan nods.

I take my £15 train ticket out of my pocket and tear it up. The London to Norwich journey took a couple of hours. Why come all the way here to see a bowl of punch and half-eaten pretty pink cake. I don't want to go home without seeing other things.

With great trepidation, I send a text to Maroje: 'I'm not coming home tonight. There's a Dancing in December event tomorrow … extra money for me.'

The lie is answered immediately: 'Where are you going to sleep?'

'Hostel.' Another lie.

'Okay.'

He doesn't say anything else. I am worried he might explode and send a helicopter to escort me home. I genuinely can't be sure what he will do, so I wait at the train station for another ten minutes, fearing that he will send a follow-up text telling me he was just testing me. It feels a little weird, actually, that I can get away with it so easily.

86

I don't sleep on the couch. After texting Maroje that I am turning in, I climb into Jonathan's comfortable bed and curl up on one side while he reads a book.

He looks up. 'I know you want to talk.'

But he doesn't know just how relieved I am to hear him say that.

'It feels like it's been two years since I last spoke to someone.'

Jonathan puts down his book. 'That bad?'

'He's not that bad. Just a little different.'

'He tortured you with relentless sex?' teases Jonathan.

I laugh. 'Uh, no. He hasn't touched me at all. Just hugs me in public, but that's to protect me.' I smile to myself. 'I think he's too romantic,' I add. 'A few days ago, he told me to stop working just because he was worried that men would flirt with me. I don't know why he's changed. He wasn't like this before.'

'Maybe you didn't really know him before. Or maybe you did know but refused to admit it for fear of being disappointed.'

I reply with a 'hmm'. Logic slap again.

'You know what's the worst?' I say. 'Yesterday he made me work at a gay sauna. He said gay men wouldn't chase me. I've lived here for a few months, and no one has ever wanted to do that to me.' I pause. 'Actually, there was one incident when I worked in, er, marketing in Soho. I returned to the hostel late at night by Tube. The carriage was pretty empty. Only a few people there. Then, an old man came up and sat next to me. He looked drunk. He asked if I wanted to be his friend, and you know what … he asked it with his hand on my breast.'

Jonathan snorts out loud. 'I know it's not funny, but you have to laugh.'

'Actually, it was really funny. At the time, I just opened my mouth in shock as he kept his hand on my chest. You should have seen him.' I imitate the old drunk. 'Anyway, I pushed the old pervert and he fell over.'

'That's must have been very traumatic for you?'

'Not really. He was completely harmless. It makes a good story.'

Jonathan bursts out laughing. 'You are so funny. And you're a very strong person too.'

'I'm Xena, that's why I'm strong.'

'Come here, Xena, let me cuddle you.'

I move in closer and let him hug me. Ah, how I miss being hugged like a normal human being.

87

Norwich during the day turns out to be very picturesque. Jonathan takes me for a walk along the sparkling river that runs through the city centre. He calls it his riverside walk. There's a bridge made of limestone, rows of medieval houses, and a city market selling plums and pomegranates. But I can also see Debenhams and Primark which somewhat ruins the vista.

As it is Sunday, we eat at a restaurant serving British Sunday roast. Tender roast beef with Yorkshire pudding and gravy. After taking pictures at beautiful Elm Hill, we walk to the Odeon cinema. Even though we don't watch a movie, we just hang out at Costa, sipping coffee and reading the horoscope in a discarded newspaper.

'Do you believe in things like this?' Jonathan asks.

'I believe in horoscopes, yes, but that's not because I'm a girl.'

'Let me read you your horoscope,' he says. He takes the newspaper and asks what my zodiac sign is.

'Libra, romance: you fall in love with someone who lives in Norwich because you think he's very handsome and hot.'

I laugh.

'Libras can't take back a "like" because Libras like forever, and their love interests are too good to be unliked.'

I laugh even more, then hit him on his arm playfully. People at the café must think we are two over-caffeinated Asians. How come he still remembers that I wanted to take back my 'like' from him?

My day out with Jonathan is the best, and I don't want it to end. Every now and then I glance at him and catch his lovely wide smile. I can't 'unlike' it.

We then return to the previous night's venue to see Dancing

in December, the excuse I gave to Maroje. I take photos of the entrance and of the crowd and send them to Maroje as proof I am here. He reads the message but doesn't reply. Something is not right – he hasn't contacted me all day, but I don't want to think about it. I can't deny that I feel more than a little glad to be away from him.

I notice that Jonathan also takes some pictures and sends them to someone.

'Your girlfriend?' I ask, but not in a jealous way.

'Another close friend,' Jonathan answers lightly, trying to sound like it wasn't a big thing that would make me jealous.

'The one in America?'

He nods. I forget he has many close friends, and it isn't just me – that is to say, if I am even included amongst them. As he said, he has his priorities in life.

'I want to see her,' I plead, but not in the tone of some crazy girl … which of course I am.

Without hesitation he shows me a photo of a woman. Oh, okay. Despite her pretty face, she doesn't look the kind of woman who takes selfies. She looks very smart, kind of normal too but reeking of wealth. And seeing that makes me feel very embarrassed.

'She's pretty,' I say with sincerity.

'She's okay,' Jonathan replies nonchalantly. He doesn't sound overly proud.

To be honest, I didn't think Jonathan was the kind of man who could get such a pretty girl. He's not like Maroje at all. By that I mean Jonathan's not very handsome or dashing. Of course

I like him, but not because of looks, rather because he is funny, charismatic and smart. I mean, if he can win over a girl like that, he'd need to be more than just funny like he is with me. Perhaps he simplifies his thoughts around me for fear I won't understand. I recall him discussing complicated topics with the other Indonesians in the pub. With me, he's just being funny and a tease.

'Don't think too much. It hurts,' he says, as if he can read me.

'Huh, no,' I lie. 'I was just thinking about Maroje.'

'What's up with him?'

'It's strange, he hasn't contacted me at all ...'

'That's good,' Jonathan says. We sip our coffee quietly for a while.

'I'm so glad I got to spend time with you,' he says after a while. It may sound cheesy, but it has such a positive effect on me.

Someone's tongue can change your mindset in an instant. I decide to stay in Norwich another night. The price I have to pay is another lie to Maroje, this time that the Dancing in December event is running late and there are no trains back to London.

'Maybe you should rethink your relationship with him if you feel so uncomfortable,' Jonathan says, as we are about to sleep.

'So I can be the priority number 41 after everyone else in your life?' I ask bitterly.

'Aiyo, it's not like that ...' but then he falls silent because we both know that what I said is true.

'Besides Maroje, I have no one else. With him, I'm always the number one priority.' I decide to sleep. Tonight Jonathan just strokes my hair for a while without hugging me at all.

'I'm sorry,' he whispers.

88

At eight in the morning, I am already on the train to London. Just ten minutes later, Jonathan texts me: 'Missing you already, missing your company.'

I reply with a confused smiley emoji (:) Even though I really like Jonathan, but ...

***

The sky is dark and foreboding, but it's forecast to snow today and I am looking forward to it. It will be so romantic. I want to experience the snowfall with my lover in the room, drinking hot tea like a Brit. However, Maroje still hasn't replied to the messages I sent him this morning.

My worries only grow because I don't find Maroje when I get back to the Airbnb. Could he still be working at the gay sauna? Where did he go? Did he sulk and go back to Croatia without telling me? I really want to apologize to him ... and to thank him for being so kind as to provide a place to stay and for buying me food so I can save.

Unfortunately, I can't ask anyone else at the shared house because it is Christmas Eve, and it seems like everyone is away for the Christmas holidays. The whole neighbourhood is still. It is mid-afternoon but it feels like a dark evening. Then the snow begins to fall. I watch it from the window. It is so peaceful that it makes me sleepy. I turn off the lights and get under the bedcovers. I can still see the snow falling outside the window, illuminated by the streetlight. Maybe Maroje is out for a walk. He will be back.

* * *

I don't know how long I have been asleep when the door suddenly opens, the lights come on and someone violently pulls my arms back. Half-awake, I hear the sound of a belt being unbuckled. Two seconds later, I feel my hands being tied behind my back. I think it is all a dream and I turn my head to find out. I have a fleeting glimpse of a familiar, tall figure.

'Maroje,' I call softly. 'Maroje.'

He doesn't answer. Only his breathing can be heard. I see him take off his jeans, which he then uses to tie my legs together. What is happening?

'Maroje.' My voice quivers in my confusion. It crosses my mind that he is going to rape me. After all this time, is he going to rape me now? I can't think of anything else.

He pulls me off the bed effortlessly like a rag doll and sits me in a chair. Wearing only his underwear, he moves quickly through the room, locking the door, turning off all the lights except for one and closing the window blinds.

In the dimness, I can't see his face clearly, and I don't know what is holding me back from screaming. All I do is call out his name, questioning what he is doing to me.

Maroje looks confused, but I think he is also consumed with anger. Don't panic, I tell myself. He won't hurt you, I reassure myself, even though the truth is my hands are already hurting from the belt he has used to shackle me.

For a while, he just paces the room in circles. I can hear him breathe heavily through his nose, each inhale and exhale a sign of his simmering rage. Then he lunges forward, right into my face. I look into his eyes, trying to make peace. But he doesn't allow that. He raises a hand then he swings. In a split second, everything is dark, then red, then black, then I wake up and feel the heat on my cheek and the stinging on the corners of my lips.

'Help,' I groan.

Looking very frightened, Maroje circles around the room again while I try to find my voice and ask for help.

'Shut up!' he snaps. He slides down his underwear and stuffs them into my mouth.

I am suffocating. My mouth is in pain. I am choking on the cotton cloth that is halfway down my throat, acrid with the smell of urine. I am crying.

'Whore!' he screams. 'You think I don't know what you did?'

I jerk back and forth, but with hands and legs tied I cannot raise myself from the chair. I try to scream loudly and the sound emerges as a muffled cry.

'Shut up.' This time he doesn't yell, but he grabs me round the neck. Tears stream down from the corners of my eyes.

'Shut up!' he snaps, as he slaps me once more. The sound that comes out of my mouth is a reflex. His hand is so big I can feel my ears buzzing, and it feels like they are being sliced.

I am going to die. That's what goes through my head. The only thing I want to do is to apologize to my mom, for some reason. I am not a warrior princess. I am going to die in a room in London's zone three on a snowy night, gagged with dirty underwear, suffocated. I keep crying.

'I was wrong about you,' Maroje begins again. 'You're just the same as all women. A whore!' He snorts, blowing his nose like a rhino. I no longer see Maroje – the calm owner of a shy smile – I see before me a monster.

How can I express my apologies when I can't make any sound? I will just let his anger run out. I will try to survive in silence.

'I followed you, you know! You know? I followed you, where you went and what you did. You liar! And that fucking scum. You slept with that scum. You dirty bitch!' He pauses, circling the room again. Then he continues: 'Dancing in December ... dancing on his bed more like.'

Tears well up in my eyes again and I sob. Oh my God, so he's been following me this whole time.

'Please ... please ... I'm sorry ... let me go ...' is what I want to say, but all that comes out is a meaningless moan.

Maroje approaches me again. 'I will cleanse you ...' he says in a stuttering voice. Then he grabs his penis and urinates on me. I close my eyes. Muffled screaming. It turns him on; his penis swells and becomes hard. Then he exits the room and goes downstairs to the ground floor. I pray he's leaving. But he's naked. Someone, please save me.

'Help ... help ...'

I hear heavy footsteps on the stairs. He's coming back up. My tears are like a waterfall, dropping heavily. When the door opens,

I can see Maroje has something in his hand. I hope it's not a knife. Oh God, don't let him kill me. God, help me.

He pulls his underwear out of my mouth, making my teeth ache.

'Please ...' I whine, crying.

Maroje opens his hand, and I can see it's not a knife he's holding but a small glass bottle. A salt shaker. From the kitchen.

'Open your mouth,' he orders.

My mouth instinctively clenches shut. Fear seeps through my body. I move my legs as hard as I can, trying to untie them.

'Open your mouth, bitch!' He pours a handful of salt into his palm, then smears it onto my closed mouth. The salt stings my chapped lips. He is not done. He pulls my chin and forces my jaws open with his big hands. My cheeks are in so much pain. I groan and finally give in.

He holds the shaker above my face and pours salt into my now gaping mouth. The salt burns the insides of my mouth. I feel I am suffocating and nauseous at the same time. My gag-reflex kicks in and I spit salt back into his face. Maroje screams, a few grains of salt catch in his eyes. He scrambles on the floor with his eyes closed reaching for his dirty underwear. Then he stuffs the stinking cloth back into my mouth. He slaps me once, twice and continues to slap me until I lose consciousness.

89

I come to on the floor, lying in a cold, dark room. My whole face feels like a crushed apricot, and there are firecrackers going off in my mouth. My legs and arms are cramping, but the belt and jeans that tied me are gone. For a moment, all I can hear is my breath, like a broken carburettor. I want to shut down all the systems in my brain, wishing this is all a dream. I want to close my eyes again and fall back to sleep. However, of course, this is not a dream.

Wake up!

Still feeling very scared, I force myself to wake up then to stand up. The smell of urine emanating from the carpet and from my body makes me nauseous. Has he gone? Where did he go? Hesitantly, I approach the door and turn the knob. Slowly, the door opens. I worry he might have caged me like a pet, and I will be imprisoned here until death, but that doesn't seem to be the case. I turn on the light and stumble back to the window blinds. *Light, I need light. I have to get out of here!* I scream to myself. But, against my first instincts, all I do is to sit on the edge of the bed. For a second, I think about calling the police, but what would I say?

I try not to get carried away with fear. Come on, think clearly. I search for my phone and realise that it is Christmas morning. I have been unconscious all night. I force myself up again and turn on all the lights in the house, then I switch on the heating. I don't want this house to feel like a cold, dark grave. Trembling, I go to the bathroom and look for painkillers in the cabinet. I find a bottle of paracetamol and take three pills in one gulp. I strip naked and turn on the shower. I stand under the showerhead and use all the available shampoo and soap to cleanse my body from the smell of the urine. Then I sit on the shower floor and hug my legs. Surprisingly, I am not crying. I just want to get rid of the smell of it all.

After twenty minutes or so, even though I still don't feel cleansed, I step out of the shower. I leave all the dirty clothes on the floor and creep into my room. I change into clean clothes and quickly pack the rest of my gear into my suitcase. I have to get out of this grave.

I puff some baby powder on my face to cover the bruises, but it is useless. My swollen lips are bigger than tomatoes and so painful to move. I am sure that Maroje has left. I can feel that he's not here anymore.

***

After bolting the front door from the inside, I warm up some instant soup in the kitchen. I am very hungry. I must eat before walking to the station. Unfortunately, after dragging my suitcase to the station, it turns out the trains are not running on Christmas Day. What now?

It's getting colder. I don't want to be outside for long. I lug my suitcase back to the rental house. Through the windows of neighbouring houses, I can see people gathering with their families, warming themselves in front of open fires and opening gifts. They are clueless of others' misery.

I purposely turn on all the lights so that people will know that there is life in this house. After locking the front door and the bedroom door and securing it with a chair, and my suitcase, I climb into bed and close my eyes. He's not here, he's not here, I whisper. It seems that Maroje really has gone. I don't know where because I don't know what's in his head. I never really knew.

90

I wake up on Boxing Day, December 26th. Again, I head to the station with the suitcase I haven't reopened, only to find that the trains are still not operating.

I'm about to walk back to the rental house when two people approach me and ask if I want to share a cab to the city centre. It costs around £45, not too much for three people, so I agree. They don't comment on the state of my face (which still looks like a bruised fruit); they mind their own business throughout the journey. One of the good things about British people is that they are so polite they will say sorry even when someone has stepped on their feet.

The people I'm with want to go to Hyde Park to see Winter Wonderland and to ice skate. I say it sounds lovely, and it's really nice to meet them. I try to say it as sincerely as possible with my swollen lips. I get out in the Earl's Court area and pay my share. Luckily, there is still an empty bed in the hostel I've stayed at before. 'I have money,' I tell the receptionist, who doesn't seem to recognize my face at all. After paying for three days with the option of extending it later if necessary, I immediately look for a ticket to fly home.

I can buy a ticket leaving tomorrow, or even today if I want to. I have the money. But I don't want to show my face to my mom in this condition. I find a fairly cheap ticket for a flight leaving on New Year's Eve. After checking my savings, I ask the hostel receptionist to help book the ticket for me. Luckily, he doesn't ask too many questions, just a 'You alright?' to which I respond by handing over my passport and giving a weak nod. I have five days until I go home.

***

London is not as crowded at Christmas, and reminds me of Jakarta during Eid. I go to M&S to buy an ice pack to compress my face, a box of paracetamol and some reheatable meals.

The afternoon feels like any other afternoon. The sun doesn't appear at all during the following days. I pass the hours by curling up in my bed, watching the hostel guests come and go. Occasionally, I go to the TV room to eat and snack while looking at the colourful flickering lights adorning the small Christmas tree in the corner of the room. I ignore the occasional pain in my body that still haunts me.

I've tried texting Jonathan, saying 'Hi'. But he has not replied to the message.

***

For two days, I do nothing but surf the internet, check Facebook and read emails. My fingers begin to itch to comment and update statuses because there is nothing else to do. An idle hand is indeed dangerous.

'I'm heartbroken.'

I update my status on Facebook.

Several comments appear, such as: 'Poor you', 'Single now?', 'Be patient' and 'Grammar, please'. I ignore them all, but one comment catches my attention: 'Hearts are meant to be broken, anyway …'

That comment is from Oleksii. I reply to the comment with a heart emoji. My heart is broken not only because of what Maroje has done to me. I am heartbroken at all the hopes I had, it broke my trust in people. I'm heartbroken at the whole situation. Heartbroken at myself. What Oleksii says comforts me quite a bit. I read it many times over.

'Hearts are meant to be broken, anyway …'

91

Only one day left until I'm home. London is starting to get crowded again for the new year. The bruises and cuts on my face are a little less visible. I thought it wouldn't hurt to buy some souvenirs for my mom, my brother and maybe for the neighbours too. Keychains should do.

I am reminded of a song by Alanis Morissette. She said that life has a funny way of sneaking up on you, just when you think everything is fine and everything's going right. Or, when you think everything's gone wrong, it has a funny way of helping you out. Life is like that.

I head to Piccadilly Circus in the late afternoon, visiting souvenir shops to buy fridge magnets, cheap keychains, thin scarves and low-quality screen-printed T-shirts with pictures of London or Big Ben on them. I also go into M&M's World out of curiosity.

After filling my tote bag, I walk down the famous Oxford Street. The street is lined with shops and boutiques from world-renowned brands such as Burberry, Coach, Ted Baker, Zara, H&M, Tommy Hilfiger and others. It's said that this street is one of the busiest shopping streets in Europe. The shops are crammed with tourists, some just window shopping like me, others actually shopping. Not everyone is poor like me. Those who are really shopping carry their bags with panache. I just swing my tote bag around carelessly.

I wander the street for hours, watching people. I see a man distributing pamphlets near one of the entrances to Oxford Circus Tube station. He is shouting something about religion, but almost no one pays him any attention. I pop into House of Fraser and Debenhams department stores, thinking of buying some shirts for my brother but there is nothing on discount so I try John Lewis next door.

Leaving John Lewis, I consider buying some perfume for my

mom at ZARA. However, something doesn't feel right. I hear people screaming from the left side of the street. It's not clear what they are shouting. It sounds like people are fighting. I wonder if it has something to do with the person distributing religious pamphlets. But then I see people running from the direction of the underground station. It looks serious. Seconds later, two police cars pass by, sirens blaring and lights flashing.

'Run!' someone yells. Run? I stand still because I still don't understand what is going on. Like me, the people next to me are looking in all directions to try and figure out what is happening. People run past us on the pavement.

'What's wrong?' I ask someone. 'Guns!' someone shouts, followed by a woman's scream. I still stay rooted to the spot even though the people next to me have started running. I want to see what's going on, but a wave of panic from the left sweeps up the road, and more and more people scream. The word 'gun' has changed to 'bomb'. There's a bomb in the underground station … there's a mass shooting underway. That's what I hear. I see an old couple running in front of me, and when I look behind me, the department store doors are already closed. Buildings up and down the street are being locked down. People are banging on the glass doors because their friends or family are still inside. It is only now that I realize the situation is serious.

I hear someone shout 'Run!' again. That's my cue. I dash to the right, caught in the current of people thrown into panic. It's a domino effect – what starts as a trickle soon becomes a flood, overtaking those who are walking. The panic amplifies, filling the air with a chorus of screams, warnings, the cries of children, and people questioning why they should run, but they run anyway. We move as one. If there really is a mass shooter, we are a very easy target. I look to the left and right, still figuring out what to do. People are pushing and elbowing each other, and my feet are hurting from running in boots. Then I stumble and fall; my groceries scatter on the pavement but I can't save them because they are trampled on. What a waste. My hand is stepped on too. I groan in pain. Someone lifts me up. 'Run! Run!' he exclaims. I run on, hobbling now. A black car with tinted windows slows down not far from me. Is that the shooter? I am sure that I am about to die. I fully expect a window to roll down and a gun to appear.

* * *

People are ducking into side streets and alleyways in an effort to escape. I turn right down a side street of restaurants and bars. Police sirens are getting closer and louder. The black car is still following us slowly. I stop and bang on the door to a locked bar along with a few others. At first, the waiters and patrons are surprised, but they quickly usher us in when they realize what is happening. 'Everyone, go to the basement!' shouts one of the waiters, pointing to the stairs. The bar's door is locked behind us.

The basement turns out to be a private lounge with crescent-shaped leather sofas against the wall and wooden chairs in the centre of the room. In the corner are shelves of wine and spirits.

'Okay, everyone, calm down. We're safe down here,' the waiter shouts.

However, nobody is quiet. Some sob into their hands, others

are chatting too loudly, perhaps from shock.

'Terrorists,' someone whispers.

I squat in a corner, my knee cut from falling over and the palms of my hands grazed. Another waiter enters the lounge and asks us not to worry. He says he will inform us of any updates.

Everyone is feeling anxious. Some complain they feel suffocated and claustrophobic. Another waiter hands out bottles of mineral water. I can hear a girl stammering in her Korean accent, saying she is separated from her friend. She won't stop crying.

* * *

Being cooped up in the bar's basement lounge with so many people for an hour and a half is not pleasant, even with lots of wine and spirits – and quite a few people are now drinking alcohol. Every minute we wait for updates. How are things outside? Is it safe? Has the terrorist been arrested? Can we get out yet? I sit in the corner in silence. My heartbeat has still not returned to normal from the fear and the running. I may be experiencing a panic attack, but all I have in my bag is paracetamol.

I text Jonathan to say I am caught up in the terrorist attack on Oxford Street and that I am really scared. The message is not answered. I don't message anyone else.

We are released from the bar when the waiter receives the green light from the police that everything is safe. However, we are warned not to return to scene of the attack. Several roads are blocked, and the Oxford Street underground station is closed. We are advised to walk to Bond Street if we want to use the Tube. Outside, there are loads of police cars in the street, and security personnel are everywhere. There are helicopters overhead.

92

I cross the street and find a bench at the edge of a park. I feel like I can't walk anymore; my legs have turned to jelly, and suddenly my heart is racing faster than before. In the shade of a tree, I just sit and cry.

I haven't cried since my attack. I guess I have been suppressing my feelings about that day, carrying on as normal and pretending everything was fine. I thought I was fine because, hey, I am a very strong person. But everything is not okay. London is not okay. People are not okay.

'Hey, God, what's up? Look at me! I am angry!'

Unable to keep it together any longer, I remove all the screws to my emotional cupboard and let the contents gush out. Tears of anger, frustration, fury and fear pour out of the corners of my eyes. I start wailing loudly, so loud that my snot flies. My chest heaves up and down in great sobs, and I am drooling like Gollum, but who cares.

'What does life want me to do? Fuck life! Damn you! I hate you! I fucking hate you, you fuckity fucking fucker!'

This week I came into close contact with death. Not once but twice. It feels like the grim reaper is stroking the ends of my hair, teasing me, 'Come on, come on, come on ...' I am not that strong, you know! Even I have limits. So please be a bit kinder!

I continue to curse life and everything else responsible for what has happened to me. It can't be all my own fault, can it? The curses and swear words come out of my mouth like a stream of vomit. I don't care about anything else right now. This moment belongs to me. I have every right to feel this way. I swim in my emotions until I am exhausted and the sea of tears subsides. Then only a few straws of snot are left.

My phone vibrates. I pull myself together and check it. There is a message from Jonathan.

'What happened? Hide!'

That is all he says, and it makes me even more annoyed, so I ignore his stale reply. My chest hurts more and more.

After all the emotions recede, all that is left is a sense of loneliness. I feel so alone here, by the side of the road, in London, in this world. I wipe away the tears that start falling again.

My phone rings. I ignore it, but it keeps on ringing, desperately wanting me to pick it up. Through my tears, I see the caller ID. I pick it up listlessly and put it to my ear.

'Hi, I heard something happened in London ...'

I cut him off. 'Oleksii, I can't breathe ...' then, out of nowhere, I break down in tears again.

'Where are you now?'

'On the side of a road, Oleksii, I'm so scared.'

'Are you safe now?'

'Yeah, I guess,' I sniff back the tears. 'Help me ...'

'Hey, calm down. It's over, okay? It's over ... don't think

about it anymore. It's over, right? You are safe now. I'm driving, and I'm on my way to my parents' house. It's pretty far from my place, about two hours. My mother wants to set me up with a girl. I can't believe it. I don't want to do it, but I'm going anyway, to see her. My mother is a very strange person. She truly is. And I've broken up with my girlfriend. Do you remember her? Anyway, I just signed off the ship a week ago ... We missed you, especially your vomit when the sea was rough, ha ha.'

My crying starts to subside. My panic starts to disappear.

'Remember when I showed you my missile? You were very surprised, fascinated maybe? Ukrainian missile,' he lets out a laugh. 'I still remember the look on your face ...' Oleksii talks non-stop about our time together on the ship, even using funny words like bomboclat, chiki-chiki, paisano and prata. He distracts me.

'Don't worry, okay ... don't be afraid, you're very strong, you told me that. You can lift a tray full of hot soup.'

'I drink milk ...' I reply, trying to laugh. 'You should too ...'

'Hey!'

After almost nineteen minutes of talking, he hangs up.

I remain seated on the bench for some time. I am safe. I am alright. Just like Oleksii said.

***

Someone taps my shoulder, making me jump. I turn to find a woman standing next to the bench. She's wearing a striped long coat, and I can see large round earrings, hidden in her big brunette hair.

'John Lewis … is it open again?' she asks. The strange thing is that she asks me this without even looking at me, as if she is not talking to me but to herself. She keeps her eyes fixated on the entrance to the shop. I shake my head in response. I don't know.

'It looks like it's open again,' she says calmly, addressing whom I don't know. Ignoring me, she crosses the street and enters the store. I wipe my eyes. I am mesmerized by the woman. It's like she doesn't care about what just happened.

And it gets me off the bench.

93

I walk to the Tube station at Bond Street, feeling the sting from the cut on my knee. I buy a tube of Betadine on the way to the hostel and squeeze the antiseptic cream on my wound right there on the pavement.

Back in my hostel, I go straight to my room and lie down on my bunk bed. The room lights have been turned off. There are already three other people in the room – the light from their phones illuminates their faces.

I can't sleep. My heart is still pounding from the remnants of fear in the corner of my soul. However, I am done with crying and getting angry. I get out of bed to grab some water from the tap. I am about to take a few paracetamols to help me sleep when I receive a text.

'Hi, I'm in London.'

A message from Jonathan. I hesitate to reply. But finally, I type something:

'I'm going back to Indonesia the day after tomorrow.'

'Oh? We'll meet tomorrow, then.'

'Okay.'

I don't sleep at all, despite the medication.

* * *

In the morning, I go to the Earl's Court Pret a Manger, my favourite place to buy a hoisin duck wrap and to sip a warm cappuccino, maybe for the last time. Jonathan comes in and sits across from me. He offers a deep 'hi'. I continue to chew my food, ignoring him.

He doesn't take his eyes off my face.

'What happened?' his voice is worried.

'Life,' I reply. My mouth is stuffed with breakfast. 'Life happened.'

Hearing my bitter tone, he puts his coffee down on the table. 'I'm sorry. My girlfriend – I mean my close friend – came over, so I ignored my phone while she was around. I took her to Heathrow last night.'

That explains why he was unreachable over Christmas and why he is in London now. However, I honestly don't care anymore. I keep munching my hoisin duck wrap.

'Is … is it because of yesterday?' he asks again. 'The terrorist? I thought it was a hoax … the bomb wasn't found, right?'

I snort, then stuff the last big chunk of food into my mouth.

'We didn't know it was a hoax. What we felt was real. The horror was real.' It is true. It was a hoax. But we didn't know that yesterday, the terror was real. We only discovered later on the news that there had been no bomb, no shooters. I wipe my mouth with a napkin.

'I'm sorry,' he says.

I shrug.

'What about your face, then?' he asks, watching me take a slow sip of coffee.

'Well, my jealous boyfriend beat me up on Christmas Eve,' I reply casually.

Jonathan's jaw drops. He searches for the right words to say. I don't want to judge him, but I know Jonathan: he can't handle unpleasant things. It makes him giddy and confused.

'It's fine, don't give me that face,' I say, to help him control himself. 'This thing has happened, the person has left, and tomorrow I will go home ... I'm tired of crying too. It's over, ciao, adios, all in the past ...'

He nods doubtfully, feeling even more uneasy. We both know it wasn't his fault, but I think he feels he contributed to my decision to stay over in Norwich, and he seems to feel guilty. Behind his logic-driven character, he is of course a person who still has a conscience.

'Oh, Maya ...'

'Don't call my name like that.' I don't feel comfortable being pitied. 'Call me Xena or Pang-pang.' I try to lighten the atmosphere.

He forces a smile.

'What time is your flight tomorrow?' he asks.

'Two in the afternoon.'

'Stay with me tonight? Please?' his voice squeaks.

I say yes without thinking. 'Could you please carry my suitcase?'

This time he agrees.

* * *

Jonathan takes a room in a hotel in Earl's Court. A room with a comfortable and clean king-size bed, a television and proper heating that I can control.

He buys me a bag of grapes and I eat them on the bed while watching television. Today, Jonathan is extraordinarily kind. He doesn't say much but just smiles every time he sees me doing something. I love to see him looking at me. It makes my chest flutter even though I know it might not be romantic affection he has for me.

'Don't hug me, my body hurts all over,' I say, when he tries to cuddle me at night.

We are silent for a moment.

'I have to be honest,' he says. 'I really like you.'

'Hmm,' I reply.

Jonathan looks dissatisfied with my response. Does he want me to scream for joy? Or to say the same to him? I can't do that anymore. So, I come up with something else.

'Jonathan ... I know, but to you I'm just Indomie.'

'Indomie?'

'Yes, Indomie. A snack that you can get whenever you are hungry and nothing else is available. If there was better, tastier food, you would definitely ignore me.'

He snorts. 'Aiyo, that's not true ... but comparing yourself with Indomie, that's very creative and funny, you're really funny.'

'You like me because I'm the one who is here. Available. Near to you.'

Jonathan takes my hand and holds it. I hold him back.

'And even if it's true that you like me,' I say, 'I won't be your priority.'

I think we both know there's some truth in it.

'Don't you believe me?' he whispers.

'I do. I really like you. Maybe I fell in love with you.'

94

This morning, Jonathan wheels my suitcase to Earl's Court Tube station. I am about to take the train to Heathrow. I take a look around the city and bid farewell to it in silence. Bye, London; bye, Earl's Court; bye, Tesco; bye, old buildings with character. See you soon. Goodbye. I am going home.

'Maya ...' Jonathan calls my name softly.

'Hmm?' I turn to him with a smile.

'Be my priority number three, after me and my work ...'

My smile widens hearing that.

'I mean it.'

'I know,' I reply.

'So?'

'It's not about you, it's me. I believe you, but I don't trust myself. I don't believe that I won't be jealous all the time. I'll always be wondering what you're doing. You're going to be in Norwich for a long time and I'm far away in Indonesia. I'd also be curious if you have other priorities even though I'm your priority number three. I don't want to be in a relationship that worries me.'

He smiles, takes a step closer and hugs me. It is an intimate moment and neither of us knows whether it will be repeated in the future. Just let the universe do the talking. We only let go of our tangled arms and emotions when my train arrives. Jonathan waits for my train to leave so we both have a reason to wave goodbye and miss each other.

***

I am not convinced he really likes me. I think he feels sorry for me and enjoys my company. Anything to drive away his loneliness. Maybe he even feels sorry for seeing me last night. And that's why he asked me to be priority number three. His motive is not romantic. And even if it is, and it turns out I am wrong about him and that he really likes me, I don't want to make any impulsive decisions. I have learned to let time be the judge.

By rejecting him, I am making it easier for both of us. Honestly, though, I really like him. Ah, I'm so upset. It's okay, I can cry, *lah*. Heartbroken.

I update my Facebook stats: 'broken heart part 2'.

95

I find myself once again at Amsterdam's Schiphol airport, waiting for the next flight to Singapore. This time I don't pretend to be busy, posing as an exec with a laptop while reading sexy stories on Wattpad. No, no, this time I'm just sitting casually, munching on Doritos and scrolling through Facebook on my phone.

> Maya: 'Mom, I'm on my way home.'
> Mom: 'Oh, great.'
> Maya: 'I don't have much money.'

Plus, I didn't bring souvenirs because, you know, they're already in some rubbish bin.

> Mom: 'Then you can't come home.'
> Maya: 'I'm already in the Netherlands, transiting. Now waiting for the plane. I don't have money, but I have a lot of stories. I've met a lot of interesting people. I can tell you all about it later. Like fairy tales, right? Stories are precious. You used to read to me before I went to bed when I was a kid, and I liked it so much. Those things can't be replaced by money! Those stories and

those memories. They are treasures. Maybe this time I'll tell you stories about the people I met in London while you're in bed. You'll like it.'

If you really think about it, it's true. I have met so many people and done things I never thought I would. I met Erick, who taught me to be a good marketer; Josh, the handsome gay-sex-shop expert; Paul Jr, who's in the Maldives and never fails to like my status updates; Linda, who is the devil's servant; some naked Turkish men in hostels (with their trumpets); Jonathan, who calls me Pang-Pang; Maroje, who is ... confused, and many others. Humans are creatures full of surprises.

Mom: 'Fairy tales can't pay off debts.'

Ha ha, that's right.

Maya: 'Please, Mom ...'
Mom: 'Yes. What matters is that you come home. After that, you can't go anywhere else. There was a bomb scare in London a few days ago, you know that?'
Maya: 'I know. You've checked on me several times since then.'

She doesn't know I was right there in the middle of it. Of course, I'm not going to tell her now at the airport. Later, when I arrive home, and she asks me about the bruises and the cuts on my face, only then I'll give her this answer: 'During the bomb scare, I fell and was stepped on.' I won't mention Maroje. It would only hurt my mom.

Maya: 'I'm confused. I don't know what to do after this.'

Mom: 'You're always like that. Never tired of worrying about stuff.'

Maya: 'How else should I be?'

Mom [*typing* …]

Ten minutes later.

Mom: 'Maya, everyone has a void in them that they always want to fill. The way to fill that void may not be the same for everyone. Some fill it through careers, life partners, hobbies, and anything else that makes them feel complete as a person. Everyone's job is to find what can fill that empty space. Some find it quickly, some take time, and some even fail. Before they find it, most will feel insignificant, empty, unfilled. So don't stop looking until you find it, that's your job. My job as a mother is to worry about you and ask you to come home …'

I forgot how much I love my mom.

Mom: 'I need to go now, my fried *tempeh* is about to burn.'

To be honest, I still haven't found the answer to what I was looking for or what I really want in life. However, over time, I've learned many new lessons and gained a better understanding of myself through each experience, making me a more optimal human being. That is, if I care enough to look closely for lessons. With everything I've been through, I understand a little more about myself. That's not so bad, right?

The world is a very big place. I will continue to seek and try to understand.

I remember the woman in front of the store that evening after the bomb hoax. When I was still bawling on a bench in a park, and she came out of nowhere, asking if the store was open. I looked at her, and this is what crossed my mind: *So, something bad happened, a disaster. It's scary, it's dramatic, it's painful, it's horrifying. But it's done, it's over. So? And then the shop was closed for a while, but now it's open, and we can shop again.*

And now that's my philosophy in life.

***

While waiting to board, I chat with Oleksii via Messenger.

> Maya: 'I might return to the ship, but I don't know.'
> Oleksii: 'I don't know either.'
> Maya: 'I'm confused about what to do next ...'
> Oleksii: 'So, what should you do next?'
> Maya: 'Plans. Don't you have any plans?'
> Oleksii: 'Yes, I will have dinner tonight.'
> Maya: 'I mean long-term plans ...'
> Oleksii: 'Oh, that ... after dinner, maybe I will get some dessert.'

I giggle.

Maya: 'You're so cheesy.'

Oleksii: 'Ha ha. By the way, I'm going to Bali next week.
I'll visit Yanti, you still remember her, right? She's
starting her flower farming business. Said that selling
flowers there is good money. I want to see it. Aside
from sunbathing on the beach, of course. Gotta show
off these biceps! I might stop by Jakarta before that.
Want to meet?'

Maya: 'Absofreakinlutely!'

* * *

Next to my last Facebook post, where I wrote 'broken heart part
2', Oleksii has written another comment:

'Hearts break so they may grow larger. And you never
truly know who you are until your heart has been broken.'

Hearts are meant to be broken, anyway.

Acknowledgements

I would like to thank the National Book Committee of Indonesia for granting me a writing residency program in the UK to enable me to write this story, as well as the National Centre for Writing in Norwich, my UK publisher Phil Tatham, azizam Aras Amiri, and all the crew (my fellow seafarers) aboard the MV *Corinthian* during my time working as a waiter at sea. Also, my mum.

Terima kasih banyak!

Not A Virgin
by Nuril Basri

'One reason I disliked my brother was because he was responsible for me losing my virginity, which happened when he got me kicked out of my own home – even if only indirectly.'

Jakarta teenager Ricky Satria overhears his parents discussing how they would send him to live in a *pesantren*, an Islamic boarding school, to cure his spoilt nature and free up a bedroom for his elder brother. Ricky is insulted to be called spoilt and decides there and then to enrol himself in a *pesantren*, both to challenge his parents' perception of him and to pre-empt his eviction.

In this coming-of-age novel, four Indonesian students seek to discover what their future will bring and look for answers to their questions about sexuality, religion and drugs. With characters ranging from cross-dressing hairdressers, drag queens and rent boys to fanatic Muslims and low-life security personnel, the action of this tragicomedy moves between an Islamic boarding school and a gay bar in Jakarta, and in so doing illuminates the mindset and yearnings of a new generation of Indonesians.